I0769622

THE
APOCALYPSE
WEDDING

Join our mailing list at

palmcirclepressbooks.com

for news on upcoming releases, exclusive previews, and special subscriber-only content…

This is a work of fiction. Names, characters, places, and incidents either are products of the writer's imagination or are used fictitiously. Any resemblance to actual events or locales or persons, living or dead, is entirely coincidental.

Printed in the United States of America

ISBN: 979-8-9888754-4-4

Map of Jyn Designed by Peter de Jong

Front Cover Design by Terrence Mercer

Interior Layout by Rachel Newhouse for elfinpen designs

Published by Palm Circle Press
www.palmcirclepressbooks.com

THE LOST BOOKS OF JYN

BOOK TWO

THE APOCALYPSE WEDDING

LEE ANDERSON

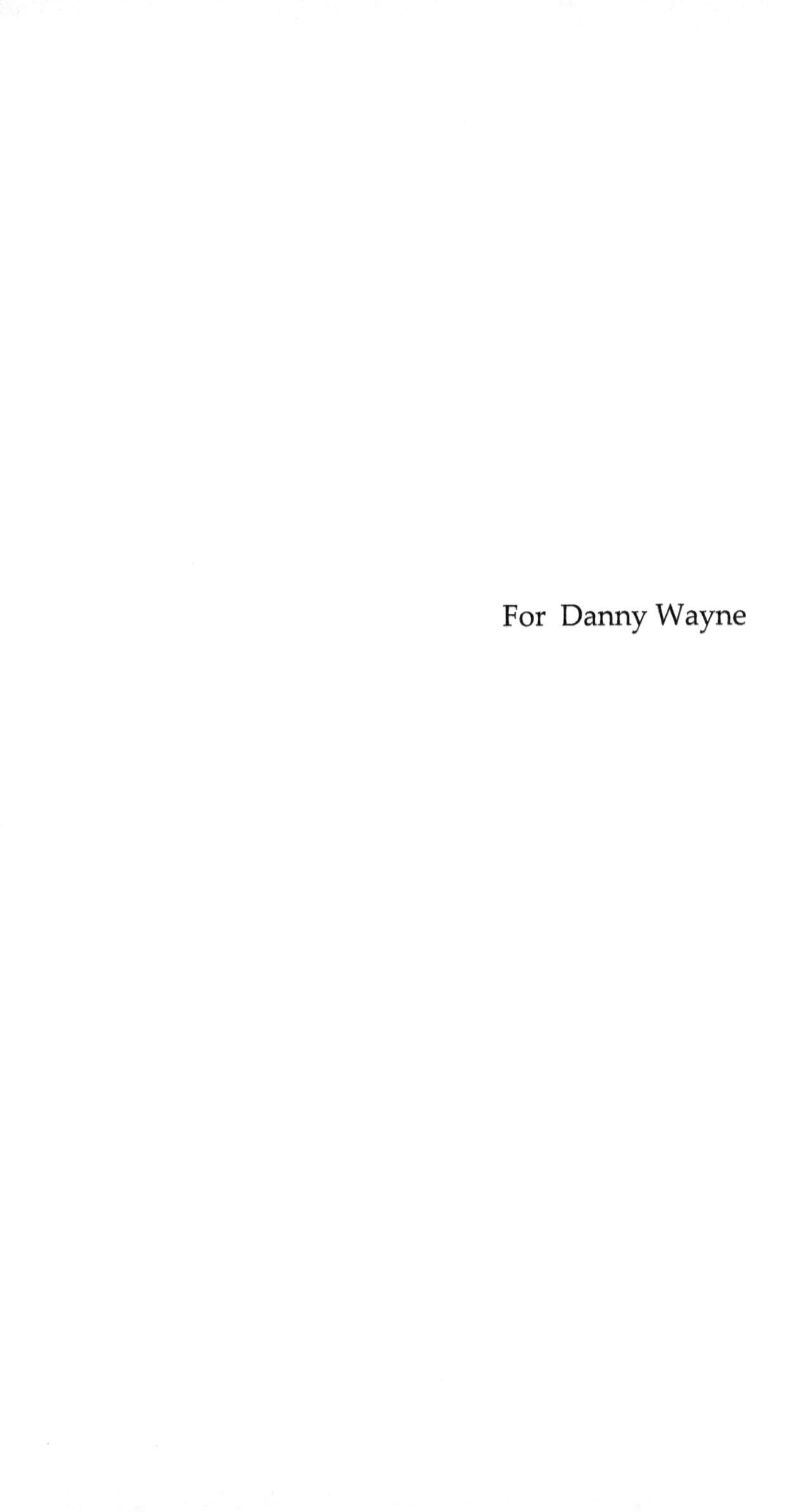

For Danny Wayne

DRAMATIS PERSONAE

~ The Kingdom of Tartaria ~

King Khilji, the former King of Tartaria, the Northern Kingdom.
Queen Abika, the former Queen of Tartaria.
Princess Sarna, daughter of King Khilji and Queen Abika.
King Shayan, deposed King of Tartaria, son of King Khilji and Queen Abika.
Ivaanjav, advisor to King Shayan.
Lalya, Princess Sarna's best friend and schoolmate.
Luca, an ex-soldier turned outlaw who kidnapped Princess Sarna.
Khilji, a scout in King Shayan's service.

~ The Kingdom of the Cathyrnee ~

Chief Arlyn, leader of the Cathyrnee, a nomadic tribe.
Chieftess Yarlaa, the slain wife of Chief Arlyn.
Khuyag, commander of the Cathyrnee military.

~ The Kingdom of Burnya ~

King Montrose, King of Burnya, the Western Kingdom.
Ozyan, former handmaiden to Queen Saraal and King Montrose's mistress.
Queen Saraal, Queen of Burnya.
General Amgelan, General of the Burnyan military.
Artemis, Burnya's Gold Master.

~ Shamans, Warlocks, and Beasts ~

Baal, a deity of the ancient underworld, known for demanding ritual sacrifice in exchange for good fortune.

Corsika, a female Ghe-sui shaman, once loyal to Chieftess Yarlaa.

Drakksuk, flying, lightning-breathing reptilian creatures with bat wings.

The Magshaa, slain Master of the Ghe-sui, a shaman cult.

Momaset, leader of the Ghe-sui, spiritual authority second only to the Magshaa.

Seelskan, a high-ranking warlock of the Dark Shulam, a branch of the Ghe-sui devoted to its darker side.

Ulaan, a female Ghe-sui shaman, once spiritual counselor to Queen Saraal.

Yelkin, man-eating giants from the Oroo Mountains.

~ Terminology ~

Babsulisk, a popular narcotic fruit juice, extracted from the babsulisk tree.

The Great Awakening, a sudden, mysterious growth spurt in philosophical knowledge, engineering advancement, and psychic abilities.

Ha'wiih, a respectful way of addressing any Cathyrnee leader.

Joppa, a curse word, often used to express anger, frustration, or amazement.

Sünsü, a mysterious energy appearing in Jyn as part of the Great Awakening.

As could be imagined of a mythic world, the people of Jyn did not speak English, but a language called Xhenkhel. It was the official language of Jyn and the most widely spoken, best-known member of the Xhengolic language family. Speakers across every dialect numbered close to fifteen million, including the vast majority of Jyn civilians and many of the tribal residents of the outer plains and mountains.

While it was possible to recover more than eighty percent of the implied connotation of the text, translating Xhenkhel to English encompassed centuries of specific idioms. Special skill was used to maintain allegiance with the intent and meaning of the original books. However, modern English vernacular was used where appropriate.

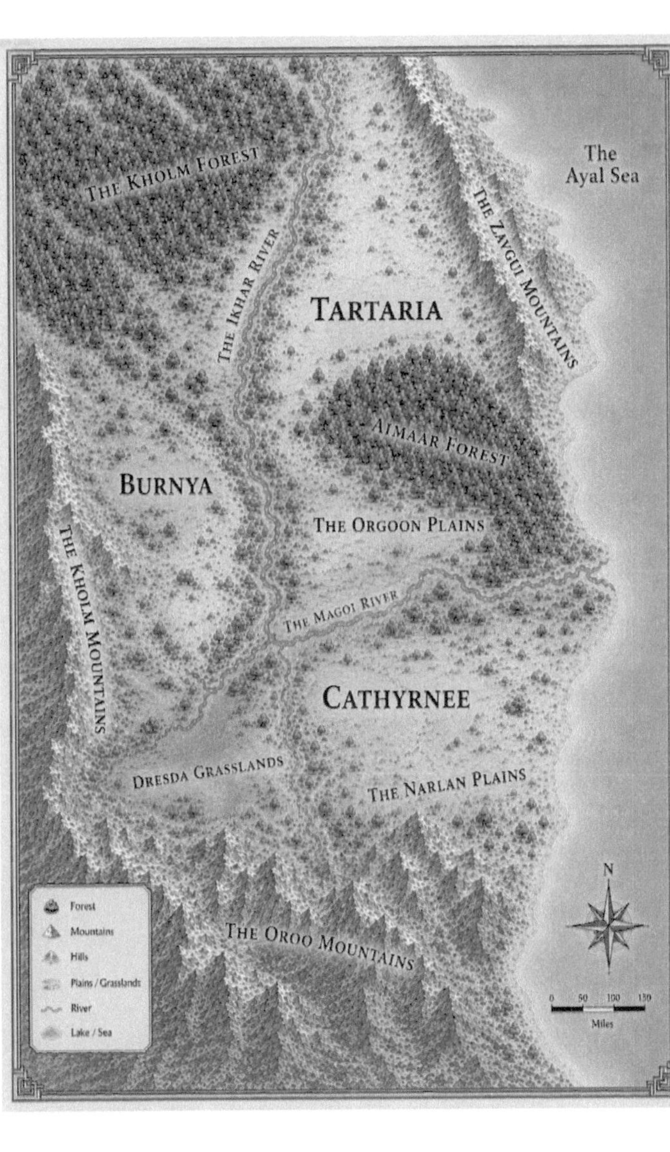

THE KHOLM FOREST
The Ayal Sea
THE IKHAR RIVER
TARTARIA
THE ZAVGUI MOUNTAINS
AIMAAR FOREST
BURNYA
THE ORGOON PLAINS
THE KHOLM MOUNTAINS
THE MAGOI RIVER
CATHYRNEE
DRESDA GRASSLANDS
THE NARLAN PLAINS
THE OROO MOUNTAINS
Forest
Mountains
Hills
Plains / Grasslands
River
Lake / Sea
N
0   50   100   150
Miles

SARNA

She held her arms firmly around Luca's waist. He steered the horse northward, with an auburn haze on the horizon. High above, clusters of clouds hovered beneath a pair of thumbnail moons, the smaller moon peeking from behind the larger, its surface radiant and blistered.

Sarna's frayed tunic flapped against the horse's backside. Her exposed forearms and ankles prickled from the evening chill. They'd been riding for over an hour, and her inner thighs pulsed from the discomfort. She craved rest and yelled as much into Luca's ear. She was sure the horse needed rest as well. And to eat. Luca was pushing them too hard.

He ignored her. Sarna felt him leaning forward more, kicking the horse to go faster. Though he had his moments, Luca was a stubborn fool. She considered the possibility that she hated him.

Their destination was the kingdom of Burnya. The bandit and the princess simply had nowhere else to go. Their kingdom had been leveled. The Ghe-sui had fled to the Kholm Mountains to save themselves. While hiding at the Magshaa Temple for over three months, Sarna had no idea which of her family members were dead or alive. There wasn't even much hope that she or Luca would live much longer. Not in a flimsy, poorly-sanitized hut.

They headed to Burnya despite being unsure of where Burnya's allegiances lay anymore. Her father and King Montrose had always despised one another, so Sarna doubted the Burnyan king would show her much sympathy. Still, they had no choice. The realm of Jyn was overrun with unthinkable dangers, namely the drakksuk—flying creatures that breathed lightning. Also, the temple was out of food. They needed civilization with fortitude and walls. They needed consistent meals and water.

Besides, the remaining shamans had chosen to embark for the Kholm Mountains weeks ago, joining the rest of their kind. They'd insisted that the two of them keep the horse since Luca had stolen it.

Sarna pressed against him, their cheeks bouncing together. "We should stop!"

"Not yet!" he barked. "I want to make Burnya by tomorrow afternoon!"

"The horse is exhausted! I am, too!"

Luca remained focused on the path ahead. His long locks smacked her face.

After a while, he said, "There should be a river up here! We'll rest there, all right?"

"How far?"

"A few leagues! Twelve, I think!"

"No, no, no, that's too far! It's too far! Stop!"

He pulled on the horse's reins, far more forcefully than necessary. The animal grunted and dug its rear hooves into the ground. Sarna was nearly flung. She managed to hold on by squeezing Luca's ribs. He cried out.

She went to scold him for nearly tossing her, but Luca held a finger up, signaling for silence. He swung his right leg forward and over. He slid down from the horse. He kept one hand on Sarna's knee, the other on the reins. He surveyed their surroundings, alerted by something unseen. A half-spherical hill bulged from the south, shingled with shards of granite. On their right stood a thin row of thick trees. The wind flattened the high grass in waves.

"What is it?" she whispered.

He shook his head.

She went rigid, listening for what worried him. She heard nothing but the wind until…voices. With Luca's help, she slid down from the horse to join him. The insides of her thighs throbbed, nearly sending her to her knees, her legs numb and noodly from the long ride. Thankfully, Luca caught her. He motioned for her to follow him as he led the horse into the shadow of the trees. Once there, Sarna stared with him in the direction of the voices.

The tribesmen appeared over a hill, less than a hundred yards away. She counted seven men in loincloths, doused head to toe in tribal paint. The luminous tint of the twin moons revealed the men in stark detail: Their legs and hips were black with a blue band around their waists and abdomens, turning to white over their chests and bald heads. They held spears. Their eyes smoldered with an orange phosphorescence, like hot charcoal, and Sarna realized these were not men at all. Her stomach dropped.

She and Luca held completely motionless as the strange beings walked closer. They spoke in a language punctuated with clicks and whistles, their cadence sounding far from melodic, but at a much higher timbre than she might've expected, considering the pure evil of their appearance.

Inevitably, the horse snorted and brushed its rear leg against a tree. The seven strange beings stopped and went quiet, their spears pointed.

Luca took a deep breath and stepped out from their hiding spot. He held his hands up in surrender. "Hello there," he said to them.

Sarna wanted to scream. Luca's recklessness was beyond comprehension. However, the befuddlement of these beings seemed to be what had momentarily saved him. They appeared as astonished as she was.

"Didn't mean to scare you," Luca said. He dropped his right arm but kept his left raised, as if swearing an oath. "I'm with someone very important." He nudged his head in her direction, then apparently lost his mind because he told them, "This girl here is the princess of Tartaria. I'm trying to get her to Burnya."

The nearest being growled, a low-pitched, demonic rumble.

"We wish only to pass on our way," Luca added, his voice faltering, likely regretting this plan already. "Do you understand? Are we all right?"

No one moved. Caught in a moment stretched from terror, Sarna noticed their spears were thin yet heavy-looking, made from what resembled volcanic rock. One of the beings pointed at Luca and said something in a jarring, idiosyncratic meter.

"Do you speak Xhenkhel?" Luca asked him. "I'm sorry, but I don't understand you."

The being with charcoal eyes straightened his back while sucking his bottom lip, an image so unsettling, Sarna felt sure she would remember it for the rest of her life, however short that might be. None of these man-things appeared happy to meet them. In fact, as a group, they appeared more than willing to slay them both for the first reason.

The same being who had spoken turned and spoke to the rest of his group. They resumed their advancement.

"What are you doing?" Luca asked. "Whoa! Wait! We mean you no harm!"

The beings increased their pace until they charged

with their spears leading the way. They made no noise, no battle cry, only those glowing eyes narrowed with focus. The wish to kill.

Luca drew his sword, and the beings paused, off-guard, as though it hadn't actually occurred to them their foe might be armed.

The same being shouted at Luca.

"I have no idea what you're saying!" he responded. "Now back off! All of you! Let's please talk this out!"

Sarna held her breath and stepped out of the shadows. She stood next to Luca.

"We mean you no harm," she said, and saw no choice but to behold how dumb she was being herself now. They couldn't understand her! The only hope left was that they might at least interpret her tone favorably. Show mercy to a female.

They blinked at her, puzzled but interested. She took this as a good sign.

"Hey, friend!" Luca shouted. "Friends! Let's be friends!"

The being did the odd thing with his lip again, and he yelled. He raised his spear over his head, prompting the others to do the same. They continued their charge, their mouths open, revealing rows of slobbery fangs.

"Oh,...," Luca muttered. "Oh, no."

He advanced to meet them and was surrounded in seconds.

A veteran of Jyn's Great War, Luca had turned to banditry to survive. Both endeavors left him a fully skilled swordsman. Against his current aggressors, he used his long sword to slice along diagonal lines. He protected his sides while following through in a figure-eight motion, looping as he pivoted. Having such a long sword, he was able to cover himself and Sarna from multiple directions. Luca moved like a dancer, separating body parts in rhythm. The high grass became stained with gore.

Still, he was outnumbered. Sarna could see that maintaining such a whirlwind of movement required incredible energy. Luca feinted to one opponent while striking another. Unfortunately, while shielding against the first, or even a third, blow, he went to his knees repeatedly, which slowed him. Even worse, despite losing limbs, many of the strange man-things kept attacking, unbothered by being limbless.

Luca blocked a thrust from a jutting spear but was knocked onto his back. He tried to get up and stumbled. He fell to his knees, inadvertently giving his blindside to them—the worst thing that could've happened. The three remaining beings closed in. The fight was over.

Sarna stepped forward. She'd only meant to make herself a flimsy barrier between combatants, but the world went white. A torrent of energy fountained upwards throughout her body, sparking through every nerve ending, webbing them with lightning, joined in concert. A cosmic sneeze erupted from her core, an all-consuming, uninhibited release of control. Her back arched and her feet bent, Sarna exploded. She floated just off the ground and gradually went higher. The ashes of singed grass curlicued in the wind around her.

She noticed Luca staring up at her, stunned and gaping. The strange beings were gone, even the ones already dead, reduced to smoldering stumps. Their spears lay about in scattered shards. A musty, sweet smell wafted in the wind—gases created from charged air. Sarna felt her hair standing straight out from her head, each strand repelling the other.

"I killed them," she said to Luca. She spoke slowly, entranced. "Every one of them. Did you see that?"

Luca remained on his back, trembling, his eyes locked on her floating figure. She recognized that look. She was becoming far too familiar with it from absolutely everyone.

He was terrified of her.

2

SHAYAN

King Shayan first believed the boy was handing him a flower. The object was white, tubular, and curved into a sharp point. But it was hard to the touch. Turning the object in his fingers, Shayan judged it as the tooth or claw of an enormous animal. The king and his small group of men stood atop a raised contour of rocky terra firma, horseshoed by dense woods.

"It's a drakksuk's tooth," said the boy, touching his arms behind his back. He grinned sideways, sheepish. "I wanted you to have it, Your Highness."

The boy was one of nine volunteers on a quest the king had organized. The goal was to scout what was left of their former kingdom, setting out from their refuge over a hundred leagues away. Shayan wanted to check whether any survivors were left behind and how they were being treated. His crew was comprised of a fair cross-section of Tartarian outcasts: two older farmers and their four grandsons, and two ex-soldiers. Shayan knew there were far better soldiers and scouts that he could've brought, but his military training had taught him the importance of keeping reserves, saving them for the bigger fight. This quest was largely reconnaissance in nature, so a smallish, amateur crew should've been enough.

Still, just in case, they were joined by General Harloog, a thick but battle-experienced man with a beard like a lion's mane who was never without his smelly pipe. He was the only one who had dared to voice concern over this quest. Their home was gone. Taken. There were fewer than a thousand survivors from a former kingdom of millions. It would take generations before they possessed the means with which to counterattack. In the general's opinion, this made their mission largely pointless. They would observe their decimated kingdom from afar, and do what about it exactly?

But King Shayan had insisted. No one had to come with him who didn't want to, and plenty wanted to. He'd even been forced to reject around forty other volunteers. He chose these nine simply for their youth, experience, or stamina, or what he could judge of it on the spot. He was in no position to be terribly choosy since most survivors were women and children. Most male survivors had been maimed beyond use. He believed it best to keep their group small anyway. Easier to avoid detection. Easier to stay light and fast.

He held the tooth up to the sunlight, and it shone iridescent, almost glass-like. "Where did you get it?" he asked the boy. He couldn't recall his name.

"Found it on the street while I was running. During the attack."

"And you stopped to pick it up? Despite everything happening around you?"

The boy nodded. The rest of the crew sat around, resting, using the smoother rocks as seats. Many drank from their flasks.

"A drakksuk tooth is magic," the boy said. "It kills whatever you stab it with. No matter what."

Shayan snorted. "Just like that? Anything?"

"So legend says, Your Highness."

"This is quite the gift, then. I'll treasure it." Shayan tucked the palm-sized weapon inside a pouch fastened to his waist.

The boy bowed. When he looked up again, the king flinched from realizing how young the kid was. Barely old enough to shave. He wondered at himself for having chosen him, done at the urging of the boy's grandfather, who had come as well. Shayan was new at ruling people and inwardly reproached himself for not being more discriminating. Too easily influenced by the opinions of others.

Following a few moments of rest and drink, the crew trudged eastward. They traveled slowly over a terrain of jagged rocks, their holes and ridges filled with rain puddles. Later in the day, the rocks gave way to a clearing carpeted in tall, yellow grass. The sun shone bright and hot through an empty blue sky.

Harloog reached Shayan's side and asked to see the tooth. He took it out of his sack and handed it to him.

"How do you think it fell out?" he asked the general.

"Their teeth fall out all the time. They've got bunches of them."

"It's yours."

"No, Your Highness." The general handed back the tooth. "It was given to you. Seemed as though it meant a lot to him."

"I don't much believe in magic, I'm afraid."

"I didn't either once. It's a bit difficult to deny these days, no?"

Once more, Shayan admired the tooth in his hand. He tried imagining it inside the cavernous, triangular mouth of an actual living drakksuk. He winced at the memory of just such a beast incinerating his father's funeral procession, barely three months ago. He tucked the tooth away again.

At midnight, they made camp, and Harloog insisted on taking first watch. Claimed he wasn't tired enough yet. While everyone unpacked their sleep gear, Shayan watched them. The deposed king of Tartaria had come to feel relatively comfortable with life in the wild. Though it was a far cry from his days as a castle-dwelling prince who slept in silken sheets with a fresh outfit to wear at every stage of the day.

Oddly enough, he didn't miss it. He preferred the comforting simplicity of the forest. He found the roughness and cruelty of nature to be reductive, lacking frivolity. Time was no longer filled with fox hunts, social events, bejeweled cloaks, or philosophy lessons. It was food, water, and shelter now.

The next morning brought a sparse breakfast of air-dried donkey meat, then Shayan's party resumed their hiking. He expected them to be within eyesight of their former kingdom by early evening, but he'd miscalculated. At midday, one of the teenage grandsons spotted smoke and cried out. Shayan went to quiet the kid, but his grandfather beat him to it, slapping the poor boy to his knees.

As they kept on, increasingly careful to stay silent in the woods, Shayan occasionally paused on tiptoes to check the column of black smoke, a dark line across the lower sky. He saw the smoke as evidence that their kingdom was still smoldering, all this time later.

Everyone walked as Harloog had shown them, lifting their feet and pointing their toes at the ground, making it less likely to get snagged. When connecting with the outer edge of their foot, they rolled the rest down until the sole became flat. They matched each other's pace while breathing quietly and steadily through their mouths. Even the slightest amount of forced air through their nostrils was too much noise.

Before long, the once mighty kingdom of Tartaria came into view. Shrouded in ribbons of dirty mist stood the crumbled walls of Shayan's former home.

A feeling of bleak shame crept through his gut. Tears spilled, and he couldn't stop them, not caring in the least if his men saw. He heard a sniffle and turned to see Harloog crying as well, despite the noise it made. The king hadn't expected that seeing Tartaria again would hit him like this. It was devastating.

Harloog caught Shayan's eyes. Harloog gripped his elbows, then pointed towards the kingdom. It was a hand signal asking, "How close did you want to get?"

Shayan shagged his own hair with his right hand. The signal for: "Not sure." He thought about it, kept his hand flat as he chopped it forward: "Closer."

He led his crew towards the next gathering of elm trees. He decided they would stop between the edges of each clearing to assess the threat level of their position. They would do this until reaching a spying spot. However, before entering the next expanse of trees, he observed a slender, dark shape darting upwards into the clouds, spearing through the smoke. Everyone halted to watch as the shape went ever higher. When the drakksuk's wings fanned out as the creature prepared to level, Shayan felt his blood freeze. He sensed every man holding his breath, feeling the panic shudder through every joint and ligament.

The creature dove towards them.

Shayan ran, and his men followed. He felt the approaching wind from the thrusting of the drakksuk's giant wings. The advanced displacement of air lifted the king and several of his men from their feet. Shayan tumbled forward and was only able to stop himself by grabbing fistfuls of grass and soil.

He flipped onto his back and spotted Harloog's face nearby, pale with panic. The creature filled the background behind him, a black tarp of scales punctured by pink, sparking eyes, the pupils shaped like keyholes.

Shayan heard sobbing and noticed the boy who had given him the tooth. The kid lay across a large rock while embracing it, his face pinched red with hysteria. The king scrambled to his feet and resumed running while intense heat mushroomed from somewhere behind him. The tops of the surrounding forestry turned yellow, bright with flames. Burning leaves floated like fireflies.

He dove into a field of rocks and landed hard. He prayed the nonflammable stones might offer a survivable amount of protection. Also, there was nowhere else to run. The drakksuk had assailed them with unbelievable speed. Shayan folded his arms over his head and waited. He heard more screaming and reflexively lifted his head. He saw one of the soldiers ablaze, running, his arms flapping. One of the old farmers collapsed to the ground in three pieces, serrated by lightning from the creature's thorax—a spray of energy that sliced or detonated everything it touched. The entire area became netted with super-hot light.

A few yards away, Shayan noticed a low rock shelf.

He rolled towards it as the drakksuk's enormous shadow passed over. More bright flashes. More screaming. He pressed the entire length of his body under the rock shelf. Harloog sprinted towards him, likely hoping to do the same. The two men met eyes as a white cone of light swept through the gap between them. Shayan's last war general convulsed from the electrical currents forking his body. Skin and muscle melted from bone.

The king wiggled in an attempt to further press himself under the rock shelf, yet he remained halfway exposed. His lungs emptied, the air no longer breathable. His tears sizzled on his cheeks. Wood crackled as it exploded. He shut his eyes and waited to die. The darkness behind his lids turned orange from the flames drawing closer.

CHIEF ARLYN

The entire northern perimeter of Tartaria had been erased, replaced by a fuming landscape of displaced, broken stones and lumber. High above, Chief Arlyn sat on the bed of what was once the castle's royal bedroom. Below, the castle's courtyard buzzed with construction, the chief watching from a hole in the wall. Sizeable slave crews of captured Tartarians worked on most of the rebuilding. Hammers pummeled rock. Cartwheels ground over mud. Horses whinnied and men shouted instructions. These were glorious sounds to Chief Arlyn's ears. They cheered him up.

Every building in central Tartaria had been damaged in one way or another. In the kingdom's surrounding districts, nearly all development was erased. Only in the furthest outskirts had any buildings gone untouched.

During the first stages of restoration, Arlyn had focused on the most pressing problems, such as rebuilding infirmaries and establishing schools as humanitarian aid stations. Rebuilding would not be easy. The specialists needed for such an undertaking had largely perished in the attack. Though the kingdom had mostly returned to a life of peace, theft and rape persisted.

Since the end of the siege, Arlyn spent most of his days in the former bedroom of his enemy. He wore the same red, T-shaped tunic he'd found in the closet, not even sure if it belonged to the king or Queen. He wore it regardless, enjoying the absurd perversity of it. Since losing his wife, he regarded life as not much else anyway.

Despite the cracks, the gaping holes, the numerous layers of dust, he could tell the bedroom had once been the modern Jyn standard of luxury. Black walls stood trimmed with white borders, complemented with white bedding that now lay torn and dulled with soot. A pronged chandelier remained miraculously dangling above shattered ceramic planters. A portrait of King Khilji and Queen Abika leaned against a far wall, propped in its ornate brass frame, bordered with angelic engravings. Someone had seen fit to slash the painting once across its middle in a single plunging stroke.

Khuyag entered without knocking, a habit Arlyn noted was becoming more frequent as he failed to protest it.

"Checking on you, *ha'wiih*," Khuyag was already saying. "I'm worried about you. A lot of us are."

His new military head was adorned in a relatively clean tunic and sandals, obviously opting for such dress since his duties were more diplomatic these days. Made of hardened leather and iron, the armor was laced onto a fabric backing. His clothes were the cleanest Arlyn had seen on anyone in weeks.

"Aren't you pretty," Arlyn said to him. "I'm happy to see at least *someone* enjoying the spoils of victory."

"Begging your pardon, *ha'wiih*?'

"What do you want, Khuyag?"

"I was just visited by the tribal assembly."

"To criticize me, I assume."

"They are growing a bit skittish. They're afraid of these…," Khuyag looked heavenward, drew a breath, "*things* that keep flying over."

"Anyone who wishes to return to the plains can do so. Return to living like hunted deer. I no longer care."

"*Ha'wiih*, the drakksuk are getting bigger. And they're changing colors. No one knows what to think of it, honestly."

Arlyn rose from the bed and walked to the padded,

high-back chair in the corner. He gathered the bottom of his tunic into his fists and sat hard.

"Forgive me for bringing you more troubles," Khuyag said with a bow after realizing Arlyn had nothing to respond with. "Those creatures killed a *lot* of people. In minutes. Everyone is grateful for this new kingdom, but they're also traumatized."

Arlyn motioned at the opening in the eastern wall. "The Cathyrnee are safe. Tomorrow is promised. That's all they need to know. Go tell them if you need."

Khuyag nodded. He covered his mouth with his hand and sighed. He dropped the hand and faced his chief. "It's the opinion of your assembly that you should give such a speech yourself. Explain what happened. Your side of things. Why you did what you did."

"I don't have to explain myself to anyone."

"But without any word from you, speculation has become far too imaginative."

"*You* give the speech then. I have other matters to worry about."

"I know you've been concerned about this… *magician*. I assure you there's no need."

Chief Arlyn exploded. "A magician? Did you call that diabolic thing a *magician*?" He froze, alarmed at himself for getting so emotional. More calmly, he said, "He was a sorcerer. A real one. Incredibly dangerous."

Khuyag appeared unfazed, though he swept his

eyes around the room as if searching for a way out. "You still fear this warlock," he said, half-question. "I thought you killed him."

"I did," Arlyn said, his voice even lower, suddenly exhausted. "But he will return for his revenge on me. I have no doubt of it."

His military head crossed his arms and grimaced. Arlyn could see him mulling over the right words to use. "Pardon my ignorance, Chief," Khuyag said, "but that doesn't make sense. If you killed him…"

Arlyn stood and went to the hole in the wall, the same hole through which he'd pushed the warlock Seelskan. The chief gazed down at the spot where the warlock had fallen, only to vanish moments later.

"He's dead, but he's still a threat," Arlyn explained. "Men like him, you can't just kill them."

Khuyag carefully examined his nails. "So, you've been planning a defense…from a ghost?"

"I underestimated Seelskan. Or misunderstood. The warlock wasn't looking to conquer and rule. He genuinely wanted to kill every man, woman, and child of Jyn and start over. The Dark Shulam want to create an entirely new world."

"Yes, according to them, *we're* the evil ones."

An ear-stabbing scream sent both men to the floor with their fingers plugging their ears. Khuyag drew his shortsword and rushed to Chief Arlyn's side to protect him. A purplish-green creature landed atop a nearby cathedral buttress. The drakksuk flapped its large, bat-like wings before folding them to its sides.

Its reptilian face carved open into a wide, glistening-red mouth fringed with rows of golden teeth. Its serpentine body was a translucent mass, its circulatory system mostly visible. Arlyn stared frozen at the sight of the drakksuk's heart, a churning shadow inside its narrow ribs.

When the creature flapped its wings again and regained altitude, its entire body turned jet-black. The drakksuk flew west over the kingdom as people cried out below, some running, others falling. There would be no getting used to them. The Cathyrnee had seen what these creatures could do because the evidence lay everywhere. How could you ever trust such an abomination?

"*Joppa*," Arlyn whispered.

A smell reached his nose, stirred skyward by the creature's wings. The chief knew that smell—burning bodies. Burnt human muscle emitted an aroma like beef and fat in a frying pan, the iron-rich blood like copper. Months after the attack, bodies were still being discovered under the rubble, then piled for burning.

A knock at the door made Arlyn cry out, his nerves shattered with raw agitation. "Enter!" he shouted.

The door still ajar, a Cathyrnee warrior walked in. Arlyn recognized him as a captain from the pair of red circles painted with plaster onto his forehead. The warrior bowed. "Queen Abika has been found," he said.

"Alive?"

"She was hiding in an underground waterway."

"Bring her to me."

The captain made a small sound in his throat. He would no longer look at Arlyn. He breathed heavily, winded from either the stairs or what he had to say. "They killed her," he monotoned.

The chief licked his lips. "Who did?"

"A group of warriors. They dragged her out." The captain swallowed hard. "They sodomized her with a dagger."

Chief Arlyn backstepped and collapsed back into the chair. "Anything left of her?"

"Her head."

Arlyn raised his own head, still attached. He touched it to make sure. "Do they still have it?"

The captain nodded. "They do have it, yes. They've brought it for you."

Khuyag stiffened. "Keep it out of here. Get rid of it."

All Chief Arlyn could do was shake his head. What had he turned his people into?

"By the gods, yes," he whispered, "keep it out of here."

But the captain was already gone. The two men left in the room stared at the closed door.

"And that's why the drakksuk don't attack us," Arlyn said to Khuyag. The chief set his elbows on the arms of the chair and let his hands dangle from the ends.

"Because we're the same, *ha'wiih*?"

"Actually, I do believe we might be worse." Chief Arlyn thought about it and nodded. "Yes, we are much worse.

3

SARNA

Her vision filled with a deep and blue liquid. She saw blue trees. There were blue hills. Luca still lay on the ground while looking up at her. And what a sight she must've been! A smoldering energy pulsed from her eye sockets. She felt ablaze with energy, but it wasn't enough. She wanted to glow brighter. Allow her light to swallow the world and evaporate all aggressors. Devour the darkness plaguing life, then enlarge herself further. Always further. Increased in strength until she was no longer human, but a pure essence of love so beautiful with intensity, yet terrible in its heat. She wanted to embrace the universe as she chewed it to pieces. Sarna had lost control, and she welcomed it, savoring energy from the chaos.

She floated in a sizzling sphere of blue sparks, nearly twelve feet off the ground now.

Luca shielded his face as he got to his feet. He said her name. He shouted it, but she couldn't hear him. Threads of visible static crackled from the bottoms of her feet. Her hair stuck out from her head in an affrighted globe.

A small voice inside her head pleaded with her to hold back. Come back to him. She'd been floating up there for hours. If she went large as she wanted, there might be no turning back. Yet the temptation for such an impulse was mighty. Conflicting thoughts piled on her. She should vaporize this pathetic, stupid man. He wouldn't let go of her. Luca kept prohibiting her from her destined path. He'd kidnapped her, ripping her away from her home and family, snuffing out any chance she might've had to protect them, or at least die with them. Luca had also been physically abusive towards her. And he'd caused her to lose sight of Lalya! He'd even stolen Sarna away from the Magshaa and his teachings. Thanks to him, her days of confusion and helplessness were endlessly extended. All because of this uneducated, brutish thug who believed he had a right to her. Sarna decided she would be manhandled and manipulated, not one minute more.

"Please," Luca said, though she had to read his lips, "where are you? What's happening?"

"I didn't ask for this," she wanted to say, but when she opened her mouth, a blast cone of gelatinous air rammed Luca back to the ground. He rolled. His arm twisted into an odd angle, only loosely connected. He came to a rest on his stomach, face down. When he turned his head, she saw his face had changed into her father's—King Khilji. She held him in her mercy, but it was a hollow feeling. King Khilji returned to his feet, never taking his eyes off her. He grinned, except he had no teeth. His mouth opened until his head peeled inside-out, and his visage became the exposed fleshy tunnel of his throat.

The background distended, and Sarna lowered slowly. The terrain behind her father ranged from hilly to mountainous. A panhandle of grass stretched northward, another eastward. An icy breeze kissed the bridge of her nose. She felt the crackle of burnt leaves beneath her feet as she landed.

It was no longer her father standing there, but Luca again. Seeing the fear still in his eyes, she couldn't help but pity him. Their union had not been without pleasure. He had been an important teacher in his own way. He'd taught her wilderness survival. He'd introduced her to her own body. These were lessons she'd never been allowed, and likely never would've otherwise. She was at least grateful to him for this and always would be.

She took a few steps and touched his face. He smiled at her. He appeared to be greatly relieved by her gentle touch until a vine of fluorescent light left her fingertips and entered the muscles of his face. His brow compressed with pain. He screamed as his face liquified. His arms flailed, but he could do nothing to stop what was happening. Chunks of flesh dropped like wet clay, collecting at his knees. Ringlets of white smoke sprang from his hair as his head caved in.

Sarna loved him in a way. He was her teacher, her tormentor, her first lover—evaporated until no other part of him existed, except the hand she was holding. She brought the severed hand closer to her face, noticed the bloody, smoking end of it, the exposed bone, and singed meat. Coming back to herself, she screamed and flung the appendage into the high grass. She hugged her stomach and tried to throw up, but her stomach was empty. She heaved, but it was useless. Sarna straightened and checked around for Luca, the wind blowing her hair around her face, rather unhelpfully. She was alone in the exact middle of nowhere.

ULAAN

Ulaan awoke. The bright, late morning sun lit up her cabin bedroom, reflecting off its stone walls. She raised her head from her pillow.

She turned, then held still. Incredibly, the spirit still slept next to her. He lay on his stomach, facing away. His muscle-wrapped shoulder blades swelled gently with each breath. His wavy dark locks covered his neck. She marveled at his basic physical presence. So odd to witness that even a powerful spirit required sleep. A dream world with which to interpret the real one. She would've never expected it.

As if sensing her eyes on him, he opened his own and looked at her. The instant intensity there made Ulaan squirm and sit up. She planted her back against her bamboo headboard.

"Was that a dream last night?" she asked him.

He cleared his throat. "Which part?"

"All of it? The past few months? Where have you been?"

He leveled his eyes at her. "Waiting for the dust to settle," he said. "This realm has suffered."

She tried to read his face but saw only a handsome young man with long black hair. She admired his chin and jawline, so angular yet symmetrical. His body was statuesque and nearly hairless. He resembled someone more fit for a painting or statue than here in her bed.

"I was sleeping last night," she said, "then I woke up, and you're there. Out of nowhere. Who are you?"

The spirit used his elbows to scoot up, and he joined her in sitting against the headboard. He hugged his left knee. "I'll leave if you want."

"Of course not. I just don't fully understand what you're expecting from me. You are Baal, no?"

Again, he gave her those narrow eyes, green as glass and deep as crystal. She remembered the first time she'd seen those eyes, while fleeing the carnage. Here was the same man who had kept appearing over every hill as she ran, smiling at her, saying her name like he'd known her since birth. She didn't know where else to go, so she went back to life on the farm. Was just getting comfortable with it again. Next she knew, she lay naked in her bed, this man moving in and out of her while she pressed the insides of her legs against his hips, vibrating from the ecstasy of his movements. Her fingers had dug within his hair, pulling him to go harder. As she neared orgasm, in her head she heard the screeching of those flying monsters, the last desperate wails of people as they burned alive.

And now it was morning. Like that. The next day. Another one. The entire realm and her world within it were completely changed, but it didn't much feel like it.

"What are you?" she asked him. "Be straight with me. You're not a person."

"You know what I am."

She snorted. "I honestly do not."

"Don't say that." The spirit tilted his head back, looking down his nose at her. He touched her chin. "I'm going to need you, Ulaan."

"I rather doubt that. Why would someone such as you need me?"

"Because I love you, Ulaan. And I was summoned here to help you. To help everyone. I exist for nothing else."

She leaned away from his touch. She looked him up and down. "I've never met an angel, but I'm still fairly sure they don't look like you."

The spirit frowned. He scratched his collarbone

thoughtfully. "I'm not an angel, no. But I am the savior."

"Funny. That's what The Magshaa used to tell us."

"And where is he now?" The spirit laughed, incredulous, then sauntered to the nearest window. He parted the curtain with a finger, taking in a partial view of the eastern farmyard. He sighed as though he meant to say something more, but he didn't.

"Where do you come from?" Ulaan asked him. "Can you at least tell me that much?"

"Why should that matter?" He turned his attention back inside. When they met eyes again, he laughed. "All that matters is that I'm here, and I'm going to make everything better."

"The Magshaa warned us you were coming," she said. "About how you were invited here. Conjured. It was Chief Arlyn."

The spirit dropped his hand, deflated at hearing the name. "Chief Arlyn is a good man. You're going to get to meet him, actually."

Ulaan lifted her robe from the floor. "Everyone I know is dead." After getting both arms into their sleeves, she tucked her body inside the robe, tying the cloth belt around her waist. "Thanks to you."

"Those Ghe-sui needed to die," he said, calm and even. "They're greedy and petty. They're hoarders of magic, and you're better than them, Ulaan." He reached over and took her hand in his. He kissed the back of it, but she remained facing away. "Look, Jyn has become nothing more than a land controlled by corrupt monarchs who live off the backs of the people they starve."

"And what do you do so differently with your fire and death and monsters?"

"I use the tools I have, Ulaan. Think you can save the world with speeches and gifts?" The spirit sidestepped, placing himself in front of her. He touched her chin again. "I am truly going to need your help."

"I won't help you kill people."

"I wouldn't dare ask that." He grimaced and shook his head, wounded by her words. "What kind of monster do you believe me to be?"

"The Magshaa told us you were here to destroy the world."

"Of course, he would say that." He touched her forearm, and a warmth spread throughout her body like a sedative.

He moved a strand of her hair around her ear, and she wished to remain inside this small, serene moment for eternity. His jewel-green eyes beheld the entirety of who she was within a heartbeat, and he loved her for it. Adored her. She had never experienced another person looking at her like that. She craved more of it. And more and more.

"How could I possibly help you?" she whispered. "I am nothing."

He kissed her hand again, letting his lips linger. A depthless darkness spread from his mouth and swallowed the room. Ulaan felt herself outside this universe, breaststroking across a shimmering landscape.

She felt a sudden spiritual breakthrough, a greater understanding of existence and her place in it. Her love spread outside the cottage, reaching the trees, the wet soil, the plants, the animals. She didn't only love them: She *was* them. They were connected, each of them part of a single being. A great battery. She felt saved. Protected. How had he done that so easily?

"Ulaan," said the spirit, "you are far from nothing. Go look at yourself."

"What do you mean?"

He nudged his chin at the small mirror atop her wooden cabinet, the only item of furniture in the room apart from the bed. She wasn't in the habit of keeping many mirrors around her cottage, especially as her appearance had begun to deteriorate from using the Sünsü so much. She'd done this all for the sake of her Highness Queen Saraal and her endless need for fortune-telling.

"You want me to go look in that mirror?" she asked. "What for?"

"Don't be scared. Just go."

She held still. She grew nervous. Though it'd been days, her last few mirrored glimpses of herself had revealed the full damage she'd inflicted on her appearance. Her own image frightened her. The Sünsü always took what it gave, so the Burnya Queen's demands on her had sapped her soul, aging Ulaan terribly.

She heard the farm outside. It was spring, the season of new life. Normally, she would've been milking the cows about this time, tending to the sheep. There was gardening to be done. Potatoes and corn to pick. Water to pump, manure to clean. She sat there and stared at the mirror, but it wasn't large enough or close enough to see anything.

"Do it." The spirit nudged her with his elbow. "Go look at yourself. I want to see your reaction."

After a long breath, Ulaan went to the mirror, prepared for anything but what she saw.

4

KING MONTROSE

The King of Burnya stared at the intricate, crystal chandelier dangling above his head. He considered the ramifications of its suspension unraveling, the whole contraption plunging onto him, glass and brass slicing and stabbing his body and face. The barbed spindles beneath each candleholder would undoubtedly puncture his torso in several places, the weight of the chandelier smashing his bones, caving his face in.

Thoughts of calamity pleased him, distracted him from the ceaseless shame he felt. An entire kingdom in flames, his Queen incinerated before his eyes, masses of people turned into black ash, the sweet, pungent smell of charcoaled flesh. The king rarely slept anymore.

The royal bedroom he occupied held black walls trimmed with white borders, matched by the white bedding. Tall flowers with shield-sized petals drooped from golden planters positioned in each corner.

Occasionally, Montrose called for subjects to be brought in, whom he would subsequently torture. Watching his guards inflict cruelty on the innocent and helpless improved his mood—a sublimation of the shame he suffered. Though he had survived the attack on Tartaria during King Khilji's funeral, Montrose was far from unscathed. After finding him amid the chaos, Chief Arlyn had Montrose marched back to his kingdom naked, the message "Love Me" written in mud across his large belly. This followed Chief Arlyn commanding that Montrose surrender the Kingdom of Burnya. The Cathyrnee Chief and his army of beasts and monsters would be coming for them next, except that was over four months ago.

Naturally, King Montrose returned home and did no such thing. Once inside the safety of his kingdom walls, he had the Cathyrnee warriors captured and executed, an action much celebrated by his people, galvanized by their king's defiance. No one could threaten their home and get away with it! Their mighty king certainly wouldn't allow it. The Cathyrnee would pay dearly for the humiliation they had made their king suffer.

However, they hadn't seen what he had seen. They

stood little chance against a horde of flesh-eating creatures who could fly, or what other supernatural beasts might be launched at them. It was hopeless. The end was near. He wasn't even sure what they were waiting for.

Lying there, King Montrose decided that he couldn't stand to be alone anymore. He wanted Ozyan back. He could still smell her hair on his pillow, like some fragrant wooded plant. If he couldn't have his Queen, he at least wanted someone to spend his last days with. Wallowing in the shadows of doom, the king repressed thoughts of how much physical damage his chandelier might inflict on him. He decided instead that all he wanted anymore was love. Yes, by the gods, he wanted his favorite mistress back.

"Enter," King Montrose snarled at the sound of someone lightly tapping the bedroom door. A pair of teenage girls stood shivering and naked at the foot of his bed, cowering at what he might order them to do next.

Artemis walked in. He paused at the sight of his king with two young girls hiding their nakedness with their arms. The younger of the two fluttered her eyelids, as though seconds away from fainting.

"My Lord," asked Artemis, a surprised lilt to his voice, "what are you doing?"

"Fuck it all," Montrose growled, "gawking like you've never seen this before. Go away!"

The Master of Gold cleared his throat. He folded his

arms behind him and rolled on the balls of his feet. "Am I to understand that you want the money to reinforce our defenses?"

"Artemis! Do I look like I'm in the mood to discuss economics right now?"

"Not in the slightest, My Lord, but what you're wanting to carry out will require a fortune." Artemis looked at the girls, torn between helping them and addressing this larger picture at hand. "Unfortunately, Burnya has an outstanding debt more than six times the annual crown revenue with interest rates far above what you seem capable of managing, My Lord."

"Either suck my fat cock or get out. I would murder you if you stood closer."

"With Tartaria destroyed," Artemis continued, nonplussed, his eyes still locked on the two young girls, "our wool exports are stopped, and local market rates have plummeted. Our banks were already weakened as it was. The only reason Burnya hasn't collapsed already is because of loans secured by physical goods. With import duties and estate—"

"Not another word!" King Montrose jabbed his finger at the door. "And don't ever come back talking this nonsense to me. Not even once."

Artemis instead crossed the bedroom to an armoire by the eastern window. "My Lord, a banking crisis when we're on the verge of an invasion leaves us quite vulnerable."

He removed a pair of hemp blankets from the armoire, appearing to know they were already there. Artemis walked the blankets over to the girls who snatched them and covered themselves, still shivering.

Montrose rolled onto his side. "Print more money then. Problem solved. There. Was that hard?"

"The annual production of coins is simply to pay the army," Artemis replied. "Once they've finished defending the kingdom, you can debase the coinage. That's what Tartaria did."

"And how well did that turn out for them?" King Montrose sat up and noticed the girls staring at him, their eyes wide and wet with absolute horror. He yanked a ruby-encrusted ring from his index finger. He removed every ring from every finger, overhanding the rings onto the floor where they bounced and rolled between Artemis and the two girls. "King Khilji threw himself out a window!"

Neither girl moved. The room was silent.

Artemis recrossed the bedroom and opened the door. Without an encouraging word to do so, the girls fled through the door and were gone.

"Find Ozyan," said King Montrose. "Bring her back to me."

"That handmaiden?"

"You know who I'm talking about."

"May I ask why?"

"Because I want her. I want her standing in front of me. Today."

Artemis nodded his head slowly and smirked. He

remained at the door. "Will this calm your mind and help you focus at last, My Lord? Stop you from kidnapping young girls from the street?"

"I'm their king."

"Keep abusing the populace, and they're likely to stop believing you're so wonderful."

"I want Ozyan here before sundown."

"I will personally see that it gets done." Artemis performed a full bow. While bent, he noticed a ring on the floor. He lifted the ring and tested its weight in his hand. "You have my word on it."

Artemis gave the king another exaggerated bow, and he left the room.

SARNA

She flew. She made sure not to look down, nervous from the great distance between her and the rolling hills beneath her. Her arms held straight out, she maneuvered the wind with an agility graceful in its simplicity. She kept her body parallel as she planed with enough speed to feel weightless. Movements as subtle as shrugging or pointing her toes to stretch her feet carried a significant impact on her speed. Sarna was in complete control, experiencing what should have been the purest form of serenity. Instead, she began sobbing. She was freezing.

Surprisingly, this increased her speed. The friction of air against her body made it into an even harder surface. She redirected the wind across her torso and descended. Sarna steadied her hands out and landed softly on her feet, the wet soil mushing between each toe. She looked around at where she found herself. A wavy carpet of green hills stretched into the far distance. The land and sky lay separated by a jagged line of mountains.

She wiped her nose and gathered her wits the best she could. Her royal education had taught her enough to know that the Kholm Mountains lay west. Keeping them in sight would lead her in the general direction of Burnya. That was the goal anyway.

After coming to terms with the fact that Luca was nowhere to be seen because she had murdered him, Sarna had flown away, launching herself skyward, propelled by the angst, regret, and confusion pulsing through her nerves. She had killed Luca. Like he was nothing. Smothered out with no more fanfare than an insect.

She walked. She hugged her elbows and tried to recover from the frosty, elevated air, which had left her skin pimpled. However, after only a few meters of the sharp twig and pebble-strewn ground punishing the bottoms of her feet, she decided to take flight again. Too many thoughts here on the ground. Too many dangers. She needed to flee. She held her arms out and inwardly commanded the magic energy to launch skywards again.

Nothing happened. Keeping her arms out, she concentrated for several minutes on retaking flight yet remained where she stood. The power had abandoned her. She was still freezing, so she dropped her arms to hug herself again. Sarna realized she was starving. She had not only flown away from the scene of Luca's death, but from their food and supplies. She had also left the horse behind.

She rubbed her eyes. She tried focusing on the act of flying once more. She went onto her tiptoes like this might help if she only stood tall enough. She went nowhere.

From a thick patch of undergrowth to her right, she heard a growl. She ran away, and the prairie grass whipped her knees and thighs. The lavender sky ahead of her resembled a velvet screen pockmarked in crystals. The twin moons shone dull like the murky orbs of a toad, the smaller moon now partially eclipsing the larger.

She grew tired and slowed to a trot, then walked. She kept glancing over her shoulder to check if she was being chased. She walked for so long that she lost track of time, and the balls of her feet became inflamed. She had no memory of how she'd lost her sandals, possibly while flying. Without the cushioning of decent footwear, walking barefoot proved increasingly brutal.

At the base of the distant mountains, Sarna thought she could make out a faint brightness to the northwest, so she headed in that direction. Caught in a carapace of shock, fear, and exhaustion, Sarna kept this faraway light as her only objective anymore.

5

SHAYAN

Nightfall and his sinuses still burned with the acrid, toxic scent of burning wood mixed with roasted flesh. From behind his lids, the brightness intensified. He opened his eyes and saw flames devouring the canopy of tree branches above him. He lay surrounded by black, the entire area incinerated. Among the charcoal lay his dead reconnaissance party, a few of their bodies fused together. The king found his feet and checked for the quickest path to safety. He spotted none whatsoever—only dark pillars of chalky smoke, enough to smother out the moons and turn the stars bloody.

He could no longer hear or see the drakksuk, which he didn't take to be a good thing. He needed shelter immediately, yet he stood where he was, still dazed from the ferocity of the earlier attack. The charged air made breathing difficult. He resisted the urge to lie down again. To fall unconscious and sleep away the stress.

The sky screamed. He knew without looking that the drakksuk had spotted him. He had only seconds to save himself. Maybe less.

Shayan noticed a high hill to the north, capped with stony embankments. It appeared unscorched, but it was too hard to tell from below. And it didn't matter. There was simply nowhere else to run. He took off, not looking back because he could hear its wings. He felt the massive suction of air as the creature closed in, and there was nothing he could do about it. Nothing except run and wait for the end.

"Your Highness!" The voice came from his right.

It was one of the elder farmers. Next to him ran one of the teenagers, likely his grandson. Or someone's. They had appeared from behind a wall of granite boulders. The grandson reached Shayan first. He embraced him by looping his right arm around his king's neck, nearly knocking them both over. Shayan shouted at him to let go, but the elder farmer caught up. He tugged on Shayan's tunic, and together they dragged him towards their hiding spot. An enormous shadow blocked out the moons. As the creature plunged by, the farmer and his grandson shoved Shayan beyond the rocks. Their hiding spot was a shallow cave, barely formed by the slightest, water-warped groove within the granite.

Shayan planted his feet and stiffened his legs, resisting their push. However, he was too weak from the smoke he'd inhaled while running. They were able to hold him.

"You'll burn," he tried shouting, but his voice wasn't there. He wheezed instead, then choked.

Shayan stopped fighting them. He looked at the teenager's feet behind his own. He fixated on the kid's knee-high shoes laced around the front, revealing him as a common villager.

"You're going to both die," Shayan managed to squeak. "You should've stayed hidden."

"Our mission is to protect you, Your Highness," said the old man. He stood hunched, his arms like bowed sticks, weaponless.

This was suicide. How could they protect him? The three of them were cornered. The man and his grandson had revealed their hiding spot and would now die for it. Shayan wanted to yell at them more for being so stupid, throwing their lives away over some misguided sense of loyalty. Because their lives simply were not worth as much. He noticed the pair were singed in numerous spots, blistered everywhere. Shayan felt certain he appeared every bit as pitiful. The kid visibly trembled, his entire body detonating with twitches, breaking down from the sudden and persistent closeness of death. Shayan had seen the same look on soldiers during battle. Make a man fight for his ultimate survival long enough, and the stress would demolish his mind.

Noticing them off guard, Shayan shoved his way past the farmer and the teenager. He sprinted for the hill again. Elevated and exposed, Shayan knew it was no time to stop and look behind, but that was exactly what he did. He didn't see the drakksuk anywhere, only a landscape of towering, black plumes, veined in flames. There were also more rocks, but far more scattered now. Up ahead, a dense lump of forest bordered the bottom of the hill.

Another scream pierced his eardrums. The sound was so loud that it rattled between every organ and bone inside Shayan's body. He watched the creature slicing upwards through a lower cloud bank. The drakksuk tucked its wings and nosedived.

Shayan kept running, but the creature was too fast. It rounded the summit and was on him. The king dove and flattened his body against the ground as a cone of energy sprayed from the creature's mouth. The energy, webbed between tree branches, ignited the leaves. The trunks collapsed into burning timber. Large fiery spheres bloomed in every direction, lighting up the sky. Shayan used his back muscles to press his entire body into the soil. He could smell his own hair burning. He heard screaming, which reduced to moaning.

Another familiarity of warfare was knowing what the screams of the dying sounded like. He knew that what he heard was the old man and the kid perishing in fire.

MOMASET

The shaman awoke much later than normal, his fur blankets dampened from the morning dew. His newest disciple lay beside him, her leg hooked over his waist. He grasped her leg gently, nudged it aside. He rose from the bedding and stood a moment to stretch, his fingertips nearly touching the felt-covered ceiling of his hut. He lifted his white robe from atop a low wooden table and put it on before leaving. Outside, the direct sunlight caused him to squint. Shading his eyes, he could make out the rocky hillside below, the land speckled with other huts and tents pitched by his fellow shamans.

Though the Ghe-sui were long ago considered nomadic, this had changed in recent years with the construction of the Magshaa's temple. The Great War had made traveling too hazardous. Now here they lived, driven to exile by the greed and violence of kings and warlocks.

Momaset began each day as he did now—on a ledge above an encampment of the remaining Ghe-sui. He took in the full sight of them. There were at least a hundred still alive, though after so many months of exposure and cold, illness had killed even more of the shamans.

Their diet had become limited. Many seeds taken from former farms along the Magoi River could find no purchase in the low moisture soil of the mountains. Though they were still able to grow carrots, radishes, potatoes, beets, and sweet corn, the harvest was slow. The high winds of the mountain wilted many crops.

He spotted a young female shaman walking up the hill towards him. As she got closer, he saw that she wore a shiny blue tunic, the front apron covered with drawings. The patterns of snakes and lizards revealed she was the young shaman Corsika. In her left hand, she held an oval membrane drum, rimmed in fur and rattling rings.

Corsika was a shaman whose role in the end of their former world was well known to all yet uniformly forgiven. She was never to be blamed, only loved. She had also played a part in invoking the evil spirit Baal, but her intentions had been good. She hadn't known what she was doing. It was the Ghe-sui way to forgive all.

She made it to the foot of the hill, the swell of which rose and became the ledge he stood on. Noticing she was winded, struggling with the climb, he trotted down to meet her. He took her hand and guided her back down a ways until the ground became level enough to stand on.

"It's time for morning prayer," he told her. "We will go together."

"Why are you leading me away? Did someone share your bed with you last night?"

"Yes."

"A woman?"

He laughed. "A woman, yes." He looked at her and noticed the disappointment in the way she lowered her head. "I understand that some of my ways make you uncomfortable, Corsika, but making love with my followers connects me with them. It connected you and me, didn't it? Don't you understand?"

She nodded but still wouldn't look at him.

He tightened his hold on her hand as he resumed leading her downhill, their new makeshift temple coming into view. The front doors faced east while a wide set of stairs led to a spacious porch filled with offerings. The roof held three peaks, with the highest in the middle. "What can I do for you? Tell me."

"You promised me your door was always open to me. To all of us."

"Have I not kept that promise?"

She punched his arm with her drum, and it made a quick, discordant jingle. She stopped him. "Why won't you let me come to your bed anymore?"

"Because there's someone already there. Why would you want to?"

She punched his arm with her drum again, lighter this time. "I need you," she said. "I'm scared."

He placed his arms around her and held her. "Tell me."

"I'm afraid of the punishment that awaits me when I pass from this world. I'm trying my best to forgive myself for what I caused, but how can I go unpunished?" She stepped back. She laced her fingers with his and pulled his hands up to kiss their knuckles.

"Please, help me. Please."

"Dearest Corsika, this world is only a school for our souls' development. The spirit world holds no punishment for anyone."

"Is that why there's so much evil?"

"Evil is only the conscious overshadowed by impulse. Those who do evil will spend their afterlife repairing their energy. And they will do so for as long as it takes."

"Then how do you explain someone like King Montrose?"

"Some souls get damaged beyond repair. The only solution is to return the soul to its source, stripping away its identity. It's an extremely rare situation."

She laughed, a childish titter. "You are so wise. How do you know all this?"

"I have seen it, Corsika." He took her other hand, leading her in the direction of the temple again. "I have even seen my own death."

"Old age, I trust?"

"No, I will be killed in Burnya."

She stopped, all her mirth instantly drained. "You know this?"

"Unquestionably."

"Then why go?"

"It is my path."

She shook her head. "Let us help each other," she said, her voice hushed. "I know you're trying to be the Magshaa and sacrifice yourself, but you're not the Magshaa. Don't be. Don't get killed, too."

He felt certain her words were not meant to be as insulting as they sounded, but they stung all the same. He responded by hugging Corsika again, tighter this time. "You are one of my most treasured disciples."

"No, you are the treasure, my love."

Momaset broke the embrace and placed an arm around her. They resumed downhill. "But not everyone is on my side."

"Most are. And they would die to protect you."

"They?"

"We."

They passed a pair of shamans who bowed. A third shaman stood from milking his goat to bow as well. Afterward, the three shamans followed Momaset and Corsika towards the temple.

"You feel bonded with me because I've made you more yourself," he explained to her. "I've removed every false idea you had, Corsika, every wrong emotion that was hurting you."

Every shaman they passed fell in line behind them. An old woman looked up from where she knelt on the ground. When he made eye contact with her, she clamped her hands together in prayer and began weeping. Having their world taken away, even people of magic were left defeated and malleable.

The shamans chanted his name. He and Corsika halted from the growing size of the crowd around them. Hands reached out to Momaset from every direction. Soon, the uneven force of everyone shoving to get closer created a swaying current of bodies. To alleviate the pressure of feeling trapped, he jumped up and down. The impromptu celebration was entirely unexpected, but he accepted it. He lifted his hands and flapped them, gesturing for all to join him, which they did. The shamans mimicked him by jumping joyously until they were dancing, caught in a feverish, euphoric trance.

Corsika beat her drum in rhythm to their chanting. His name became a song.

Enshrouded by dancing shamans, Momaset reflected deep within and considered that he could be the new Magshaa after all. How else to explain this common outpouring of spiritual agreement? This collective belief in him? Though many of the Ghe-sui had perished, still many felt Momaset had shown them hope. His speeches galvanized those who were younger and fuller of fight. They looked up to him.

The shamans danced for so long it became the entirety of Momaset's sermon, this physical gyration of transcendence and freedom. They were alive. They were the strongest among them. They would make it.

On a bounce that took him above most of their heads, Momaset caught a glimpse of three elders, watching nearby. One wore the headdress of a deer, the middle shaman a wolf, and the third a bear with antlers. Their footwear matched with deer hooves, claws, and bears' paws. They observed the sudden celebration with an unmistakably high degree of concern, especially the wolf.

Momaset smiled and waved on the next bounce. The elders averted their eyes and turned their backs.

ULAAN

She could not look away. Within the small, brass-framed mirror she held, an entirely new Ulaan stared back at her. Instead of sagging cheeks, bulging neck, and dark-ringed eyes, she saw high cheeks, a slender neck, and cat's eyes rounded by a waterfall of jet-black hair. She was a goddess!

She looked down and saw her body transformed into a firm hourglass of nude, glossy-brown skin. She trailed her fingertips along her hips and belly, enjoying their smoothness. She cupped her breasts.

"You did this?" she asked the spirit standing behind her.

"Are you happy?"

"I don't have the words."

"See what I can do for you, Ulaan? Look at yourself! How could someone who's supposed to be so evil conjure such beauty?"

"I never said you were evil."

"You didn't have to. I know the Magshaa has brainwashed you. Would he have done this for you?"

"I never asked him to."

"He was destroying you, Ulaan. The Ghe-sui are selfish, and they're cowards. They're a fake religion."

"Fake?" She couldn't tear her eyes from her reflection. "No, I don't know about that."

"They're so convinced they're the only authority on truth. That they're the only ones deserving of power. They worship and serve themselves and no one else."

Stunned and dazzled, she meandered to her dusty, wooden dress stand. She lifted her burgundy farm dress from there. She pulled it over her head, then turned to face him. "Is this the way everyone sees me?" she asked him.

Baal closed his eyes and nodded wearily. "This is who you were all along. I only brought it out of you."

He smiled, and she dissolved, lost in the serenity of that perfect face—yet she couldn't help it. She also felt dread. Everything about this spirit-man was too good. He wasn't real. He was Baal—a being manifested from the underworld. A being whose name wasn't even permitted to be spoken at the Magshaa Temple. Ulaan suspected she might've been dreaming, having either lost her mind or become trapped in a spell far more encompassing than merely appearing beautiful suddenly. This could've been a dark, delirious fantasy for which she would later be punished. The value of vanity was always fleeting. Still— why did power always have to be about servitude and responsibility? Perhaps, as he'd said, this was simply the person she was always meant to be.

Maybe Baal was right about the Magshaa having repressed this warrior-witch goddess she saw in the mirror. Wasn't it obvious he'd wanted all the power to himself, that universal desire of all men, no matter how holy?

No! No more shame. No more servitude. No more weakness. This was where she belonged.

"What do I do?" she asked. "I am yours."

"No, no, no, you belong to no one," he told her. "Isn't that what you've always wanted?"

"I want freedom, yes."

"And that's what I'm here to deliver. It's the only thing I want for everyone. It's why I was called to Jyn in the first place. For the salvation of its people." He closed the gap between them, and Ulaan couldn't help but back up, taken aback by his height. Baal moved with a grace and swiftness bordering on hallucinatory. A bluish blur trailed his movements. He took her hand and placed it over his penis.

"What are you?" she whispered. "You're not real."

"I'm you, Ulaan. You are the reflection, but I'm the original."

"An angel who shepherds monsters that incinerate people?"

He rolled his eyes, barked a short laugh. "I'm the first person you've ever met who fully understands you, and you know it. The Magshaa understood you, but in a more fatherly way. You and I are soulmates." He lowered his head, but kept his eyes connected with hers. He ran his hand through the side of her hair, fluffing it, as though admiring his work. The hand moved to her shoulder, and he kissed her forehead. "I will use my powers with yours to achieve your potential."

"I'm old enough to know there's always a high price for such power."

"As you've been raised and trained to believe, sadly. The only price is an unfrustrated life in a beautiful world of never-ending peace." The spirit Baal walked around behind her. She waited for his arms to enclose her, but when that didn't happen, she turned to find him at the window again. She heard her farm outside, the workers shouting to each other, the thoughtless muttering of pigs and chickens.

"The Ghe-sui have allowed you to make your weaknesses part of your innate spiritual identity," Baal said. "But what you see in the mirror is not just you, but you as a whole. I'm delighted I could do this for you." He touched the window's glass. "I want you to go outside and show those men who you are now. Do it for me."

"What do you mean?"

She knew exactly what he meant. Modesty made her ashamed of the idea, but she also felt obligated to do as he wished. Ulaan left the bedroom and went to the front door of her cottage. She opened it.

Ulaan expected all activity to stop, but it didn't. The herding of animals with the tilling of land for harvesting and seeding occurred unabated. Not even the chickens noticed her.

She spotted her head rancher, Lomen. He stopped digging a garden row to wipe his forehead. Lomen had worked on the farm for as long as she could recall. He'd been like an uncle to her when she was much younger. She knew he would see her first. He always had. He went back to digging.

Ulaan stepped back into the cottage. She found her vegetable-tanned goat skin shoes and slipped them on. For extra warmth against the morning chill, she covered herself with a blanket stuffed with rabbit fur. She entered the farmyard, holding her head up. After only a few feet, several ranch hands noticed her. They stopped working and stood, skirting her notion that Lomen would see her first. She walked in a straight line towards him anyway. The other men blinked at her. A couple of them dropped their tools.

Noticing the lack of movement or noise around him, Lomen looked up. He saw her. "Ulaan?"

"You recognize me?"

"I...I don't know. It's you, no?"

The workers did not appear pleased, as she had anticipated. They appeared mortified, scared witless by whatever witchcraft they were witnessing.

"Everything is all right," she told them. She lowered her voice. "Lomen, tell them to stop looking at me like that."

"I think they're...they're confused."

She frowned. "I scare you? Don't be scared."

"Times are dark, miss. A lot of these men had relatives in Tartaria."

Ulaan laughed. "But a fresh, beautiful world is coming to all of us." She bundled the blanket tighter around herself. She turned to address the other workers. "You should rejoice in what you see! A better life is coming."

A dog barked from the far side of the farmyard. Everyone turned to see a Bankhar dog sprinting towards them. The canine, bred as a livestock guardian, closely resembled her old dog Noknok. Sadly, she'd been forced to kill the pet when he'd mysteriously attacked her. As this dog came closer, she saw he had a large, star-shaped spot on his side, exactly as Noknok once had. This dog was him, except that was impossible. Her dog was dead.

The men mumbled in fear and backed up.

Ulaan could see Noknok wasn't running to attack them. No, this was his happy bark. She felt momentarily overjoyed. Her beloved Noknok was still alive! The dog came directly to her, the animal caked in mud from where he'd been buried. Noknok's eyes and mouth glowed red, as though his innards were made of magma. A fractured bone punctured the skin of his neck, grotesquely tenting it. His skin was gray and patchy, missing hair in places, skin in others.

She kneeled to embrace him anyway. Noknok had always been there for her. He'd served as the most enthusiastic, giving, loving friend she'd ever had. Her bond with him was massive. Ulaan had nearly grieved as much for Noknok's death as she had for her own husband's.

The dead dog lapped at her hands.

Ulaan only looked up when she heard her ranch hands running away. Speechless, they sprinted for the road that led over a hill. The dead dog jumping against her leg, she stood and watched as they fled the farm, even Lomen. Some lost their hats but didn't stop to retrieve them.

A smaller band of workers wandered up, having arrived from further out in the field. They had seen the other farmhands fleeing and had understandably come to find out what had happened.

"Don't be afraid," she told them, keeping her voice as warm and benign as she knew how. "It's all going to be okay. It'll be wonderful. Our world is going to be so much better. Be happy."

The men collectively spotted something over her shoulder. She turned to see Baal standing in the doorway of her cottage, nude, his brown skin glistening in the morning light. Noknok barked, and his lower jaw dropped off, so the dog's bark became a winded but guttural bellow.

Ulaan turned back around. The last of the men follow the rest, passing from sight over the hill.

She understood them. She had to. The new appearance. A zombie dog. It was a lot to take in. But they would understand someday. She was sure of it. Everyone would.

Baal gestured for her to return inside. The sight of him warmed her to her core. She walked towards him, exhilarated by how quickly her old life had been extinguished.

Besides, she thought, she'd outgrown the farm anyway.

6

CHIEF ARLYN

Early morning, Chief Arlyn walked along the crowded street, accompanied by two thick-plated guards with longswords. This created a six-meter-wide wedge through the people as they pushed in, fighting to get a glimpse of their leader. As determined as he'd been to leave the castle, he felt nervous now. It was the first time in almost two months he'd been seen among the Cathyrnee, his people.

He wasn't sure what type of reaction he'd anticipated once recognized, but this wasn't it. After initially spotting him, they appeared nothing less than gobsmacked, halting in whatever activity they were doing, then approaching in droves. Some wanted to yell at him, while others simply wanted to touch him. It created an odd mix of idol worship and rage.

Chief Arlyn normally felt empowered by crowds, especially those coming in so close, but this crowd confused him. No one smiled. Few made eye contact. When he reached an intersection packed with shopping tents and vegetable carts, he ordered his guards to halt. He went forward without them. Arlyn figured the optics of having guards were antagonistic. Let the people loose, and they would back off.

They did not back off. The people crowded in on him tightly. Some chanted his name. Others shouted at him, mere centimeters from his face. He shoved at them. He checked over his shoulder. He saw that many from the courtyard were still following, while more people pressed in. He looked for his guards but could no longer see them. The Cathyrnee Chief shoved his way forward until the crowd parted, split by a small bread shop. Next to the shop stood three warriors, each holding salted fish and a small swath of dark oat bread. More than a dozen empty babsulisk bottles lay at their feet. Even more stood propped on a bench.

Chief Arlyn could see in the faces of these men that they had been waiting daily for him to show his face. Multitudes of soldiers and commoners had sought an audience with him over their problems, and he had declined them all. Now he would be forced to suffer them all at once.

The tallest warrior was shirtless and bald. His chin sprouted a thin beard braided into sections. His chest was tattooed with ancient Cathyrnee script, the ink likely made from bark and eggs.

"Ha'wiih," the warrior said. The man bowed and curtsied in an exaggerated manner, making fun of it. "So delighted to learn of your resurrection. Done with making spells, we hope?"

Arlyn unsheathed his sword. "How dare you take that tone with me."

The warrior gazed at the tip of Arlyn's sword and shook his head sadly. "You used to be my hero. Since I was a boy. I actually used to pretend I was you."

"I've let you down, have I?" Arlyn met every eye around him that he could. "What exactly is so offensive to some of you? The safe home? The availability of food? You're only alive because of me!"

A scattered cheer went up but was soon replaced with discontented murmuring.

"That so?" asked the smaller of the three warriors. He used his remaining two upper teeth to bite into his fish before tossing the bones into a pile, already seething with flies. "When are we invading Burnya? How many more of us do you intend on getting killed?"

Chief Arlyn went to speak but was caught without words. He felt astonished that news of his plans would've spread already, except of course it had. People were perpetually bonded by big news, especially when it involved a worrisome future.

The tallest warrior stepped forward. "Thanks to you, we stand here conquerors of a destroyed kingdom. Allied with demons. With beasts! And we're supposed to thank you for this?"

"The Chotgor are not beasts," Chief Arlyn said. "They are living beings exactly like us. They only want what we want. Peace and health."

"Peace?" asked the third warrior, the oldest, his white beard and sideburns still flecked with black. His facial tattoos were faded and green, dented with wrinkles. He wiped the wet from his mouth. "You claim you want peace, yet you prepare us for war. Which is it, *ha'wiih*?"

"The Chotgor are raping our women, Chief," added the smaller. He stroked his complicated beard. Arlyn noticed his other hand inching towards the dagger on his belt. "They're savages. They're not like us at all."

Seeing Arlyn's befuddlement, the oldest warrior chortled. "You should get out more often. Have a peek at what's really going on."

Some people laughed but were silenced by Arlyn's glare. "Enlighten me then."

"No one supports more bloodshed. We're done!"

The crowd applauded, apparently more uniform in this opinion.

Arlyn flinched. There was a time when he couldn't have imagined such a collective agreement against him. He supposed backlash was inevitable in any leader's life. He straightened himself, projecting as much confidence as he could manage. "I have led us to victory! I have done what had to be done to protect us. And I will do so until my last breath."

Silence.

"We have witnessed what your victories look like," said the smallest warrior. "Flying creatures who breathe death and savage beasts who now share our world? We're not interested."

Arlyn still addressed the crowd at large. "Do you miss living out on the plains? Being hunted by the yelkin? You prefer the suicides? The disease? Please, tell me which part you miss!"

"We saw women and children burned alive, *ha'wiih*." The taller warrior squinted as he ran his fingers over his bald head. "By siding us with darkness, you have turned us into darkness."

A ripple of agreement spread through the crowd. Chief Arlyn understood he had avoided his people and this confrontation far longer than he should have. He had lost them. "It was war," he said, his voice breaking. "It was either them or us, and I chose us."

He swept his eyes at the mixture of villagers and merchants still surrounding him, again meeting as many eyes as he could. The chief felt cornered and frustrated. He had lost his wife. Lost his best friend. Meanwhile, his people still drew breath, thanks to him. What more could he give?

The warriors each unsheathed their daggers. Arlyn recognized the weapons as being made by the Chotgor. He'd heard from Khuyag that they'd become the favored weapon of most fighting-aged Cathyrnee males. The daggers were cheap, yet sharp enough to slice brick. Though his people didn't wish to mix socially or culturally with these "savages," trading for their advanced weaponry somehow remained permissible.

Arlyn felt a nudge from behind. He resisted the reflex to turn around. Instead, he raised his sword and charged at the three warriors. He tackled the tallest, judging him to be the greatest threat. They crashed together into a small table propped by a cluster of vases. None of the vases broke, but they prevented Arlyn from regaining his feet. All three men dove onto him. Arlyn felt a blade entering his abdomen, then a blazing-sharp pain blasted through every nerve. His body seized from the shock of having a foreign object inserted where no such object belonged. He howled while kicking his legs to free himself, but could only turn onto his stomach, leaving his back exposed. He felt a second blade pierce his left calf. A third blade entered somewhere around his right arm, but he couldn't tell exactly where yet.

OZYAN

She felt a discharge running down her left leg. She stood in the living area of her childhood home and, with the help of her younger sisters, struggled into her chemise. Even after her miscarriage, the weight had stayed on. There was also the occasional discharge.

Ozyan could feel nausea from only *remembering*

that night. The blood-rinsed sheets, so much blood it squished. The cramping in her womb as large clots of tissue spilled out of her. It had happened twelve weeks ago, yet the sickness and pain had only recently subsided. She could only eat bread or rice and felt constantly fatigued. Her breasts ached, swollen from milk glands rendered useless.

Once dressed, she thanked her sisters. She plopped onto a cushion made from folded and piled blankets. Her leg still slick with biofluid, she set about washing green beans, preparing to relieve her mother at the market that afternoon.

The home was made of bamboo with a dirt floor, and its inhabitants were Ozyan, her two sisters, her mother, and both her grandmothers. Everyone slept on mats made from a flat knapsack stuffed with flowers and straw. It was less than ideal, but more than what most had. The death of the Queen, added with the threat of invasion, had sent the kingdom's economy into a panic. Currency stopped moving and, as usual, the lower class was the first to suffer. To support themselves, Ozyan's family sold potatoes, cabbage, and green beans at the central market but ended up eating most of the produce themselves. One of the sisters "dated" the landlord's son, which kept rent affordable. Sooner or later, Ozyan knew she would be forced to lie with one of the other sons. Village women did what they had to. Meanwhile, they lived well enough, despite the sporadic lice infestations.

Ozyan snapped the green beans before tossing them into a wicker tray. Her oldest sister, Zylee, sat with her and watched her without helping. Ozyan nudged the tray closer to the sister.

Zylee shrugged. "Too bad you don't work in the castle anymore. You would know everything that was really going on, I bet." She picked up a green bean but only looked at it. "Do you miss being there? Inside the castle?"

Truth was, she had evaded all thoughts of her time as King Montrose's mistress. The proximity to so much power had certainly been an intoxicant. At the end of it all, she did love her King Montrose. He made her feel beautiful, which in turn made him sexually attractive to her, despite his obesity and avarice. The king knew how to make her feel secure, understood, appreciated, and supported. He was a man of ultimate authority, so his choice of her was the ultimate compliment. She often couldn't bear to face how far she'd fallen. From silken sheets and down blankets to a patch of wool over a dirt floor. Being the king's lover, she had fooled herself into believing she was special. Instead, she'd been discarded like garbage at the Queen's command.

While working, Ozyan balanced a book on her lap and returned to reading rather than answering Zylee's question. It was a book about the history of military struggles in the age before the Great Awakening. Her favorite part so far concerned a long-dead female warrior named Jind Kar, born into a regent of the Ageocron Empire. Jind Kar was famous for her beauty, strength, and intelligence—exactly the type of woman Ozyan wished to become. A fierce woman who never had to raise a blade. Her weapons were her words.

Conquered by what would soon become the Cathyrnee Empire, Jind Kar's power and influence grew until she was imprisoned, then exiled. She remained an inspiring figure for freedom and female empowerment throughout all of Jyn, no matter the kingdom.

Across the room, a minor bickering between the other sisters turned hysterical. Ozyan yelled at them to go outside, knowing that both grandmothers were squatting by the well there, washing the first batch of beans. They would put both girls to work within seconds.

However, when the youngest opened the front door, she gasped and stepped back. A man in a light tunic with a burgundy breastplate entered without invitation. She recognized him as Artemis, the Master of Gold for the entire kingdom.

He removed his helmet to address them. "My pardon for disturbing you, ladies." He looked at Ozyan. "Get your belongings together," he told her. "The king has ordered that you return to the castle."

Ozyan exchanged a look with Zylee. Such an incredibly odd event, considering what they had just been talking about!

She saved her place in the book with a finger and

uncrossed her legs. "What if I don't want to go?"

She didn't have to look at Zylee's face to see the shock there. What was she *doing*?

"But this is a command of our highest royal lord, and you must obey," said Artemis. "You're coming."

She barked a laugh, which made her sisters jump. "His Majesty comprehends his mistake."

The Master of Gold waited. When he realized she was expecting an actual response, he muttered, "Please, get your things together and come now."

"I'm comfortable here. I don't want to go."

Artemis appeared taken aback, though his expression didn't come close to her sisters.' Their faces fell forward, their eyes like eggs, shocked and embarrassed by their oldest sister's haughtiness.

The man gestured at the door with his helmet. "There are two men outside on horses," he said. "If I'm not back out with you in a few moments, these men will come inside and take you physically. Nobody wants that, especially with you being pregnant."

She did indeed hear horses outside, but people rode by on horseback all the time. The Master of Gold could have been bluffing. "Why doesn't the king come here himself to ask me?"

Artemis dropped his arm, the helmet hitting his thigh. "Because that would be insane."

"Says who?"

"My lady, you're going to make me do this? Please, don't. You're pregnant."

The king still believed her to be with child. The idea that she held this knowledge over him, this unintentional deceit, filled Ozyan with a sense of power. Other than that, she had no idea what she was doing or why. She only knew that her reputation was already ruined in this village. Queen Saraal was immensely popular, even more so since her violent death. People hated Ozyan, so she might as well go back. Find some measure of control over her fate and the fate of those she loved. But what would the king do when he discovered she was no longer pregnant?

Ozyan couldn't help it, though. She wanted to be taken. She wanted the king to hear about how she had fought and resisted. Like Jind Kar would have.

Artemis gazed around their small bamboo house, likely assessing which strategic features might withstand a physical conflict. He looked back at her. "I beg of you. This isn't a debate."

She got to her feet and folded her arms. She glared at him. "You wouldn't dare touch me. You'll hurt the baby."

Her sisters continued to gawk at her like she had grown a second head.

The Master of Gold frowned and bowed. He turned and went to the door. He opened it halfway and poked his head out, speaking to someone else, standing just out of sight.

Here we go, she thought.

7

SARNA

She stopped running because she couldn't anymore. A large shadow passed over, and Sarna sprinted left to the closest tree cover. When she checked over her shoulder, she saw the drakksuk reverse its flight, doubling back towards her. It was too fast. The trees were too far away. She wasn't going to make it. She'd made a careless mistake by traveling in the open, and now it would cost her life.

As it descended, the drakksuk arched its spiny back and went sideways, its black scales sparkling with sunlight. Its beaming, almond-shaped eyes focused directly on her. Sarna resumed running, her arms practically windmilling, the hem of her tunic preventing her from taking the larger steps she needed. She could only hope that when the creature breathed death or tried lifting her with its claws, it missed.

Surprisingly, Sarna made it to a narrow gap of trees, bracketed by low hills. She thought she'd gotten lucky until the shriek of a second drakksuk split her ears, loud enough she emptied her bladder.

The second creature came into view, circling a few meters behind the first, appearing every bit as big. She was going to die.

And she deserved to die! She had murdered a man for no reason. She was evidently not good for this world. Her powers were an abomination, and she—the dark princess—needed to be put away. Exiled. A cautionary tale for girls feeling too full of themselves.

While running, Sarna concentrated hard as she could on flying, doing her best to use her pumping legs to launch herself. She figured she could lose the creatures inside the clouds. Outfly them. However, all she accomplished was to insert a ridiculous hop in her gait. Not only was she not taking off, but she slowed herself down.

Both drakksuk closed in. The enormous shifting of air from their wings shoved her to the ground, then covered her inside a swirling avalanche of leaves. She rolled into a ball, her arms covering her head. She thought she could even feel the intense heat from their bodies, growing hotter as they drew near. She closed her eyes and waited as a backdraft of wind sprayed her face with dirt, leaves, and pebbles. She coughed and sat up, reflexively struggling to clear her eyes and lungs from the debris.

She shielded her eyes and looked up. She saw the drakksuk's tails as they finished soaring over. Both creatures flew in a loop until doubling back. Even from that distance, she made eye contact with the closest one, its ice-blue eyes locking on hers, cutting through her. The drakksuk broke the gaze, and the creature veered towards the northeast.

A third creature dove in front of her, impossibly fast, and she screamed. This one came out of nowhere and landed with enough impact to lift her. Sarna rolled away, then crawled. When she tried standing, she slipped and fell again, her tunic slick and glossy with mud. The princess swung her hair off her shoulder, and it moved as a single, clumped mass.

"You would be wise to hide right now," the drakksuk said to her.

Sarna stood there, shocked, having no idea these creatures could talk. The drakksuk's voice was deep and amplified enough by its enormous thorax that she could feel its voice inside her chest, rumbling her joints like thunder. The drakksuk appeared as an enormous silhouette, barely visible through small spaces in the trees behind it. The only way she might've known the creature was even there was by the luminescence of its eyes, which lit the bridge of its long nose.

"Can you understand me?" the drakksuk asked her. "Do you speak Xhenkhel?"

She swallowed a few times to find her own voice. "I understand you."

"There's a pair of yelkin to the south. They probably smell you already."

"Why-why are you helping me?"

The drakksuk grunted. "You're a young female."

"I-I'm not…I don't understand."

"It's a simple rule of agriculture. Females reproduce, so you don't kill them. We can't go running out of food, can we?"

She wanted to speak, a thousand questions on her tongue, but the massive absurdity of the event kept her words suppressed. Instead, she stammered, making whimpering noises inside her throat. She noticed a small cloud of gnats circling the drakksuk's ear.

The creature shook its enormous head, and the gnats scattered. "I'm telling you that you need to hide, though. You don't have much time. That's all." The drakksuk flapped its wings, sending another gust of foliage into Sarna's face. She flinched and turned away. When the sound of flapping faded, she lifted her head again. The creature was gone.

Sarna meandered back through the woods. She had only traveled a few meters when a belch of thunder rumbled from down the valley. The sound kept rolling until she soon understood it wasn't thunder. A vibration shimmied from the ground and up her ankles, reaching her knees. Through a larger break in the forest, she saw two tall, slender shapes in the distance as they crossed a large opening. They stood fifteen to twenty feet tall with spindly, red bodies and long, thin arms. Their claws nearly reached the ground. Their legs bent backward like the hind legs of an animal. Their mouths peeled back into a perpetual grin, showing rows of yellow fangs inside black gums. Their upper faces were hidden by a pair of tumorous horns, sprouting from their temples.

She had grown up hearing about the yelkin but never imagined they were so mindlessly vicious-looking. She didn't know much about them, except they were man-eating giants who lived in the Oroo Mountains. They often ventured into the lowlands to eat any living thing unlucky enough to find itself too far south of the Narlan Plains. These monsters were the reason her father had called for a second wall to surround their kingdom, even before the war.

The two giants spoke to each other in a language she'd never heard. Judging from the way their speech overlapped, it appeared as though they couldn't even understand each other. Their speech resembled a form of Xhenkhel, except grunted into gibberish.

The ground pulsed from their footsteps.

Sarna considered whether to hide or run away. Meanwhile, the giants looked in her direction, as though most definitely aware that something else alive was just beyond the trees. She had little doubt that they, unlike the drakksuk, would be absolutely fine with her as a meal.

8

KING MONTROSE

He finished his business in the royal garderobe. He heard his name called as he walked out. Ozyan had arrived. Montrose already knew it. He could sense her. Also, it was about damn time. He had ordered her to be brought to him hours ago.

He followed the voice into a hallway where he met a royal page speed-walking his way towards him. The king halted him with a raised finger. "I know, I know. Bring her to the Great Hall."

The king went directly to the Hall himself. He sat at the long dinner table there, choosing the table's head, so Ozyan would be reminded of his power. His immense importance. While waiting for her to appear, he got up and paced the room, rehearsing the things he would say to her. He saw her in the doorway and jumped. She'd been standing there, watching him pace and talk to himself. He began explaining, but she shushed him.

"You rehearse conversations before having them," she said. "I do the same."

"Tell no one."

"Wouldn't dream of it, My Lord."

"You enjoy your secrets, don't you?" he asked, though it wasn't a question. He looked up and became glued by those eyes, the built-up hurt there, the quivering. She appeared every bit as nervous and excited as he was.

For a full minute, they faced each other, neither speaking. Wide motes of dusty-golden light spilled around her figure. Behind her stood Artemis and the two knights who had escorted her there.

"Why did you do that?" Ozyan asked him.

He reseated himself at the head of the table. "Do what?"

"Have me thrown out."

"I was a fool," he whispered, then louder: "It was a mistake."

She went to the chair next to his. She scooted it out and sat, almost touching knees with him.

Montrose became aware of an assortment of extra eyes watching them. "Leave us," he said. "All of you."

Artemis and the knights left, replaced by a small group of handmaidens, likely called there by no other reason than news of her return. Like him, they stood in awe of Ozyan's presence, awash in the entirety of her glorious, delicious beauty. He recalled how the low birth and simple manners had once made her so alluring to him. So innocent and corruptible. She represented something so much more now. She carried his child!

"Why did you bring me back?" she asked him. A single tear spilled from her right eye, leaving a wet line over her cheek.

"I've been sick without you," he said. "I'm not the same man."

"I thought news of your child would make you the happiest man alive."

"I have no explanation for my behavior. I went mad."

"So, the Queen is dead, and now I'm good enough?"

He stood and walked to her. He embraced her. "I missed you. I missed you. I missed you. Please, stop being angry. Let's turn the page. Move forward." He touched her stomach. "How much longer are you?"

She placed her hand over his. "How did the Queen die? Is it true what I heard?"

Montrose winced. "I'm afraid to ask what you heard."

"That Burnya is on the verge of an invasion."

"Yes."

"And the Queen was killed by an actual drakk-suk. They really exist. And the chief of the Cathyrnee controls them."

The king pinched a wedge of fabric from her tunic's sleeve and held it between two fingers, transfixed. "Everything will be fine, my dove. We have the finest army in Jyn. In five hundred years, no army has ever broken through our walls."

She crossed her arms. "I assume we will get married then? I will be the new Queen and give birth to your first child."

"Nothing could lift the spirits of this kingdom more."

Ozyan turned away. "But it's my child. And you threw us away. Maybe we don't need anything from you. Maybe we were fine where we were."

"Don't play games."

"Your men had to drag me from my home. Did you know that?"

"That was not my command."

"I don't know whether to believe you."

"I don't care. I needed to have you back, my dove. And now I do."

King Montrose dropped to his knees and hugged her around her waist. He pressed his ear to her womb. When he felt her fingertips gliding lazy circles through his sparse hair, he wanted to weep with euphoria. "I'm sorry," he whimpered. "I'm so incredibly sorry."

"Make me the Queen of Burnya," she said. "And we're even."

"Whenever you desire."

"I desire in five days."

He raised his head. "Five? My dove, the people will be furious with me. They'll hate you. It's too soon after Queen Saraal."

She took his plump cheeks between her hands. "I don't care about that, not even a little bit. I want to rule by your side. Help you take this kingdom back to where it belongs."

"It's already where it belongs."

"Are you sure?"

The king stood, his girth making this a challenge as usual. He looked down at her. "Fine. Five days. We'll be the most powerful royal couple ever."

"You forget, your Majesty. I have lain by your side on numerous occasions and listened to you lie to people through your teeth. With complete ease."

"Because those people are idiots. They are not my new Queen."

"They will be delighted when they hear we're having an heir?"

"And they'll get used to you. They'll have no choice."

Yes, let the demonic forces of Chief Arlyn try their best, he thought. Burnya would resist. They would fortify. They would fight. Tartaria had fallen so quickly because they'd suffered a surprise attack. Chief Arlyn would have no such advantage over Burnya. Also, Burnya stood surrounded by a series of defensive stone walls built by Montrose's great-great-great-grandfather. As the kingdom grew, a double line of walls had been added, making Burnya even more impregnable. These walls had already saved the kingdom from numerous tribal invasions.

Feeding from the strength of his fresh resolve, the king wouldn't stop looking into the divine face of the next Queen of Burnya. He took her chin and gently steered her into standing with him. He kissed her, and her lips remained closed. They gradually warmed and moved against his. For this small moment, the king allowed himself to feel that everything was fine at last. Nothing bad was ever going to happen ever again.

SARNA

The giants walked within fifty meters of Sarna. The nearest had only to turn its misshapen head, and it would see her. She tried crouching into the bush, tucking her folded knees beneath her chin, her best effort at making herself as small as possible. The nearest yelkin stopped, causing the other to do the same. She heard them both grunting and sniffing. She knew they could smell her because she could smell them, their scent dense and musky, like that of an enormous cow after a hard rain.

She peeked through the foliage. The nearest yelkin looked over its shoulder at the sky, sniffing harder. Sarna checked where it was looking and spotted a dark sliver against a backdrop of milky, orange clouds. Within seconds, the sliver grew larger. The drakksuk cried out as it swooped in.

Both giants emitted throaty howls as they ran, the ground shuddering from their weight. They moved with a speed she would've never predicted from their size. They bounded with the grace of deer while long ropes of slobber trailed between their mouths and fingers. The yelkin both disappeared into a forest of thick-trunked trees lining the other side of the plains. The treetops swayed from the giants' passage, telegraphing their route.

The drakksuk reversed its wings to slow its descent. Sarna covered her head with her arms. She protected herself from the onslaught of debris, though most of it was already blocked by the trees. The immense creature landed as light as a bird.

She recognized the drakksuk as being the same one who had spoken to her earlier. She couldn't see its entire head through the awning of branches and leaves above her, but she could sense the drakksuk looking directly at her. It moved closer, half-walking, then hopping. She could even smell the creature's breath, like charcoal mixed with baked garbage. She also felt the heat from its center, warming her as it drew nearer.

"Come out of there," it said. "I told you I wouldn't kill you."

Sarna considered fleeing through the forest but was halted by the obvious futility. She felt exhausted, starving, and weak. If this was her death, then be done with it. The gods knew she certainly deserved it. She needed to be put a stop to.

The princess held her head up as she stood, then stepped out from her hiding spot. She walked further out from the tree cover where she found the drakksuk perched on its back legs, gazing down its snout at her.

"I told you there were two yelkin nearby," the creature said to her. "I told you to hide, and instead you walked right over to them. Why would you do that?"

She went to speak but realized she didn't have an answer. She had no clue why she had walked towards the giants rather than hiding or running. She had simply wanted to see them.

"I don't know," she said. She sounded strange to herself. Her voice cracked. "I'm lost. I don't know what I'm doing. I don't even know why I'm still alive."

"Go find more of your kind to be with. Or you won't be alive much longer."

"I'm headed to Burnya. Or trying to."

"I would go anywhere else but there, actually."

"Why don't you go ahead and kill me then?" She felt the tears coming but swallowed them back. The overpowering presence of this mythic beast, so close. She trembled.

"Because that would be a waste," the drakksuk answered, its voice dropping, as though it truly pitied her.

She blinked up at him, stupefied again from the self-awareness that she was having a conversation with an enormous entity that wasn't human.

The drakksuk used its long neck to swing its head around to nibble briefly at an itch in its scaly side. The creature brought its head back around and lowered its face to her, close enough she could make out the mucousy condensation around its snout. "Go ahead to Burnya then. There's no other chance for you, I suppose."

"Is something bad about to happen there?"

"The apocalypse, probably. But stay too many nights out here and something hungry will eventually find you. That would be a much worse death."

"Will you fly me there?" she asked, her voice lilting, desperate. "Can I ride you?"

The drakksuk narrowed its serpentine eyes. "Keep me in your presence too long, Your Highness, and I don't think you'll enjoy what happens."

"You know who I am?"

"Of course I do."

"How?"

"I know everything."

"Everything?"

"Ask me. I want you to."

A disbelieving laugh escaped her. She felt her chest ballooning. She tasted sweat from her upper lip. "What do you mean?"

"If you could know absolutely anything, what would it be?"

"Is my family still alive?

"I didn't mean personal things. Ask me something bigger."

Her shoulders sagged. "I don't know. Why do we exist then? Where did we come from? Like that?"

The drakksuk lifted its head, gazing down its snout at her again. The creature blinked slowly, pondering its words. "The universe and all of its concepts are born from the workings of the great cosmic consciousness.," it told her. "Beyond physical matter, there exists a vast celestial intelligence that is the source of creation and the main force behind all facets of our existence. Everything that exists does so as a consequence of the universal mind. Do you understand?"

"Sure, I think so."

"Dwell on it. I'll allow you one more question."

"What's going to happen to me when I get killed?"

"You'll meet dead friends and relatives, travel to your past, and walk down a street you once lived on. Meet with guides, so you can learn from them and teach others. You can solve big problems, or you can lie around and hallucinate. Or travel through the universe and explore other worlds. Whatever you choose."

"And that's it forever?"

"Until you're ready for your next life."

"And the Great Awakening? What caused it? Where did the Sünsü come from?"

"Magic comes from the lands and the air around you. It was here all along. The soil and atmosphere are charged with an energy that only certain people are sensitive to."

"Why only certain people?"

The drakksuk made an annoyed groan and flapped its wings. The wind blew her several steps back. She kept from falling by clutching onto a tree. Within seconds, the drakksuk appeared as a ribbon in the distant sky. Still buzzing from the encounter, Sarna watched the sky even though the creature had long disappeared.

She held her stomach. Her hunger had become an animal that threatened to leap out of her. She needed food, shelter, and rest. Why hadn't she at least asked for directions? The drakksuk was right about one thing as much as others: She wouldn't survive too much longer out here. The princess resumed walking towards where she thought she'd seen the light the previous evening.

Towards what she hoped was Burnya.

9

CHIEF ARLYN

He lay in bed, heavily bandaged. He touched his ribs where the first blade had entered him. The second dagger had pierced his left calf, which predictably caused him extreme pain when he tried walking. Though the wound had missed a major artery, it still bled profusely. He knew from field experience that his leg would never have the strength it once had. He would need crutches for the first week or two of the wound healing. After a few weeks, he would still require a cane to get around.

Arlyn wasn't sure why his third assailant had failed to finish him off, electing instead to merely slice his upper arm. A last-second impulse of mercy for his once great leader was the only explanation. Either way, Arlyn felt thankful his assailants had fled, shocked and remorseful at seeing Chief Arlyn on his back, hemorrhaging within a cluster of large vases, blood mingling with the dust.

After getting stabbed, Arlyn had turned onto his stomach and coughed up a goblet of phlegmy blood. He'd gagged, then terror as another breath failed to follow. He choked and his vision watered, yet he managed to rise to his knees. His breath returned, and he went to get up, but the agony of his wounds folded him over. He returned to his back, wheezing. He blacked out.

The Cathyrnee Chief awoke here in the royal bedroom. A young male shaman applied something moist to his wounds. Arlyn drifted back to sleep for the rest of the day, where he blended between agonizing wakefulness and feverish nightmares about monsters. The next morning, following a slow, painful effort, he found the strength to lift his head. A different, older shaman used two sticks to apply maggots to Arlyn's serrated arm and calf muscles. Despite understanding the maggots were there to eat away at dead skin and infection, he flinched. The shaman cooed and shushed him into relaxing until Arlyn settled back.

After the worms were full, they were replaced with honey, spread over the wounds using the same two sticks.

By the end of the day, the pain in Arlyn's side eased. Alone, he slid from the bed and hobbled to the window. There, he watched as his people went about their lives, either oblivious or uncaring that their chief had nearly been assassinated. His one venture out of this room since conquering the kingdom, and his life nearly ended. There it was. His people hated him. He'd brought them a new home but burned it down first. He'd gifted them with ashes, bringing an incomprehensible malignancy into their lives. Monsters flew overhead without attacking, but who knew when that might change? Their presence was terrifying.

By nearly being killed, Arlyn understood he could no longer remain in this room and out of sight. Word of his attack would have spread to every corner of the kingdom. He absolutely could not allow a story of weakness and vulnerability to become the prevalent narrative about him. He needed to convalesce at a superhuman rate. Walk among his people again. He had to show them he was still alive and, therefore, undefeated.

With great effort, Chief Arlyn tottered to the door and opened it. The two guards there jumped, startled witless, unprepared for their leader to make an appearance so soon. They stepped aside and watched in awe as Arlyn took a few wavering steps down the hall. One of the guards reached out to steady him, but Arlyn slapped his hand away. He made for the stairs and could feel their eyes on his back; both guards locked in confusion over whether they should interfere.

He kept a hand on the wall as he descended the

mid-hall stairway. The throb in his side caused him to swoon, and he stopped, nearly somersaulting headfirst downwards. The pain was excruciating, but it didn't matter. He wouldn't be cowed. He took a tentative step down, then another. He reached a landing where he rested. He looked up to find both guards at the top of the stairs, watching him, still puzzled over whether to allow this, or if they even had a choice.

His bare foot landed on a sharp rock, leftover debris from the castle's takeover. The tiny but sharp sensation tilted his foot, and he barely caught himself in time. This brought the guards running.

Chief Arlyn accepted their help in regaining his feet, then shoved them both away.

"I can walk!" he barked.

A female voice scolded him for his foolish temper. It was Yarlaa, her response burned into his hearing, despite being long dead. He often talked to her in his mind. Could hear her responses, as clearly as if she were right next to him. He could imagine her shaking her head at his slow progress, asking how he intended to ever make it back up to the bedroom.

Helped along by gravity, he reached the courtyard, though this took over an hour. The sky appeared cloudy, yet he flinched from its brightness. He walked while shielding his eyes.

"*Ha'wiih!*" came another familiar voice, this one male, this one behind him.

He turned and saw Khuyag. His new head of military had changed his clothing to crescent-shaped gorgets of silver gilt, an indication he was "on duty." Arlyn hadn't directly chosen the man, but he had been next in rank to Gish. Khuyag had started behaving as the military leader, and no one objected, especially Arlyn. He knew Khuyag came from a small family, had led a life of extreme poverty until joining the military. Stories of his bravery during the Great War were well-known. Captured by a Tartarian battalion, he'd been held in chains around their camps, entertained by his personality. One night, inadequately guarded, Khuyag killed the sentry by choking him with his bare hands and escaped.

Khuyag carried himself with an ease that Arlyn found agreeable. He could sustain a dialogue with the chief as easily as he could with any blacksmith. Very little was beyond Khuyag's expertise.

"Are you all right, *ha'wiih*? You don't look good."

"I will be."

"Next time you venture out into the public, you must make sure I'm with you the entire way. We're lucky to still have you."

Arlyn looked up at his window, a black dot high up on the main keep. "Are you?" he asked. "Khuyag, I fear that I no longer know how to live this life of peacetime. War is all I know anymore."

Khuyag stepped closer. He looked up and searched for what held the chief's attention. "Indeed, it will be difficult adjusting to this new way of life. I don't know anyone who isn't aware of this."

"Once we're ready, I still plan on invading Burn-ya." A silence followed, and Arlyn looked at him. "You're going to tell me the Cathyrnee are tired of war."

Khuyag grinned but averted his eyes. "I believe we can establish dominance over Jyn in a different way, Chief Arlyn."

"I'd love to hear it."

The military leader looked up and down the court-yard before turning back to Arlyn. "We can marginalize regional tribes, force them onto our side. Make King Montrose completely dependent on us by controlling all the trade routes. There's no need for more death." Khuyag stepped back. He touched his fist over his heart. "So you know, *ha'wiih*, I have always been on your side. Some uneducated villagers may question the morality of what you did for us, but never me. You did what saved us when nothing else would. The Cathyrnee owe their lives to you."

Arlyn placed a hand on the man's shoulder, not only for physical support but also because he didn't want to weep or hug the man. He cleared his throat. "Thank you."

"I also deeply regret what happened to our Chieftess Yarlaa. She gave her life for us."

Khuyag offered Arlyn a comforting pat on the arm, right where he'd been stabbed, a thoughtless gesture. Both men winced and drew back.

Khuyag's eyes popped, mortified. "I-I'm so sorry, Chief Arlyn. Forgive me."

"Fine, it's fine." He did his best to appear unfazed. Strong. "There's something else you should know," Arlyn said, his voice strained, not fully recovered. "There's a warlock who wishes to kill me."

"Yes, you have mentioned him several times. The one you killed."

"I pushed him out of that hole in the wall up there, and he fell." He nudged his chin at his window up high. "He's going to show up for his revenge when I least expect it. I'm sure of it."

He saw Khuyag still looking up at the window. He watched as his eyes lowered until he was gazing sideways at Arlyn. It was a look of skepticism.

"I've destroyed everything," Arlyn said under his breath.

The chief couldn't help himself. The need to cry came from nowhere. The self-awareness of how utterly out of character this was for him only made the grief deeper. The great Chief Arlyn dropped his head and let the tears flow. The release felt nothing less than cathartic. He covered his face with his hand and shivered with weeping.

MOMASET

The new Ghe-sui Temple stood on one of the few flat areas of ground available. This temple was a cruder version of the original, largely due to the lack of dense forest cover the Ghe-sui had once enjoyed at lower elevations. In the Kholm Mountains, the climate was far less giving. It was cold and windy, which prevented too many trees from growing, creating mostly grass and shrublands. Trees up here were thin and reedy, so it took the work of many men, many hours to collect enough wood to make a temple.

As with their own homes, the shamans combined the wood with stretched animal hides to make six angled walls with pyramidal roofs, approximating a round shape. The main gate of the temple grounds, which Momaset had deemed "the Gate of Purity and Plenty," bordered the southern end, alongside a memorial archway in the front. A rugged path lay worn through the grass from its entrance, created by the passing of so many carriages during construction. The encampment lay connected by several such paths.

Within the temple, Momaset sat in a state of serene alertness—cross-legged, his arms resting on his knees. Palms up, eyes closed. He rested atop fluffy pillows stuffed with reedmace seed heads. Sitting this way normally freed his mind but keeping a clear head this morning proved difficult. His meditation unraveled from worry.

He'd once hoped to effectively build a new life for his people, to keep the spirits and the unity of his tribe intact. It had been the whole point of leaving Jyn. However, life in the mountains was harsh. Sickness was a ceaseless issue. The altitude sapped their powers. The change in environment had transformed not only their clothing, but even parts of their philosophy. Their need for warmth, especially during the bitter nights, had led the Ghe-sui to modify their stance on killing animals. Their lighter tunics were replaced with pelts, coats, and fur hats. There were animal hides everywhere now.

Worse still, Momaset sensed a collective damage to each shaman's soul from having abandoned their Magshaa and those who stayed and fought to the death with him.

While news of the Magshaa's violent demise had shocked them to their core, it ultimately shouldn't have. It was understood that he would be killed. Yet, for the Magshaa, death was better than deserting his home. Better than living in the mountains.

Momaset was beginning to see that His Holiness had been right. Anything was better than this.

After learning of the Magshaa's passing, many shamans wept openly for days. Although peace was held central to their religion, many of the Ghe-sui turned against one another. Bitterness and blame spread through the tribe like another virus, fracturing the group into smaller groups, each with its own leader who stood against Momaset.

So much for forgiveness being the Ghe-sui way.

To restore his mind to a meditative state, he conjured the image of a thriving, powerful community of healers and helpers. He listened to his breath and formed a single word in his mind. The word "calm."

He allowed the word to float there in front of him, but the word kept getting replaced by images of his fellow shamans dying. Placidity had brought them nothing but suffering. It had killed their beloved Father. Peace and love had left them banished and useless.

Try as he might, the mental stillness wouldn't come. Momaset stood and walked the length of the temple's main building. He stopped and rested his hand against the belly of a bronze statue of The Magshaa. Momaset gazed upwards into the serene, frozen face of his former master. He resisted the urge to embrace this cold, stone facsimile, knowing it offered no true comfort.

He yawned and stretched, having been awake most of the night. After a morning bath in the nearest stream, he headed back to the temple. In the chilly predawn, however, he changed his mind and decided he would go for a walk. Beyond the animals eating and people farming beneath a blood-orange sky, he found himself alone.

He allowed this fact to intuit a profound connection to all that transcended thought. As he'd told his disciples, the time had come for them to harness their potency. Destroy the old tradition of non-aggression. He would never be The Magshaa, but he might become someone even greater. Become the leader the Ghe-sui needed. These shamans were stalwart, well-intentioned people deserving of life. They didn't belong in a land above the clouds.

"My love?"

Momaset turned to see Ona. She'd been following him, and he hadn't noticed. Her headdress was an array of deer feet, wing feathers, and bear teeth, topped by a pair of goat antlers, her tiny frame wrapped in a tunic made of wolf hide. The brown skin of her legs and arms were darker than most, which meant she was from the old country.

Ona bowed.

"How can I serve thee?" he asked her.

"I've been elected by the Council of Shamanic Elders to speak with you."

"There's only one council now?"

Her eyes widened, startled by his uneasiness towards her. He watched her recover, her back straightening. "Some of us have true concerns about rumors we're hearing."

"You come to me about rumors? Since when have we become the holy heralders of gossip?"

"We're well aware of the pressure you're under."

"Why did you follow me out here, Ona?"

"There's talk of many women sharing your bed. Nightly. There's talk of you leading us into violence to take our lands back."

"It's like you've been reading my thoughts. Are these ideas so outlandish for you?"

Ona swallowed hard. She blew her hair out of her face. "We're not sure what the solutions to our problems are, my love, but we're fairly confident it's not a womanizing warmonger."

He laughed but stopped himself.

Her cheeks shone in the morning light. Her watching eyes waited for him to respond. He admired the way her soft skin formed a divine face of such soft beauty above such a hard jawline. Her small mouth was made from fleshy, pink lips.

"I have tremendous news, my love," he told her. "The Ghe-sui will soon return to power. I have seen it."

She took a moment to digest what he'd said. "Return to power? We are a people of peace."

He closed the space between them. He took her face in his hands, cupping her cheeks in a way that barely touched her. "I love you," he said. "We are all a family. We will always be a people of light, love, and happiness. But I believe it's time to return home. This is not home."

She licked her lips and touched one of his forearms near her face. She squinted at the ground a moment before raising her large eyes to meet his. "Many of us do still love you."

"But it's the elders, isn't it? They feel threatened."

"They feel abused. Jyn has brought them nothing but betrayal and punishment. Everyone hates them there, so why go back?"

He threw his arms up, frustrated. He walked back towards the encampment. "We deserve to be hated. We profess to be heralders of magic yet do nothing with it!"

Ona caught up to him and hooked an arm through

his. "I will lead you to meet the Elders. Please, do it."

So, they were already waiting for him? He would give them no such pleasure.

As they reached the encampment's outskirts, Momaset noticed a group of shamans nearby. They had stopped speaking to watch them pass. This happened to Momaset a lot lately.

"The Magshaa chose me to be the next leader," Momaset said, making sure to project his voice, "because he knew I could handle this. And I will, Ona."

"That would be...." She touched his sleeve. "That would be good, my love. Where are you going, though? Come with me to meet the council, no?"

"Your council can wait. Tell them they know where they can find me. I will never fear them, nor should they ever be afraid of me."

"If you're going to leave, go ahead. Many will go with you."

"What about you?"

"Me?"

He stopped walking. "Will you come with us?"

She looked around, as if to check if anyone was listening. He checked with her and was caught by the view. He felt how much he might come to miss these mountains someday. Seeing the stars so close often made him wish time would stop so he could stare at them forever. The twin moons appeared more glorious, more luminous. Watching the sunrise and sunset from such an elevation made their beauty even more miraculous.

Ona breathed deep, looked at him straight. "Of course I will go with you," she said.

"I will tell the elders we intend to leave. I owe them that much."

She dropped her gaze and touched her heart. "They will stop you."

"They will try."

10

SHAYAN

Shayan hid in a cave until nightfall, this one far deeper than the other. This should've made it safer, but he felt sure there was something in the cave with him. Thankfully, the something seemed small, at least judging from the compactness of its maneuverings. However, he wasn't entirely sure of this since he couldn't see more than a half-meter beyond the light of the cave opening.

He decided he would spend the entire day here anyway. Move only at night. The last thing he wanted was to lead the drakksuk back to his people.

As far as he knew, every single member of his reconnaissance party had been killed; his own survival was only made possible by the extra protection his crown afforded him. And that protection was gone. For the first time since the morning of his father's funeral, he was completely by himself.

By mid-afternoon, hunger overwhelmed him, and he stepped out carefully. The fires had reached all the way to the stone embankment above him, but a lack of combustible material had choked the fires out. Shayan crawled on his stomach to the top of the hill and peered over the other side. Below, the landscape unfurled as a charred, smoldering expanse of blackness, dimpled with rocks.

Shayan slid down the other way, not stopping until reaching a plane level of soil. The king side-walked the rest of the way down the hill, then rested beside what was once a hickory tree. Exhausted and scraped -up, he drifted to sleep. When he awoke hours later, he tried to get up, but the pain stopped him. Tree roots and loose rocks had beaten his legs ruthlessly. The balls of his feet throbbed. His shoulder clenched up, hurting from where an arrow had entered all those months ago. He felt his lips covered in a sticky and stringy material—spider webs. He spat and coughed, slapping the webs from his mouth.

Feverish from too many crisis hours, he stripped down to his breeches, which relieved the abrasiveness of his clothing against his wounds. With agony in every muscle, he used the tree's trunk to pull himself up. He tried running, but his left knee went stiff, and he had to hop. He managed to walk but could only do so with a heavy limp. How was he ever going to make it back like this?

He hobbled on, but without direction. He caught himself going aimlessly and halted to break a branch from a tree. He used his bare hand to strip off its bark. After finding a large enough clearing, he drove the stick into the ground. He scratched the tip of the stick's shadow with a rock, marking west. The direction of home. He headed that way, using the occasional tree trunk for balance. Shayan kept on until his legs gave and he fell forward. He turned onto his back and lay there. He stared at the twilight sky, filled with flickering stars surrounding the twin moons, swollen discs of amber and red.

In his periphery, Shayan spotted a hazy column of grayish-white smoke, barely visible through a slight spacing in the trees. He forced himself up once more and staggered towards the smoke, praying this was from civilization of at least one form or another. The friendlier the better. He figured it was his only chance.

ULAAN

For the second straight day, she lay wrapped in his arms. At this farm. With this spirit. Someone she could trust enough that she slept under his protection, consoled by the notion that no harm could ever reach her again. How long had it been since she'd possessed that?

Outside, the farm was silent, abandoned. The animals needed to be fed, yet she didn't hear them. She heard nothing. A soft wind pushed the curtains around, the windows letting in cuboids of warm, yellow light onto the floor. No, something was wrong. It was all wrong.

"It's time." He touched her nose with the tip of his finger. His black hair curtained his sculptured forehead and cheeks, interrupting the tented line of his eyebrows. "I was waiting for a few strategic events to line up, and now they have. Ready to help me create a paradise?"

"We've spent so much time already in this bedroom together, I was beginning to fantasize we would do this forever. The two of us. For me, this is paradise right here."

He laughed, but his face darkened. "I've enjoyed it as well, but we can't be selfish with our pleasure, can we?"

"I'm ready," she said, though she wasn't sure if this was true. She touched his forearm and noticed it was hairless. His flesh was pliable to the touch, indenting like dough before easing back into shape. Or was this her imagination? "All of my ranch hands ran away at the sight of you," she said. "I don't think they're ever coming back."

"They ran away at the sight of your dog."

"Because he was running around, still alive, even though they saw me kill and bury him."

His face scrunched, quizzical. "I thought you wanted your dog back. So I brought him back."

"That's not my dog anymore. You should show mercy and kill it."

He shrugged. "As you wish."

She sat up and crossed her arms beneath her breasts. She went to cover herself, but the heat from his body warmed her enough that she let the blanket drop. Ulaan went to speak but was cut off by a scratching noise at the bedroom door. Ulaan thought she'd heard the same noise earlier, but it would always stop.

It became louder. It was Noknok, wanting in, either drawn by their voices and feeling lonely or summoned supernaturally.

"Open the door," Baal said to the dead dog.

Noknok nudged the door open and hobbled into the bedroom. One of his front paws had broken off but remained, dangling loose inside its skin. The dog's black tongue hung through a tear in his cheek. Ice-white eyes bulged blue in their corners.

"Do it," Ulaan whispered, choking up. "I can't take it."

Noknok collapsed onto his stomach and didn't move. Ulaan sat frozen by the sight of her beloved pet, lying there so still. Her closest friend, once a bouncing bundle of unconditional love and joy, was reduced to bones, hair, and teeth.

"I don't believe you're good," she said. The words sounded as though they came from someone else. Her new body and face had created a new Ulaan. Or unveiled the old one. "You're going to have to work hard to get me to believe you're good. What I've witnessed. And this. It's horrifying."

The spirit got out of bed. He held his arms straight out and puffed his chest, half-grinning. "I am good. You'll see." He leaned forward, intent. "Ulaan, I am the enemy of lies. I am the answer. Accept it. I am only here on a mission of pure love." He walked over to her. He placed one knee on the bed's edge and bent over her. "And I am truly sorry about your dog. I thought it would make you happy."

He smiled again. Knowledge and confidence flowed from this man…on her bed, having given her sexual pleasures like she had never known existed. More importantly, his answers to her questions sounded truer than any she'd ever received from anyone else in her own dizzy search for enlightenment.

Through his stare, she heard his voice inside her head, and there was no question he spoke to her, though his mouth remained unmoving, that smile never flinching. *You are mine,* he said. *You have nothing left, and you don't know what to do. You're a shaman of the Ghe-sui who have hoarded power and saved exactly no one. Queen Saraal is dead, so no more royal payments for your seerseeking. The Magshaa is dead. Many of your Ghe-sui friends are dead. What choice do you have but to accept your situation and do as I tell you?*

Ulaan took his hand. "I will obey. I am forever your servant. It would be the honor of my life to help you turn Jyn into a paradise. A land in which everyone is equally honored and equally loved. No more monarchs. No more nobles. Let's do it already."

As if agreeing with her. Noknok barked, and his upper jaw crumbled off, spilling about his paws.

Ulaan screamed.

11

MOMASET

He had a dream of sitting at a long table, covered in a silk cloth the color of rich milk. The table stood within a room with ceilings so high that they stretched out of sight. The shaman looked around at the others seated with him and saw that each was only a shadow figure, their faces made of smoke. Here and there, a face showed, but it would dissipate when he looked directly at it. The seated figure was adorned in plush robes and golden crowns.

Momaset touched his head to discover he possessed a crown as well. He took it off and dropped it on the table as he stood. He went to speak, but the table melted, and the room liquified, and he was floating. He looked at his feet, expecting to see them dangling through space. Instead, he saw nothing. He was no longer a part of the universe, but the entire universe itself. He heard people but didn't see them.

He stood on a hill, surrounded by the Ghe-sui, every one of them, all bowing in reverence to his wisdom and glory. He swam in their basking, delirious joy. They loved him and would do anything he told them. This made his purpose clear. A part of him had always suspected he was the supreme leader of humanity, born to save it from itself. A messiah.

The shaman awoke and rolled onto his elbows. A thin slice of moonlight divided his hut, illuminating its animal-hide walls. From his bedding, he meditated on a small, framed painting of the Magshaa at his hut's altar, only a few feet away. The picture sat propped on an orange cushion with gold tassels. Ona lay within the bedding next to him, completely covered by a layer of pelts. On the other side of her stood a three-tiered metal tray filled with sweets.

This tray was a relic of his childhood, an insignificant trinket passed down through generations for no discernible reason other than nostalgia. Momaset came from a village so small no one had even bothered naming it. Another vision—this one of three huts, a campfire burning between them. Two men stood nearby, sharpening spears while a young boy, barely old enough to walk, knelt and watched them. To his right sat his mother, nursing a younger sister, a hand beneath her bottom, as if about to either stand or change position. Behind them danced a wall of wilderness, made gray and amorphous in the firelight.

The vision changed, and he saw only the eyes of the Magshaa, filled with rage at him. For believing so much of himself. For seeing their power as a force for aggression rather than something to be studied and heralded carefully. Momaset explained to him that this way of thinking had become irrelevant since Baal's arrival. They needed weaponry, not spirituality. Momaset telepathically told the Magshaa that he'd made up his mind to become a force for change. No, the Magshaa Bells had never rung for him, but for the first time, he considered this was because he'd evolved. The Magshaa was dead, and so were the old ways. So were the useless Atrocity Bells.

Momaset sat up and crossed his legs, resting a knee across Ona's thigh. He decided he would call a meeting in the morning with every Ghe-sui. The time had come to inform everyone that he was the supreme being now. Their destiny would be modified. The Ghe-sui didn't belong in the mountains. The refuge may have been necessary for preservation, but remaining here was not. He would give the council their meeting. On his terms.

When the sun rose, he pushed himself onto his feet and dressed. He left his tunic unadorned and intended to do so from here on out. He left his hut and crossed the encampment. He made straight for the temple's shrine room. Inside, the large, golden statue of the Magshaa sat surrounded by four smaller statues of the previous Magshaas. Behind the shrine, the walls shimmered with brightly-colored, hand-beaded curtains. A clutter of ritualistic paraphernalia hung from the walls—feathers, ribbons, ropes, bones, horns, bells, a reindeer skull.

The elder shaman Herel sat on an immense pillow, meditating, his upper face hidden by an eagle head-dress. "Good morning, Your Holiness," he said without looking up.

"Did you have the same dream?"

"That would depend."

"I've come here to tell you that I am the supreme being of all mankind. I am here to lead us to glory, Herel. The time has come for the Ghe-sui to recapture our world."

Herel raised his head, blinked. "What?"

"I need your help in calling every Ghe-sui together. Soon as possible. I must make this announcement. It should be a secret no longer."

"You saw this in a dream, did you?"

Every bowed shaman within the shrine halted their prayers. They turned their heads.

"If it's your decision to doubt me, I can understand that," said Momaset. "I would never force anyone to come with me."

Herel shook his head but kept smiling. "I'm confused, Momaset. Come with you where?"

A young woman with a mauve tunic and long, raven-black hair approached them. She bowed. "My Master," she said to Momaset. "I have shared your dream. I am Gaalyma."

"'Bringer of Fire,' so you are aware of the truth?"

"Of course. All of us are. Whether they admit it or not."

Three other elders walked up in time to hear this. They looked at one another, perplexed.

Herel shook his head. "We don't know what dream you're talking about, my love," he said to the woman.

"I am here to lead us back home," Momaset cut in. "The Ghe-sui have a responsibility to protect this world, not cower from it. I have become the End and the Beginning."

Another elder clucked his tongue. "The Magshaa Bells did not ring for you, my love. I'm not sure what you're on about."

Momaset tried to recall this elder's name, so he could address him more scornfully, but he couldn't remember *any* of their names. Because what difference did it make? They were old. Ancient. Irrelevant. Like the Magshaa, their time was over. Who cared anymore what they thought?

"If you wish to stay," he told them, "so be it. Maybe it's your time to die anyway?"

The elders chuckled together and exchanged looks again. "The world away from here is wicked," said the same elder. "We weren't banished. We left."

"Jyn is beyond saving," said the bear elder. He removed his headdress. "We've already put too much work and sweat into this new home. We have a new temple. A newer way of life. A safer life."

"Safer is useless." Momaset went to say more, but

the bear elder held a hand up for silence.

"Please, understand. For us, this is coming from nowhere. *'I am the End and the Beginning*?' What does that even mean?"

"But I have seen it!" the woman Gaalyma pleaded. "Momaset is our messiah! We must obey him."

Momaset sensed the attack the instant before it happened, but he wasn't quick enough. A blast of energy hit him square in the back, and he tumbled fast, landing hard on his chin. The impact caused him to bite his lip, which drew blood. He wiped his face and leaped onto his feet as though he meant to counterattack, except he didn't. He held his hands out.

"You didn't have to do that," he said.

The three elders were joined by a fourth. They stood with their feet planted apart while their fists pulsed with shimmering ectoplasm, plopping to the floor in chunks. A sizeable portion of other shamans in the shrine joined behind the elders, prepared to defend them. Momaset did his best to hide his surprise at this.

"What are you doing?" Gaalyma wailed at them. "Are you blind?"

Momaset took a single step forward. "I forgive you for attacking me," he told them. "I understand your anxiety. Change is not easy."

"Please, that's enough," said the deer elder, his voice strained. "The Magshaa made a grave mistake in choosing you. Many of us have always felt it."

"You've made that quite clear." Momaset couldn't

help but feel deflated from the growing number of shamans taking up positions behind the elders. His message wasn't going over as well as he'd expected.

"You should leave," the deer elder said, out of breath. "It's time, don't you think? There is no longer a place for you here."

When Momaset checked over his shoulder, he saw he'd gathered a few allies of his own. He turned back to the elders. He tilted to speak around them, addressing the other shamans.

"Look at where you are," he told them. "Living in the wilderness and hills like animals. This is where the old ways of peace and passivity have brought us. I say we use our powers to take back the lands of Jyn! Stop allowing monarchs and warmongers to spread death and evil."

As he spoke, his followers, most of them younger and far more agile, began encircling those behind the elders. The atmosphere crackled with increasing static. The temple's windows filled with pendulous, dingy clouds, rolling in with a swiftness only possible by magic. A concussion of thunder slammed the ground, hard enough to shake the temple's support beams. He noticed the focused but concerned faces of his followers, their growing apprehension. He knew their powers were no match for the elders. The best thing he could do in this moment was to show restraint. For their sake. Help the other shamans learn the truth. To feel it.

He motioned for his followers to return behind him,

and, after brief confusion, they obeyed. "What do you have against me?" he asked the old men. "I don't understand why you won't join us. Help me understand."

"The Sünsü is a gift for enlightenment," said the bear elder. "For higher consciousness and learning, not for fighting. You are not the Magshaa."

"No, I am not. I am more than he could ever hope to be."

His followers cheered and raised their fists, their entire bodies glowing with phosphorescent energy. Lightning forked the skies and flash-lit the temple. "I will not fight you, but we will leave. As you rightfully said, there is no other choice."

The wolf elder straightened his back and groaned. He winced from a pain somewhere around his neck. "Where will you go, Momaset?"

"Burnya."

The elder gave a drowsy laugh. "And you think you'll be welcomed there?"

"Probably not. Not at first."

"If you walk around in Burnya telling people you're the supreme being, they'll execute you. You do understand that."

"The Ghe-sui have been shunned by Jyn for generations. I wouldn't expect different."

"So why go? This is sheer folly, my love."

"Because it's better than here."

Momaset looked behind him to gauge the reactions of his followers. Up close, he saw many were even younger than he thought. His charms had managed to ensnare only the most impressionable among them. Momaset felt energized by their youthful passion, their motivations not yet curbed by the cynicism of experience.

They did have families, though. Disengagement would not be easy for them. Momaset told his supporters to go and prepare for the journey. They were leaving. This was it. The moment they'd always known was coming. To punctuate his intentions, he waved his hand, and the storm clouds parted, like bubbles shoved aside by running water. This brought a fresh volley of cheering and applause from his supporters, the exact effect he'd hoped for.

SARNA

Sarna chose a path that took her deeper into the wilderness and its hiding places. Meanwhile, the sun descended beyond the towering trees, casting long shadows across the dense forest. The air was thick with the scent of pine and damp earth. The only sound was the light crunching of leaves.

She followed a narrow, winding trail, exhausted but scared to stop walking should some predator find her. Meanwhile, birds chirped overhead rather tranquilly as she ventured deeper. Before long, the forest became a labyrinth of twisted trees and thorny underbrush. When darkness fell, she was faced with a daunting realization—she was completely lost.

Her hunger returned. Seeing squirrels bound from one tree to another, she recalled sitting around a fire once and eating roasted squirrels with Luca and his men. The taste was somewhere between chicken and rabbit with a nutty aftertaste, likely from the squirrel's diet. Getting kidnapped had actually taught her a bit of wilderness survival. She knew that the forest was alive with things that could be eaten, namely insects, except for spiders and millipedes. When she came upon a tight procession of large red ants, crossing the trail and ascending the side of a tree, she picked them off one by one and ate them. Ants tasted citrusy, almost lemon-like. But they weren't enough. Further down the trail, she went to her knees again and dug for worms but found only stone beneath the soil.

An hour later, she discovered a red-yellow beetle wobbling its way over a small hill of fallen leaves. She lowered her hand for the bug to walk on yet remembered Luca's warning: Stay away from brightly-colored things, even plants. If anything in the forest carried flashy colors, it was nature's way of announcing that it was poisonous.

Dropping the beetle, desperation pushed Sarna to retrace her steps and escape the wilderness. She was only getting more lost, and it occurred to her that she might never find a way out. She staggered through the undergrowth, searching for any familiar landmark. Every rustle of leaves or snap of a twig caused her heart to jump. Hours passed, and she became overwhelmed by the isolation of the wilderness, a profound disconnection from the outside world. She felt disregarded.

Sarna came to a small clearing. The light of the moons filtered through the leaves, casting a silvery hue over a small pool of water. After slurping greedily from the pool, she lay next to it, resting. Soon, she dipped her fingers into the cool, clear water, the serenity of the moment calming her. In that stillness, she found some remaining strength within her, knowing she couldn't surrender to trepidation and despair. She cupped her hands and drank again from the pool, slower this time. She felt even more strength returning. A shred of resolve. Maybe she deserved to die, but she didn't want to. Not yet.

She decided to spend the night in the clearing, feeling that to continue wandering in the dark was too dangerous. She hugged herself for what little warmth this provided, and she watched the stars above. Their neutral beauty provided a comforting presence.

Despite hearing what sounded like approaching footsteps, she decided it was her imagination and allowed sleep to take her.

12

SHAYAN

Shayan made out voices through the trees, saw flashes of people running. After pushing his way through the foliage, the new king found himself back at his encampment, standing in a worn path between huts. Sadly, any elation he might've felt from finding himself home was short-lived. Why were the refugees not mindful of their smoke? Where were the sentries? He shouldn't have been able to walk up undetected like this. He wandered among crowds of his people without even being recognized. They were too busy racing around in fright, oblivious.

After a short while, Shayan grew weary of getting bumped and stepped aside, bewildered. He stared in amazement at the path littered with filthy blankets and clothing. The stench of rotting rice and tomatoes rose from a nearby pile of ceramic. To the north, once verdant hills lay denuded, pocked with the gray-black tarpaulin sheets of makeshift shelters. The homes around him were animal hides pinned to bamboo poles, then fastened over a patch of soil. The refugee camp was an ocean of filth and stretched leather, stretching into the horizon. The hopscotch streets were filled with people running in every direction, even as far away as the hills.

Shayan stood shirtless, caked with dirt, and marred by burns. Women and babies cried around him. A fringe of flames chewed through the partitions of several huts. Someone bumped his back, and Shayan staggered forward. He turned to see an old woman, her white hair braided into tails that surrounded her wrinkled, open face. "My king?" she asked him, her brows dented. "My king!" She pointed at the sky, but no other words came out: "My king! My king!"

A boy, likely her grandson, approached. "Drakksuk," he said with an odd speech impediment. "Drak!" He pointed skyward. "Monster!"

This explained the burning huts, though Shayan thought there should have been more destruction. Why hadn't he heard the drakksuk? Where was it now? Had it followed him here?

Shayan gently moved the old woman out of his way. He dashed up the path to find a royal council member, any council member, even if only a baron. He spotted Ivaanjav, an old friend and former personal bodyguard of Shayan's father. He and Shayan had been on many diplomatic missions and campaigns together. Ivaanjav stood next to his hut, held still by the sight of so much chaos.

When Shayan ran over, saying his name, his old friend's face rose, then went slack. His mouth fell open upon recognizing Shayan. Before he could speak, Shayan was embraced by a maniacal woman, her dress ripped away at the hip, exposing her blistered skin. She tried kissing the king on his mouth, but he held her off. She struggled to hug and kiss him until he could shove her to the ground. Undeterred, she launched herself and grabbed him around his legs. Shayan would have fallen if Ivaanjav had not yanked her off. He shoved and kicked at her when she tried returning.

"Come inside," Ivaanjav said to Shayan.

He followed him into his hut. Without an invitation to do so, the king collapsed onto the nearest resting pad, made from dry grass and straw. He couldn't help himself. His body had simply given out. A young but haggard woman—Ivaanjav's wife, presumably—removed the king's sandals while Ivaanjav's two daughters stood awkwardly nearby, shocked senseless from the sight of their king inside their makeshift home, having his shoes removed by their mother.

"How many killed?" Shayan asked the children, though he had meant this question for their father.

"Only one, Your Highness," said Ivaanjav. He came over and motioned his wife to move. He sat on the cot with her. He touched her shoulder as he spoke.

"Sentries spotted the drakksuk the day after you left. Everyone ran for their lives, but there was nowhere to escape."

Shayan sat up, his feet on the floor. "How are there even survivors? Everyone should be dead."

"We noticed quickly that once the creatures caught someone, they flew away. To avoid retaliation. All they're looking for is food."

"This has been happening every day since I left?"

Ivannjav nodded. "That's when the committee and I—we made the decision to have a lottery."

"A lottery for what?" Shayan's knees hurt, so he lay back down. He would never have made himself so comfortable in someone else's home, but he didn't have the strength left for manners. Walking and running for so long had turned his body limp. He was a sack of juice.

"The lottery is for choosing who will sacrifice themselves, so the drakksuk will leave." Ivaanjav paused upon seeing Shayan's astonished face. "To fight one of these things only causes it to fight back, which means hundreds of us get burned alive. This way, the creature takes what it came for and..." He let his hand drop into his lap. "And it leaves. I know it sounds horrible, Your Highness. It *is* horrible. We didn't know what else to do."

"And you came to such a decision without me?"

"My Lord, you left."

Shayan grunted and punched the side of the cot, hard enough to cause the smaller child to cry, a low wail building into a shriek. Her older sister lifted her and carried her to the far corner of the hut. Their mother went to them, settling beside a pile of brass cooking pots. She helped try to hush her crying child.

"I don't know what to tell you," continued Ivaanjav, his voice raised over his family's. "It's how we've survived. Otherwise, this place—all these people, their shelters, our supplies—everything would be ashes."

Shayan could only shake his head. "What kind of lottery?"

The child quieted, either consoled or stunned from so much attention.

"Men draw from a sack filled with stripes of cloth," Ivaanjav explained. "There are slips of cloth inside, and one is marked with dried paste, slight enough it can't be felt, though everyone certainly tries."

"And every man chosen, they accept their fate with honor? Just like that?"

"Half run away, I'm afraid."

"Is that why there are huts on fire? Someone didn't go willingly?"

"That's my guess. I try not to watch."

Shayan sat up again but dropped his head into his hands. He wanted to join the child in weeping.

Ivaanjav stood and faced his king. "I'm sorry if our method for dealing with this has gone against your wishes. Together we can think of a better plan."

Shayan regarded the two daughters cowering in the corner. He could see that, to them, he was no king, only one more noisy, scary entity to be terrified of. He asked Ivaanjav for his sandals back.

"We have to call the committee together," Shayan said. "Come up with something else. What they're doing…a lottery. It's madness."

Ivaanjav bowed. He knelt and tried sliding a sandal onto Shayan's left foot, but Shayan snatched the shoe away. "I know how to put my own sandals on," he hissed.

His old friend nodded and folded his arms over his knees. "What happened to the rest who went with you?"

"All dead. Every single one of them." Shayan left the hut. He ducked from the low entrance.

He made his way back towards his own hut, praying it still existed. Outside, he was caught up in a roaring river of people who scurried in a frantic search for loved ones. Others moved aimlessly, dizzy with shock, none aware that their king walked among them.

He considered grabbing a random person to ask them how he could help them, but he heard it—the low, mournful bellow of a goat horn. It was a sentry warning of another approaching threat. Shayan held still, as did everyone, uncertain over what to do about it. The drakksuk screamed, impossibly close already. Shayan raced back in the direction he'd come from. He searched his clothing for a weapon and found only the drakksuk tooth still tucked inside his belt. He thought of using it in self-defense, then cursed himself for having such a useless idea. He considered even tossing the tooth away but realized he couldn't without striking someone with it.

He shouted for people to get to the ground. Their best chance for survival was to shelter in the closest or the lowest area, ideally in a ditch. Cover themselves with a coat or blanket to protect their skin as much as possible. But no one listened. Most ran for the woods. Women cried from their hands and knees as the crowd stomped over them. How much longer must this nightmare go on? The creatures were everywhere all the time now. He couldn't take this anymore.

Shayan heard a man screaming from inside a group of people. Two soldiers, dressed in piecemeal armor, dragged a man between them. The captured man was balding, rail-thin, and barefoot. He intermittently shifted from limp resignation to fierce resistance, thrashing his body, whip-like. This only angered the soldiers.

The king assumed, of course, that the man was the newest lottery loser. If there were any compliance left in this man's mind, it had evaporated entirely. He struggled with everything he had, his desire for escape nearly overcoming the two soldiers. Eventually, the man tired out and sagged in their grip like burlap.

The soldiers dragged him towards a pair of wooden stakes, driven into the dirt at the edge of a narrow, rectangular area. The drakksuk's wings could be heard, a hard, slapping noise followed by great wind gusts. Anxious to avoid getting killed themselves, the soldiers became frantic to get away from the man. One of them grabbed what was left of the man's hair and yanked him forward.

Shayan realized he was one of the few people standing out in the open anymore, but he couldn't look away. Couldn't bring himself to lie in a ditch.

The drakksuk flapped it wings sideways and caused the trees to wiggle and bend. A massive storm of leaves and twigs flew into Shayan's eyes and mouth. His last glimpse was of the creature flying vertically, stretching its mouth until it couldn't possibly go wider. Like all of them, its body was serpentine with those large-clawed wings. The head of this one was framed in what resembled fish fins, golden whiskers sprouting from its cheeks, the underbelly sheathed in silver scales that shone with a rainbow sheen in the remaining moonlight.

The two soldiers managed to tie one of the man's arms to a stake, but they were too late. Sparking branches of energy pierced the three of them, their bodies separated into large chunks that tumbled across the ground. Edges of flesh pulsed red, still smoldering. Their armor lay in a spray pattern across the ground, blown off and smoking.

The heat of so much energy made Shayan shut his eyes again. The planet shook. The drakksuk let out another scream, followed by even stronger bursts of wind from its wings. The creature regained altitude, and Shayan backed away, his arms over his head.

Silence. He dropped his arms.

The man's arm remained, still attached to the stake by a leather strap. Ripped tendons and muscles dripped fat splats of syrupy blood into a growing pool.

As people crawled out of the ditches and woods, the noise of sobbing and shouting rose. They were noticing the arm. Hanging there.

The sun broke over the mountain range to the east, shining through shelves of violet clouds. Light bathed the landscape in a pink glow that was both womb-like and putrid.

The loudest cries came from children.

KING MONTROSE

The king's banquet included bench-sized, silver trays of roasted duck, fish, turbot, and venison, all seasoned with exotic spices. The trays balanced on the shoulders of servants who placed them one by one on the Great Banquet Table. They sat on a dais reserved for the highest-ranking attendees. At the table's head sat King Montrose, surrounded by the chosen few he'd deemed worthy enough to sit anywhere near him. Before them lay golden plates and cups, with bottles of babsulisk lined atop an elaborately embroidered linen tablecloth.

The king dressed for the occasion in a well-embellished tunic with gold thread. A surcoat with his family emblem lay across the breast. Initially apprehensive at the reason for the evening's event, he now felt comforted by the regalia of so many ornamented wealthy people sparkling in the candlelight. He had even invited Artemis—the man who could poison the mood of any celebration. But not tonight! No, tonight his Majesty would announce to the kingdom his greatest news ever.

Once the dignitaries and nobles concluded stuffing their faces, King Montrose stood and raised his glass, already drunk. Conversation faded as those in attendance noticed him and applauded, a mild noise growing until it filled the Great Hall, echoing from every corner. The king's head swam. He exploded with the need to shout his news. To see the shock on their pale, powdered faces.

"My good people, the wait is over—" His voice caught, and he coughed it clear. His speech had unexpectedly come out slurred. He was more drunk than he thought. So be it. "I'm sure you're each well aware I haven't invited you here tonight for merely eating and drinking in our finest clothing."

Some mild, polite laughter. The nobles and dignitaries held their drinks. They blinked at him, spellbound. The king turned and looked up at the stone stairs, which connected the Great Hall to an inner balcony. He'd planned for the curtained doorway of the south landing to contain Ozyan. She would stand there above them all, glittering within the crystal-infused gown he'd ordered made for her. However, his beloved had either forgotten her cue or missed it. He stepped out from his chair and spoke up at the doorway. "My dearest?"

Hearing the words "my dearest" set the guests chattering. *My dearest?* Who was he calling that? What was happening?

The king was on the verge of an epic collapse filled with hysterical blubbering, but Ozyan finally appeared. He relished the collective gasps. Though she'd chosen not to wear the dress he'd forced ten royal seamstresses to make inside a single afternoon under the threat of death, he didn't even care. Ozyan instead wore a long, velvet gown braided with silk. She was a vision. Her thin shoulders were covered by a sky-blue shawl embroidered with flowery lace and twinkling gems. The gown hugged her lithe figure like a second skin. No one would have ever guessed she was pregnant.

King Montrose turned back to the Great Table. He let a few beats go by, allowing everyone to get an eyeful. "Meet your new queen. Queen Ozyan! We are to be married in four days."

A deafening silence followed, save for a single man laughing, who quickly quieted. Montrose observed with glee as his guests stood there, perplexed, many slack-jawed with eyes the size of tea saucers.

"She's already pregnant," he added. "Queen Ozyan will rule at my side, and Burnya will have its heir."

He awaited more reaction, but there was only a stillness held in place by a gaping hush. The nobles and dignitaries were plainly horrified. He could see that Ozyan, to their minds, was nothing more than a common prostitute.

"I realize the passing of our beloved Queen Saraal was much for us to cope with," he said. He stumbled over some of the harder syllables, his tongue heavy with babsulisk. "But if this kingdom is to unite and be strong, it needs a Queen. The king needs a family!" He paused after seeing how his raised voice startled those seated closest. He gave his back to them and lifted his face to his beloved. "This is truly the best way," he said quietly.

Ozyan stepped forward and touched the railing with both hands. "I humbly welcome this chance to speak with all of you. You, the most important people of the Burnya Commonwealth and Empire. I welcome each of you to attend what will be the best day of my life!" She waited, probably pacing herself. "And I plead to you, good people, for the belief that my new role is not lost on me and never will be." She paused again and sought the eyes of as many as possible. "It is especially not lost on me the enormity of the dangers our kingdom faces."

She walked to the top of the stairs, still touching the golden railing. "I know what all of you are likely thinking as you look at me. Who does that whore think she is?" The air left the room, chased out by the word "whore." Even King Montrose held motionless. "I have made it my mission to overcome what you're thinking of me," she added. "I still trust that many of you will even learn to become my friend. To think better of me and to even wish me well."

She descended the first few steps. Everyone watched her without blinking. She stopped partway down. "I may have been born low, but I was born in Burnya. I know no other land. No other king. Many of you are from lands I've never even been to. Never heard of. However, before long, I hope to know many of your homes. Your people. I wish to take the burden off the shoulders of those Burnyans who have fought, worked, and suffered to protect the childhoods of people like me. My generation."

She finished the stairs and rested a hand on the bottom banister. "I grew up on the streets of this kingdom. In areas that most of you will never have to see. Nor should you. Because I lost my father in the Great War, I come from a background of cruelty, yet I am never daunted by the hardships the Great War has left behind for us. No challenge scares me. Please, know that."

When she reached King Montrose, she took his hand, saying to him, "And thanks to our king, we have learned to rely on ourselves and no one else. He has always held that if the rest of Jyn wants to destroy itself, then we shall stand aside and take no part in it. Our most important goal will always be peace and freedom. We cheerfully accepted the high honor of standing alone and preserving the liberty of our realm."

Ozyan turned fully to those at the Great Table. She

spread her hands. "I have no doubt you're aware of the difficulties ahead of us. A threat of war from a former ally, the assassination of our Queen, taken from us by witchcraft. These are not enviable times, but my new friends, my new family, I see them instead as a great opportunity for Burnya." She walked the length of the table. She halted here and there to touch a shoulder, brush a sleeve. "I have studied our history heavily, and it has taught me that the only way to accomplish those long years of peace we seek is to hold strong and believe in each other. To hold faith, keep courage, to clutch a steel heart. We shall make this kingdom stronger than ever, freer, more prosperous, happier, and a more powerful influence for good.

"However, we must give nothing less than everything. I declare before each of you here that my whole life, be it long or short, shall be devoted to your service and the service of our great Burnya. But I simply do not have the strength to carry out this resolution alone. Only your support for me can help me make good on my vows. May they bless any of you willing to share in it."

Having circled the table, she rejoined the king's side and bowed. There was a moment of uncertainty while she stayed bent. A few hands clapped from the other end of the room. King Montrose pounded his palms together, and the rest joined in. The applause grew louder, and the king's vision blurred with tears of happiness.

13

CHIEF ARLYN

Chief Arlyn once more hobbled through the crowded, dusty streets of his new city. The scent of timber might've been overpowering for some, but it remained the comforting smell of industry for him. It was the smell of a new home.

Predictably, the chief became an object of fascination for the various onlookers who recognized him. He did his best to hide his injuries by walking normally, but this was impossible. The sharp ache in his serrated flesh crippled him. Though painfully aware of the terrible optics that such a display of physical weakness created, Arlyn had already ventured too far away from the castle. Besides, he needed this. For himself. He could do it. He would show his people that the previous attack on him had meant nothing. He was still one of them. He was Cathyrnee.

As before, the streets were choked with the grime and fumes of urban reconstruction. Again, the Cathyrnee he encountered today behaved as though torn between affection and rage. He maneuvered his way through laborers, horses, cows, and pigs. He saw men dressed in Tartarian clothing, and Arlyn figured they might actually be Tartarian. Those captured, he had ordered released. They were made to find jobs again and start paying taxes. Far as he could tell, this was exactly what they'd done.

Despite those wishing to touch or yell at him, Arlyn managed to keep moving ahead, no destination in mind. At certain points, the harassment became intense enough that he momentarily regretted having declined armed guards, unable to shake the belief that guards projected insecurity and distrust.

He passed a small group of Chotgor, the sight of which never ceased to unsettle him. These odd tribesmen with their black, blue, and white skin were so instrumental in not only taking Tartaria but also in the defeat of the yelkin. The Chotgor were rewarded for their allegiance by getting pushed into segregated ghettos. Arlyn would've considered this an unfortunate betrayal, except the Chotgor didn't complain. They seemed grateful for housing of any kind. The inferior quality of their homes made no difference to them, though he supposed the Cathyrnee wouldn't know otherwise since no one spoke their language.

The chief passed by more than a few homeless. Though some dwellings required far more repair than others, there were still enough homes for everyone, so the presence of people willfully living on the street was a mystery to him. Perhaps for some, living in the wild had become a learned way of life, preferred since access to permanent housing had lost its comfort. They were no longer familiar with what it meant to earn wages, own a home, or pay for food. They didn't want it anymore.

Arlyn spotted a young boy squatting by a crumbled section of stone wall. He'd caught Arlyn's eye from the way he'd appeared from nowhere. This was because the child looked so filthy with soot that he'd blended in with the gray bricks behind him. Also, he was emaciated. When he moved, grains of dust spilled from his body, striped with bleeding scrapes. The boy held a small pot out for passersby to drop food or money into.

When Arlyn came closer to the boy, he scurried to his feet, his bulging eyes darting for a means of escape. He'd probably come to expect only abuse from adults. The chief held his hands out and slowed his steps.

"No, no, no," he said. "I'm not going to hurt you. Easy."

The boy held still, whimpering.

"I won't hurt you. I promise it's all right."

The boy crouched and dropped the pot, which revealed itself to be empty. The boy raised his arms over his head, his eyes making white circles within a filthy mask.

"Don't you know who I am?" Arlyn meant to lower himself to the child's level, but the agony of bending his knees jolted him back into standing. He checked around to see who had witnessed this and saw a large group of curious onlookers still trailing him.

"Where is your family?" Chief Arlyn asked the boy.

The boy shook his head.

"You don't know?"

He shook his head.

"How did you come to be here?"

The boy stared.

"Can you not speak? What's your name?"

Arlyn went to brush dirt off the boy's cheek, but he flinched as though believing the chief meant to strike him. So much horror in those young eyes. The child had experienced far too much death and destruction for someone his age. The sporadic sight of monsters flying overhead was especially petrifying for someone so small. He assumed the boy's parents had either been killed in fighting or had abandoned him. The child could have even been Tartarian, though he didn't have the look. Much too feral.

The chief was reminded of the loneliness that followed him from his own youth. The life of a warrior was harsh on relationships. While training for warriorhood had provided him with many friends, all of them were now dead.

He closed in on the boy who remained catatonic.

Arlyn scooped him up in his arms and carried him back through the crowd. The onlookers parted easily enough, likely believing the child to be injured. He saw Khuyag among them. His new head of military had discreetly followed him from the castle, disobeying orders.

"I know you told me not to," Khuyag started.

He was cut off when Arlyn edged past him. Despite the stab wounds in his arm, he carried the boy without much pain. The boy weighed nothing. The ceaseless herbal treatment of his injuries had apparently done some good.

Meanwhile, the boy emitted a foul odor, making it difficult for the chief to keep his head from turning. He eventually had to.

"Who is that?" asked Khuyag as he caught up.

"I don't know," Chief Arlyn answered him. "Someone's child."

SHAYAN

King Shayan stood with a twenty-strong group of armed Tartarians. They consisted of five noblemen and three rangers, while the rest were a mix of former knights and soldiers. A second, much larger congregation of family members, friends, and concerned fellow survivors surrounded Shayan and his squad, curious and worried to see them off. The morning was already warm and alive with insects. Swampy vegetation emitted an invasive, rancid steam, which added to the weight of everything they carried.

Shayan felt most eyes gravitating towards him, as if expecting him to give a speech or to at least explain himself. But he wanted only to leave already. He observed his motley assembly with bemused exhaustion, knowing they respected him because of his father but little else. As the man in charge, they felt Shayan should've seen their disasters coming. Their lives were destroyed, and he was the leader when it'd happened. This made him responsible.

The men stood together, waiting, their backs humped with various cloth sacks of supplies and food. Swords, daggers, and water flasks hung pinned to each torso by a leather belt or two. The noblemen wore earth-toned tunics, while many of the knights went shirtless except for whatever sections of armor they had salvaged. It was far too sweltering to wear much else anyway.

The previous night, Shayan had chosen the men for his quest in an impromptu council meeting. He'd picked them for their fighting age, or proximity to it anyway. He'd also judged their enthusiasm towards the task at hand. Though most of their expressions remained flat, he argued passionately that sacrificing people for the sake of the rest was not a sustainable plan. Although doubts over the wisdom of this second journey were valid, he saw little choice anymore. King Shayan would seek the aid of King Montrose. They would travel to Burnya to plead for solace and shelter.

The perils of the journey ahead were numerous. The biggest threat, of course, was the drakksuk, who became larger and more ferocious with every appearance. There were also man-eating giants, savage tribesmen, and warlocks. There could be beasts and creatures not even guessed at, but it didn't matter. Without the protection of stone walls, the remaining Tartarians were a hunted people in danger of being thoroughly wiped out, right down to every woman and child.

Looking at the younger faces around them, Shayan felt like hugging each of them. Thanks to his father, this was the most educated generation in their kingdom's history, an education meant to provide them with solid ground for a protected life. Instead, it had brought them starvation and terror.

Ivaanjav appeared and landed a hand on Shayan's shoulder. "Are you sure about this, My Lord?"

"Yes."

"Are you sure you wouldn't prefer to travel with more men?"

Shayan spat at the ground and rubbed it into the soil. "The smaller we are, the harder we are to spot."

"And no horses?"

"There's not enough. If I can't steed all, then I won't steed any."

"I fear the noblemen are not overjoyed at this decision."

"I don't care. Besides, we don't have enough grain

for horses." Shayan turned away and raised his voice to address the crowd. "Forgive me for leaving you again, my brothers and sisters, but I simply will not bear witness to one more Tartarian murdered in the manner in which I witnessed yesterday. This is our best hope now. I'm aware that many of you disagree, but this is the decision I've made, and I stand by it. Let me die this way if it be my destiny, but I will not sit by as we get picked off until there are no Tartarians left."

"How long will the journey take?" asked one of the knights. Shayan had seen this man speaking with Ivaanjav earlier and felt sure they were related.

"At least two days," he said.

"We'll be out in the open," said another knight next to him. "The drakksuk will have easy sight of us should any fly over."

Rather than answer, Shayan turned to Ivaanjav and gripped his elbow. "I am appointing you steward in my absence. Take care of our people."

His old friend appeared dismayed. "Am I not going with you?"

"No."

Ivaanjav touched his temple. "Are you upset with me? Over the lottery?"

"No, not at all. That showed leadership at least. You took initiative, and the people followed you. You got them to organize."

His old friend straightened, heels together. "As you command."

Shayan nodded to him, then to his squad. He turned to walk away, meaning for them to follow, which they did. He headed towards the trail that would lead them out of the Kholm Forest. There had been some discussion over whether they should take the path tracing the Ikhar River since this would provide them with a water supply, but Shayan had decided the most direct path was best. It would take them through deeper, more unknown woods, but they would also be better hidden.

Focused on not tripping over any knotted roots in his way, he didn't register the female voice calling him at first. He stopped once sensing his men were not as close behind as he thought. He turned and saw Lalya running towards him. She was Sarna's childhood friend who had been kidnapped with her. He'd developed a common bond with Lalya ever since learning of his sister's ordeal through her. Lalya was the last person to have seen his captured sister, as far as he knew. She was the only soul giving him hope that Sarna might still be alive.

He watched in wonder as she came closer to him. Everyone did.

"I want to go with you," Lalya told him.

"I don't think so."

"To Burnya, yes. You'll require a nurse should anyone get injured."

"We're capable of treating our own injuries, Lalya. The answer is no."

"I won't be a bother. I promise." He wanted to cut

her off, but she grabbed his forearm in both her hands. "Please! I cannot stay here. Not one more day. Please."

"Lalya, I simply can't."

"Don't make me stay here! I'm begging you."

"Fine," he said. He resumed walking towards the trail, not knowing why he had suddenly given in to her. A woman would slow them down. They barely had enough food for the company as it was. The notion was beyond foolish. But he recalled the sight of her that day after everyone had fled the kingdom, her dress ripped and streaked with soil. She cradled an infant that wasn't hers but merely spotted by her, abandoned on the ground. He would allow her to come because he wanted her to, and that was the beginning and end of it.

"Let's move!" This time, he waited until every man was ahead of him, no one looking at him as they passed. He fell in line behind them with Lalya walking by his side, carrying nothing but the hem of her tattered dress, the same she'd worn for weeks. She didn't look at him either, as surprised as anyone that she was being permitted to go.

He turned to the rest of his people still standing there. "Anyone else?" he called, as if open to volunteers, despite this openly contradicting what he'd said earlier.

There were a few exchanged glances between his people, but no one else stepped forward. His last image before joining his men was Ivaanjav's forlorn face, as if knowing beyond all doubt that he would never see his king again.

MOMASET

Within hours of their pilgrimage to Burnya, Momaset's followers had misgivings about their journey. The first reason was the coruscating, two-headed drakksuk they spotted flying overhead, which sent them scrambling beneath a cluster of juniper trees, their scaly leaves providing barely enough cover. As with the others, Momaset had never seen an actual drakksuk before, and the sighting was far more impressive than he could have ever imagined. He'd always felt his powers would protect them from any such danger, but witnessing its size and swiftness for himself threw considerable suspicion on that idea. The creature's simple manner of just flying conveyed a level of ferocity he had never witnessed in another living being. He worried it might take everyone's powers at once to even have a *hope* of killing it.

The afternoon brought more monsters. Momaset and his followers were crossing a meadow of high grass when he felt the ground trembling. He motioned for everyone to stop. He next heard strange vocalizations, a jumble of howls, whoops, growls, and whistles. After everyone crawled into a hiding spot, Momaset watched as four, crimson-skinned yelkin strolled idly through the forest ahead. He understood these were the giants he'd heard of, though they were never known to be this far west before. There was no denying that Jyn was not the same realm the Ghe-sui had left.

Momaset considered attacking the giants, if for no other reason than to flex his own powers—but he held back. The time for aggression would arrive soon enough, and the Sünsü always took what it gave. He decided it was best to conserve their strength for as long as possible.

Once the ominous giants had passed, the exiled shaman and his followers went on their way and didn't stop until late into the night. They set up camp next to the forest's edge, hidden in the shadows, cast by the high twin moons. The Ghe-sui shared bread and babsulisk while meditating around their campfire. Momaset instructed them to each focus their energies on the safety of their journey and the radical aspirations their purpose provided them.

The next morning, he faced profound disappointment at discovering that four of his flock had fled, likely returning to the safety of the Kholm Mountains. During a breakfast of more bread and oats, he did his best not to let the hurt over their abandonment show. He even decided to gather the shamans around and ask them who else wished to return. When there was no answer, he reminded them that returning would get harder as they traveled further east. They would even reach a point at which returning would be impossible. Though he didn't wish to shame them, he didn't want more deserters either.

Momaset was especially upset to learn that one of their deserters was Ona. He had developed quite a strong attraction to her. He'd enjoyed her odd taste in humor, their private jokes, the guilty fun of them. Ona had always carried such confidence that her decision to flee was baffling.

He was aware of how his sexual behavior might have been considered immoral to some, like her, but it was the fullest expression of love he knew how to offer. Though he'd banned sex among his followers outside of marriage, he voraciously engaged in sexual relations with both male and female Ghe-sui. He detested homosexuality yet tolerated it for the disciple's own good. Sex was simply a way of connecting them to himself in a symbolic way. Sex gave Momaset control, so it was therefore his strongest tool.

The hurt and disappointment followed him into the next afternoon. He kept imagining his disciples returning to the temple, admitting their mistake, making the elders feel even more justified in their decision to expel him. The image tore at him.

Sulking, he walked ahead of the others, alone with his thoughts. Meanwhile, he tried to keep their path as unobstructed as possible, though this was difficult because the open plains were too hazardous. He remained so inwardly reflected that he nearly failed to sense Soyolmaa, a female shaman, jog-stepping to catch him. She touched his arm and said in a hushed voice, "My Master, someone approaches us. Do you feel her?"

Momaset indeed sensed the tingling ambiance of a powerful presence nearby.

"A girl," he said.

"She's alone." Soyolmaa collected her braided hair over one shoulder and stroked it. Her tunic clung to her hips with sweat, and he recalled how sensually pleasing she was—a quiet lover, but generous.

"She senses us, too," he said.

"It's Princess Sarna! She's alive."

The other Ghe-sui caught up and gathered around, curious.

Momaset closed his eyes and tried to sense this person's presence, to gauge how close she was. In his mind, he saw a female form filled with blue light, her aura unstable but non-threatening.

"She's lost," he said. "She's afraid."

Momaset ran and climbed onto the nearest large rock. On the other side, a steep slope gave way to a field of tall grass and sporadic vegetation. He spotted the waifish girl walking a mere forty meters away. She saw Momaset, too, and stopped.

"Who are you?" she called out.

Even in the dark, he could see how disheveled she was. The spun wool and intricate embroidery of her tunic showed beyond doubt that this person was Tartarian royalty. This truly was Princess Sarna. Here. Alone. In the middle of nowhere.

Momaset descended the other side of the small ledge while the pitiful girl stood, immobile with uncertainty, watching him. As the ledge became more densely wooded, his descent turned laborious. Thorny shrubs ripped at his clothing. When he reached the ground, he brushed himself off and finished walking over. Seeing her up close, he was taken aback. Her forearms and cheeks were crisscrossed with bleeding cuts. The haunted look in her ringed eyes told him the child was deeply traumatized from whatever she'd recently been through. She'd likely seen the drakksuk and giants as well, among other terrible things.

"Princess Sarna," he said.

"Who are you?" she repeated.

"I am Momaset. I am Ghe-sui."

"Ghe-sui?" Her brows lifted, and her face brightened. A boulder-heavy tension instantly left her body as she stood straighter.

He opened his mouth to explain where they were going and why they were traveling. He was cut off by the princess, who hugged him and sobbed.

Though initially off-guard, he placed his arms around her and held her tight. She shook inside his arms. He heard the other shamans making their way down the ledge behind him.

"You're okay now," Momaset told the princess. "You're safe." He didn't know if she was safe at all. If any of them were. It still felt good to say so.

Princess Sarna nodded. He smelled the hair on her little, royal head, and it smelled like mud.

14

OZYAN

Once more, she begged the king off from having sex. He grunted and rolled over, frustrated, crossing his arms. She turned away from him, his theatrics. She brought the covers up beneath her chin. Her bitterness lingering, Ozyan wasn't open to the king's touch yet. He was so much uglier than she remembered, having gained even more weight. Even his spirit was uglier.

Furthermore, she simply wasn't in the mood. Her speech that she'd practiced for hours, revising endlessly to make sure she'd genuinely used the best words possible, had been a failure, or so she felt. She'd genuinely wanted to alleviate the statehood's fears over what kind of Queen she might make. Instead, her speech concluded with every single guest leaving the castle within minutes, many not even showing the respect to greet her.

As a result, her initial excitement for the king had transformed from a warm and romantic feeling to a pressured and cold one. She also considered it was the king's earlier rejection of her. The way he had so easily extracted her. She was less than confident he wouldn't do it again, especially upon discovering she'd lost their child. It made her endlessly uneasy.

Worse, the king was so insistent in his desire for her that she often wondered if his touch meant anything except his insatiable need for copulation. Apart from sex and babies, she worried he held little value for her. Also, she hated the pressure. The pressure to be attractive, the pressure to perform. She considered that she was simply tired of being touched. Tired of not having her personal space.

Every night since returning to the castle, she'd managed to hold him off by claiming discomfort from the pregnancy. He seemed to reluctantly bide his time for now, but she could feel him watching her. Meanwhile, she gazed out the window at the night sky. She listened to the sounds of the streets below. A dog barking. The high-pitched titter of children playing, calling out to one another. Men laughing and the women retorting playfully, their voices like disconnected lullabies. The sounds of ordinary people living their ordinary lives.

King Montrose turned away and sighed heavily. He was not a man who handled frustration well.

Soon enough, he would have a psychotic episode and sexually assault her. She expected this to happen sooner than later. The night of their wedding, most likely.

She slept a while, then awoke from a damp chill in the room. She noticed the light bar under their door disappearing. It was normal for this light to be interrupted when a guard or handmaiden passed by, but this was different. This wasn't a solid interruption of light but a haze, as if from smoke. She sat up and squinted. She saw a mist entering the room through the gap under the door. She rubbed her eyes to clear them, but there was no mistaking it.

Believing the mist to be poison, she reached over to wake the king. But when she turned, she noticed the tall, black figure standing there. When her eyes adjusted, she could see the figure forming from the mist leaking into the room. Ozyan opened her mouth to scream, but nothing came out. Nothing but the rasp of her choking.

SARNA

Sarna fainted. She awoke after only a few seconds and found herself still in Momaset's arms. She stood back, shaky and embarrassed. She sniffled and wiped her nose. The Ghe-sui shaman with the white tunic and shaved head patted her shoulder and rubbed her arm. He suggested to everyone that they return somewhere out of sight. Everyone, including Sarna, followed him into the shadows of a small wood to the slight north.

There, the Ghe-sui unpacked their various pouches to eat from. Several shared their water and dried fruit with Sarna. She ate and drank with abandon, starvation and thirst overtaking dignity. Afterward, she felt rejuvenated, returning to how a normal person might feel.

The leader of this Ghe-sui pack was a man she'd heard of at the Magshaa Temple. He swore he'd met her before, but she didn't remember. Though it couldn't have been more than a few months ago, that time felt like ages ago. The shaman's name was Momaset, and he watched her eat, a look on his face of both worry and curiosity. She decided to let him. *Stare at me all you want.* The joy at learning these people were friendly, much less Ghe-sui and headed towards Burnya, brought a gleeful comfort to her, bordering on euphoria.

After every introduction to every shaman, she hugged them and had to remind herself to let go. The warmth she felt from these people came as a natural solace. They were genuinely kind people who expected nothing in return. There was a feeling of such belonging and compassion as she had not felt in years.

Sarna thanked her food and drink donors with enthusiasm, then wandered off. She found a spot on the ground and curled up there. After filling her stomach, she lay still and listened to the surrounding chorus of crickets, chirping in near unison. Within minutes, a female shaman came to Sarna and pushed a fox fur blanket at her, urging her to cover up. When Sarna recognized her as Corsika, the two embraced, rejoicing at the unexpected reunion. They hadn't seen each other since sharing time together at the temple. After they exchanged niceties, Sarna accepted the blanket from her.

The nights were cold. In its own small way, for Sarna, the plain gift of this blanket felt like the nicest thing anyone had ever done for her.

It didn't matter that Corsika appeared half-crazed, her blue tunic and leather flap hat framing her weathered face. She did her best to engage Sarna in conversation, even going into a story about her friends and mentors she'd left behind. Sarna tried listening, nodding where it felt appropriate, but the pull of sleep was too strong. When she decided to shut her eyes for only a moment, she was gone. Out cold. She occasionally awoke to find Corsika still talking, not noticing or concerned that she was sleeping as she spoke.

In her dreams, she lay with Luca again, his front to her back as he held her. She felt the intermittent warmth of his breath on her neck. She turned to glimpse him, but he was too far behind her. She wanted to apologize for killing him. He laughed and said that it was all right. He was already dead when they met. Sarna jumped awake. She lifted her head to see Momaset smiling down at her. He'd been crouching there, watching her sleep.

"Sorry to startle you," he said, his voice like silk. Low and calm. She felt her skin tingle, which was slightly unsettling. "It's such great fortune that we found you. It's providence, don't you think?"

Though she wasn't entirely sure what the word meant, she nodded. She felt sheepish in his presence. The glare of his eyes was too intense.

"I have to confess that I'm a little in awe of you," he told her.

"Of *me*?"

This was such a surprising statement because Momaset reminded her of the Magshaa, though more direct and without the same level of serenity. She could tell how much the other shamans thought of him from the way his companionship made them instantly smile. Several times, as he helped the others prepare for sleep, she had caught him looking at her.

"Yes," he said. "I've always been fascinated by royalty."

"Do I seem especially fascinating so far?"

He licked his lips. "Most certainly."

She gestured at the rest of the Ghe-sui, snuggled into their fur-lined sleep sacks. Despite the icy bite of northeastern air from the Zanguii Mountains, they went without fire to avoid detection. The wind brushed through their coverings. "These people clearly love you," she said. She nodded at their sleeping forms.

He was still looking at her. "So I understand that the Magshaa Bells rang for you."

Her attention snapped back to him. "How do you know about that?"

"All of the Ghe-sui know. Those bells only ring for one reason."

"It was Corsika, wasn't it? I asked her not to tell anyone."

"But I'm not just anyone. Plus, it was a monumental event. Word spreads naturally."

The confession leaped from her lips, as if yanked out by him. She didn't want to talk about bells. "I killed someone," she said. "I've killed lots of people."

He shook his head and blinked, joggled. "Such times call for even the most innocent among us to act with violence. It was self-defense, I'm sure."

"One person I killed for no reason. Or because I could. And it was someone I cared about."

"A man?"

"The one who kidnapped me, believe it or not. And I don't know. We became close."

"But he was bad to you."

She ruminated over the question a moment, deciding. "He couldn't help who he was."

"So it wasn't for no reason." He squinted at her. "How did you kill him?"

"I touched him."

"So it is true. You are blessed with the Sünsü. The bells were not a mistake."

"It was absolutely a mistake," she said quietly. "The Magshaa Bells did ring when I sat under them, but it must've been the wind? I don't know."

"It wasn't the wind, Your Highness."

"Can you teach me? Teach me to control myself?"

"Of course I can." He studied her, and the crickets went quiet. "I am the messiah, Your Highness. I can teach you everything."

Though she could see these shamans thoroughly entrusted in him and would follow him anywhere, do anything he wanted, she still doubted his claim. She regretted admitting that the Magshaa Bells had rung for her. How could she dare? She wasn't even sure what the event had meant. Without question, it'd been some mystical error. A cosmic fluke. She felt perfectly willing to accept this if it meant her survival. It made far more sense that Momaset would be the new Magshaa anyway. He was an adult who knew things. She was a teenage murderer.

"Do you know what's happened to my family?" She cleared her throat. "Are they alive? I know our kingdom was attacked. And destroyed. But I don't know what happened to my brother or my mother."

"Your father has perished, I'm afraid. But you knew that, didn't you?"

She swallowed hard and nodded.

"I don't know the fates of the rest of your family," he said. "I'm sorry."

"And His Holiness? Corsika told us that he died, but she refused to tell us how."

"He was slain in battle."

"Just like that? How is that possible?"

"Our beloved Magshaa was powerful but mortal."

Momaset frowned and rubbed his elbow.

"Some of the shamans at the temple resented me," she said. "Will I be resented by you as well?"

"Never. The fact that you felt that resentment explains to me why we left them. Far too much jealousy in their hearts." He stepped closer to her, leaning in conspiratorially. "Your Highness, you'll never have my resentment. Not for a second."

He gripped her arm. A gentle transference of energy traveled back and forth between them. She sensed a brightness, growing brighter. There was an explosion, then fire. The forest was aflame while the ground shook. Sarna squeezed her eyes shut, tears rolling down her cheeks. She felt the heat of unfurling flowers of flame. She could hear the shamans shouting as they scrambled for cover. She saw her father falling again. She saw her brother's face pinched with agony, her mother surrounded by strange and malicious men. She saw a beautiful, tall man with sharp, green eyes and a cleft chin, his thin lips smiling. The shadows on his face danced from the furious light of a large fire.

Darkness. She awoke from Momaset shaking her, yelling at her that the forest was on fire. They needed to escape. She had to wake up, or she was going to die. Next thing she knew, she was running while holding his hand, being led by him.

15

SHAYAN

Late afternoon became tinted by the auburn dusk. Shayan called for the group to rest, and a collective sigh moved through them, as though this moment had been anxiously hoped for much earlier. Shayan realized he was pushing them hard, but, as he'd expressed to them many times, he wanted to make as much ground as possible. They had no other chance of making it to Burnya without incident. Also, the weather had been cooperative so far. Take too long and bad weather became increasingly inevitable.

Before nightfall, they reached a summit overlooking a valley. Shayan stood with three rangers and surveyed this unexpected view of the land before them. He thought he could even see Burnya as a dark dot on the horizon, off to the west.

He pointed at it. "There," he said to the lead ranger, a slender man of advanced age, a pointy, white beard cupping his face. "Could that be Burnya?"

The ranger leaned forward, peering. They all did. "Hard to say," the ranger conceded. The ranger's name was Khilji, the same as Shayan's father. The citizenry naming their children in honor of the king and Queen was not uncommon, but Shayan still would've preferred that the man were named anything else.

The other unnerving detail about him was that he bore a striking resemblance to Zov, the advisor he'd killed with his sword, an impulse ignited when Zov insinuated they find a way to get rid of his father, the king.

Though his mother had been right to scold him for such a heinous act, he'd still done it, knowing there would ultimately be no accountability. Looking back on the event now, he felt shocked at himself. The stress of battle had made killing people far too normal. So much had happened since the killing that it was easy to forget he'd even done it. But there it was, and he couldn't take it back. He'd slain a man in his own castle. How many more men had he killed in the Great War? Far too many to count.

Even though it'd been a time of conflict, having killed people often triggered a moral conflict within him. He felt guilt, shame, and anger from those experiences. He hurt inside, though he wasn't sure why. Why should he feel bad about killing if he hadn't done anything wrong? He was merely doing his duty to defend his kingdom. Obey his father. He'd only done what every soldier and knight had done.

Still, he couldn't escape the feeling that a dark side of himself had been revealed that he hadn't known existed. It made it difficult for Shayan to see himself as a moral person. He felt isolated from other people since most of them didn't understand the experiences of having killed. It was even hard to get close to others because of always feeling the need to hide what he'd done.

Shayan shook himself from his thoughts and focused on the sight of what was, hopefully, Burnya. Even if this wasn't Burnya, it was still the direction they needed, and something large was over there. Shayan changed his attention to the more immediate landscape and how they might navigate their way down. Several segments of large stones and fallen trees blocked the way.

As though reading his mind, the lead ranger nodded to his left. "The ground slopes more eastward," he said.

The warm air was tempered by a gentle breeze, cooling them off. Shayan became aware of a presence on his other side—Lalya. She'd kept up with the men better than any of them might've assumed. At least for now, anyway. He felt glad she'd come along. Though her feminine presence caused a distraction, Shayan could feel how much it boosted the men's morale, a reminder of why they were doing this.

She remained as close to her king as often as possible. The ordeal of her and Sarna's kidnapping was something she spoke freely of, except when it came to herself. Shayan imagined this meant she had been violated, or worse. He never pressed her for details, other than about his sister.

Shayan thought about which direction to choose. He understood this seemingly small decision could change the course of their entire journey. Possibly their entire lives. He was an instant away from voicing his decision when he spotted a light down below. Then another. Four more. It was a group of people walking with torches, a few thousand meters off. In the shadow of the cliff, they needed torches to see.

He ordered the scouts to find their way down and investigate. Without discussion, they chose eastward and blended into the brush. The rangers camouflaged themselves in subdued olive-hued leather, speckled with dark greens, blending perfectly with any foliage. To keep light, they didn't sport armor but instead kept only a sallet with a nasal helm over their heads.

The rest of the squad sat eating, unbothered. Shayan smelled babsulisk and noticed three men sharing a flask. He angrily ordered the narcotic to be put away. He was about to command the men to pour the babsulisk out but changed his mind. He knew their spirits might desperately need it later. Besides, Shayan had brought his own babsulisk, so the hypocrisy was avoidable.

The scouts returned.

"Those aren't people down there." The lead scout, Khilji, looked at the ground as he spoke, as if ashamed by this news. "It's those savage tribesmen, the ones seen at the siege."

Another ranger spoke up, bursting with his reason to address the king. "They have red eyes that light up," he said, as though Shayan wouldn't have remembered this.

Shayan went onto his stomach and crept to the ledge. He peered over and saw the strange beings in more detail as they came closer. A few more steps and they stopped, sensing that they were being watched. The beings slid their spears from their shoulder slings and held them.

The king considered their next move. These tribesmen had shown themselves to be adversaries in the recent past, and here they were coming towards them with weapons drawn. He noticed a pair of them following something along the ground.

"They've picked up your trail," he said to the rangers.

"Impossible," the rangers responded in near unison.

Still, Shayan could clearly see, even from this distance, the muddy depressions the rangers had left in the ground. Footprints were a treasure trove of information for an experienced tracker. And these beings certainly appeared to be. They inspected snapped branches, even squatting for the smaller bushes, looking for broken spiderwebs, and likely finding them everywhere. In his mind, Shayan cursed the rangers for having been so careless. No wonder they had gotten back so fast! They were poorly trained, of course, but the best Shayan could find.

He slapped Khilji's shoulder. "Take positions."

To his surprise, when he glanced back at the strange tribesmen, he spotted a large section of tree branches being jostled behind the first group. This meant there were more of them. Possibly dozens.

Meanwhile, his men darted into motion. They were outnumbered by the beings. Also, Shayan feared his squad's lack of skill in the field would make the fight unwinnable. They had only one advantage—the integrity of their perimeter. They would maintain and use a forward defense despite the woods' thickness, which prevented them from spreading out. They could still use the forestry for retreating and counter-attacking.

The king scrambled back and forth, checking every man, making sure each was ready. He pushed those out of place into a better spot. In the process, he nearly ran over Lalya, who stood statue-still, turning white, frozen with worry. Exactly as he'd dreaded.

"Are we going to die?" she asked him.

"Hide there," he said. He guided her into the nearest carpeting of kudzu, the leafy vines enveloping her protectively. "Stay right exactly there," he whispered.

He rushed back to the front of his men and hid with

them, their swords and daggers drawn, ready to spring. Shayan knelt behind a crooked tree, its base replete with mushrooms. With the day's hike catching up to his joints, he began to hurt from holding so still. The starch in his limbs throbbed.

Where were these things already? He worried his men might get stealthily flanked from behind, especially if these creatures were climbers. He peeked around his tree and saw the first silhouettes. That was exactly what they were doing!

Shayan flattened himself against the tree as a spear sang by his ear, close enough that he felt the air. He ducked and rolled away. The nearest knight leaped from his bushy hiding and skewered one of the strange humanoids through its stomach, the blade piercing its back, coated in black liquid. The knight tried withdrawing his shortsword for a defensive aversion, but his sword was stuck. He became set upon by three of the beings who hacked at his torso until he fell, bending around every blow.

The rest of the squad cried out and charged from their hiding spots. Their king fell in with them, placing himself inside their assault wedge. He parried and transitioned into a counter swing. He sliced downward through his opponents diagonally in the opposite direction. As did most of the men, he kept his stance wide to protect against a counter-swing or a hard downswing. Each time a creature lunged at him, the king countered by turning his body. He made their vital organs his main target.

Finding the full rhythm of his swordplay, Shayan held off two at once while waiting for one to make a mistake. The beings fought with spears made from chalky black rock that caused considerable damage to their blades. He swung at their forward legs, but both had a defense for his every move. The humanoids' fighting skills were honed. They possessed a defense for every move, and Shayan began to tire. He found himself slowly retreating as his opponents combined their strength over him.

Using the last of his energy, he stood his ground between a row of trees; however, the tighter jabs of their spears gave them increasing dominance. He was outmatched. Gradually retreating towards the ledge, he soon stood with his right heel inches from a hundred-meter drop.

In a last gasp to preserve his life, he swung his sword up and arched his back to avoid the humanoid on the left. He stabbed his sword forward, crisscrossing their spears together. His blade entered his left opponent's side between the second and third ribs. The being dropped its sword and clutched its wound, though its face remained expressionless. He noticed that though some had lost limbs, they didn't stop fighting.

Shayan pivoted and slung his sword back the other way. This beheaded the other being, his blade's trajectory catching the neck at the ideal point of softness. A gooey, glowing liquid gushed from the being's shredded jugular. Headless, it swung its spear aimlessly. The king slashed down across the being's torso and exposed its chest cavity, where a moat of red light flickered free and went out. The being went to its knees.

The king maneuvered away from the ledge and about-faced behind them. He swiped his sword back and forth, chopping at them until their flesh and limbs sliced free, in some cases somersaulting; yet they kept moving, still motored by some post-death reflex. Anywhere a piece fell off, more red light shot through the gap.

Shayan felt hands on his shoulders. An ambush from behind! More hands grabbed him. Pulled him. He jerked loose and swung around, prepared to face his new enemy. He saw Lalya on the ground where he'd left her, spread-eagled, halfway out of the kudzu, as if something or someone had dragged her out. She lay with her arms folded over her face.

"My king, it's okay, it's all right, my king," said one of the beings in a soothing tone.

Shayan shook his head to clear it. It was a man speaking to him. These were men.

"We got them," the man said. It was Khilji. "They're all dead, My Lord."

He struggled to regain his breath. He held his sword up, still prepared to fight against anyone. He didn't care. He felt lathered in sweat. It pooled between his clothes and skin, plentiful as rainwater.

"I'll kill them," he wheezed, trembling. "I'll kill them all."

16

ULAAN

Though he'd told Ulaan he would be gone in the morning, she still felt dismayed upon opening her eyes and seeing that the spirit Baal was indeed no longer there. He'd told her he would meet her in Tartaria, though he wouldn't appear in the same form. He claimed she would know it was him when the time came.

Of course, she'd wanted to ask him why she couldn't go with him, but the question felt too large. She felt naïve and silly for not knowing the answer. He had his reasons, and she was no one to question him.

Regardless, after so much time together, she felt a yawning vacancy in his absence. A momentary doubt surfaced over whether the past three days had even happened. The only confirmation she needed for this was the mirror. Her new appearance. She felt vaguely aware that this was a work of evil seducing her. She was headed down the wrong path. But look at her! She was the personification of feminine grace and power. Why hadn't the Magshaa, in all his mightiness, ever done something like this for her? It was only everything she'd ever wanted.

Ulaan got dressed and opened the front door, prepared to check on the state of her farm after it had been unattended for so long. Instead, she found Lomen standing there with his hat in his hands. His face went slack at the sight of her, as if seeing her for the first time, or as if expecting her to have returned to her original form.

He swallowed hard, and Ulaan felt pity for the man. He was a good soul, and she'd once held a special place in her heart for him. She suspected he felt the same, but never moved on his feelings, likely out of respect for her father. She imagined how he was regretting this now.

She gave him her best smile. Lomen returned the smile shakily.

"Good morning," she said. She made sure to sound friendly because she could clearly see he was anxious. "Lomen, it's all right. You don't have to be afraid of me."

"Right. Um, I know. Only came to tell you I fed the livestock and did a beetle check on the eggplants. We have pigs in three different paddocks, and their water will need to be filled before the end of the week. We're good on feed, though. The horses will need hay before a day or two. The hens—"

"Why are you telling me all of this? You're leaving?"

"N-no, course not. There's too much left to do! I'll be going into the village to get some lettuce and some radishes now. Maybe garlic scraps."

She frowned. "The other men aren't coming back?"

He shrugged and became fascinated with the toe of his boot. "I can try to find more." His knuckles went white from holding his hat so tight. "I mean, if that's what you want."

Ulaan wished she knew how to make the poor man relax. She could only imagine how this appeared from his perspective. Men like him were from the old country. They were simple farmers. Unfamiliar with magic and the mysterious ways of the universe. They only wanted to live off the land and raise their families. Protect them from getting sick, murdered, or from starving to death. She was relieved to no longer share a common purpose with them.

"Why did you stay?" she asked him.

He lifted his gaze and took in the entirety of the farmland around them, anything he could do not to look directly at her. "I've known these lands since before I was ten. I know it better now than my own body."

"So you have nowhere else to go. That's the only

reason?"

"I suppose."

"I understand what's happened is a lot to take in, Lomen. I know it's frightening for you."

"Oh, I'm not frightened."

She searched his face. He was clearly mortified. "I have good news, though," she said. "The world is about to change, Lomen. And it needs me. I'm needed again."

He nodded at the sacks and satchels stacked on the table behind her. "That's why you're taking a trip?"

"Yes, and I will need a horse. I'm riding to Tartaria to meet with Chief Arlyn. I have a message to him from Baal."

Lomen grimaced. "Who?"

She laughed a little. She couldn't help it. How to make him understand? "Never mind," she said. "Fetch me a horse, please. Would you?"

Grateful to have an activity, Lomen jogged towards the stalls. A short moment later, he secured her belongings to the horse. The animal showed no signs of strain since he'd made a point to bring her the strongest steed available.

Ulaan hugged Lomen. She felt him hesitate but return her hug, albeit stiffly and with one arm. She reached into a front pocket of her dress and handed him the keys to the cottage and stables, though he already possessed his own. Hers were made of iron, with a kidney-shaped bow and a simple bit that formed a right angle with the shank.

"These are yours now," she told him. "I don't know if I'll ever be back."

Lomen nodded and accepted the keys. He showed no reaction. He helped her onto the horse, his hands pushing against her back to lift her. When she reached the top of the northern hill, she pulled for the horse to stop. She guided him sideways and saw Lomen watching her ride off, gaping at her. Of the woman she had become.

He looked deeply concerned.

KING MONTROSE

The Royal Castle of Burnya held a Grand Ballroom famous for its size and complex, ornate spanglings. Immense, swooping swaths of blood-red satin curtained the impossibly high windows. Their stained-glass tinted sharp shafts of light that pierced through, the far wall swimming inside a pinwheel of color.

Whereas the other evening had seen this room buzzing and flowing with two hundred guests, most of them nobles and heads of state, the room now lay empty, save for the king and the Queen-to-be.

Ozyan paced, fingers laced behind her back. Her nakedness stood hidden by only a small slip, which would undoubtedly cause a scandal with the servants and staff. It was unbecoming of a Queen to wander the castle without formal clothing, let alone, barely clothed at all. Her lower-class values were showing themselves, which was simultaneously un-nerving and arousing for the king.

Montrose pushed himself up from his chair and walked over to her. He noticed a servant girl nearby, completely unseen to him earlier. He recognized her as Ozyan's social equal, no less than a few months ago.

"What are you doing here?" Montrose snapped at the young girl who blinked at him. "Stop staring at me!"

The servant girl rushed out of the ballroom, speed-ing away as though he had thrown something at her, or expected him to soon enough.

"Don't talk to her like that," Ozyan snapped. Her face was stone.

"You need to put some clothes on, my dove. You can't walk around like that anymore." He checked the Grand Ballroom for anyone else listening. Seeing no one, he turned back. "You're not that person any-more."

"What person?"

"A servant."

She looked at the door where the girl had vanished. "That was Zylee." She cut her eyes back at him. "That was my sister. I want her around me at all times. I'm moving my mother into the castle as well."

"I noticed you've also brought in several containers of books."

"Those are mine. I like to read."

"Why so many?"

"Reading is important, My Lord. I would hope my future husband reads when he can."

"You could teach me."

"Teach you what? To read?"

He rolled his eyes. "When do I have time to read?"

"Wait, are you serious? You're a king! How can you not know how to read?"

"It's difficult for me."

She touched his face. "My poor king. Yes, of course, I will teach you."

"There are thirteen libraries inside this castle, my dove. There's no need to bring in more books."

"But these belong to me."

"And they're heavy. Why must you tote them over like trophies?"

"To share, My Lord. I intend to read every single one and give them away. We can even have a festival."

"A festival, yes. I adore festivals." Montrose said flatly. He felt his cheeks warm. "Who were you talking to last night?"

"When?"

"In the middle of the night. Last night."

"I don't know what you mean."

"I saw you. Your eyes were open, and you were talking to someone."

"Who would I possibly be talking to?"

He considered this. "So perhaps you were talking in your sleep. But I still demand to know who you were talking to."

"Zylee!" Ozyan called at the door.

The servant girl reappeared, which baffled the king. She'd run away so fast, he hadn't expected her to still be so close.

Zylee frowned and went back into the room until she reached her sister. Ozyan squeezed her cheeks together, causing her lips to form an hourglass shape. "Don't be shy," she told her. "Just do it. Do it for me."

"Do what for you?" Montrose grunted. He felt like a child. Emasculated. His temper swelled, and he searched the Grand Ballroom for the nearest breakable object.

With her head bowed, Zylee approached King Montrose. She untied the sash of his robe and opened it.

"What do you think you're doing?" he asked her. He looked at Ozyan. "I thought this was your sister."

Ozyan gave a small smile and nodded.

Zylee went onto her knees in front of him. Before he could protest, she did something that nothing in his physical power could stop her from doing. He shut his eyes and lost control of his breathing. He considered that those nobles, heads of state, and sycophantic dullards might also learn how to properly fellate him. At the end of it all, he didn't care one bit what they thought of his new bride. They would come to accept her, or they could resign, and he would kill them.

A tongue traced his earlobe, and he jolted, surprised, his eyes opening. Ozyan laughed at seeing him jump. "I want to meet Amgelan," she whispered into his ear. "When can I?"

"Amgelan? The general? Why?"

"I have some ideas to discuss with him."

"Shouldn't you concentrate on the wedding, my dove? It's in three days."

"The wedding is in the hands of the Lord Chamberlain now. He's already promised to make our wedding the largest this kingdom has ever seen."

"Tell me your ideas. If I like them, I will pass them on to Amgelan when I see him."

Ozyan took his pudgy, bearded cheeks in her fingers, just as she had done with her sister. "I want to meet him myself. Please?"

King Montrose laughed, a throaty chortle. He couldn't help himself. Her brazenness was astonishing. And more than a little farcical. He loved her.

"It's very important," Ozyan added. "Almost as important as the wedding."

The king winced, and his legs weakened. He touched the crown of Zylee's head. "Yes?"

"Have Amgelan brought to my chamber," she said. "And you, my king, can have *all* of my sisters should you desire them."

He couldn't answer. Her request was simply too outrageous to cope with in this moment. This joyous, unexpected moment. He could only think: *Yes, this was going to be a different sort of marriage altogether.*

17

SHAYAN

The king and his men paused at a small clearing in the forest, created by a small hill of jutting, granite boulders. They swatted at random places on their bodies to kill whatever subspecies of insect crawled through their clothing and hair, some even seeking the deepest refuge of their crotches. When he found Lalya, she was hopping on one foot, inhaling sharply while she scratched her calf. Like everyone, she appeared heavily fatigued. The need for stealth while traveling was incessant and exhausting.

They had succeeded so far in keeping light-footed, an accomplishment made possible by soft-soled shoes. Shayan inwardly thanked himself for insisting on this footwear for everyone. It allowed them to feel the ground and avoid twigs or other noisy debris. He used the wind and the racket from rushing falls to cover their other, more unavoidable sounds. The king had also insisted on tight clothing since baggy fabric could get snagged.

After a small meal of oats and dried pork, he ordered everyone to push forward through the forest ahead, ensuring they moved at a glacial pace, excruciating as it was. He was experienced in traveling undetected enough to know that their worst mistake would be moving too fast, especially during dead silences.

The toughest hazard to combat was their smell. Side-stepping a predator's nose was practically impossible. Still, Shayan had to get his men to at least try. Every stream they came across, he ordered everyone to wash themselves, but without soap, since this would merely create an even stronger smell.

Continuing, he kept their path under ridges and hills, using as much thick cover as he could find. As night fell, Shayan did his best to keep the twin moons at their backs since a smart fighter always battled with the light behind them.

They rested for the evening at the base of a large ridge. Before sleep, he conferred with Khilji and insisted they collect sap and use it to stick leaves and branches to their clothing. Enhance their camouflage. Shayan could see how unpopular the idea was with the other men, but he ordered they do it anyway. Anything to help their chances.

After molting himself in vegetation, but in a way

that wasn't obtrusive to movement, he noticed Lalya having a hard time. The sap wanted to cling more to her fingers than anywhere else. He walked over to her with a small vine he'd yanked from the ground.

"I'll help you," he said.

Lalya hesitated. "As you wish."

She spread her arms out, a silent invitation to do his best. He used the sap already dotting her tunic to attach the vine around her midriff. He took more sap from his own fingers to apply a handful of brown and green leaves to her shoulders and arms. He stepped back to assess his progress.

"Where did you go?" he asked her while looking all around. "I can't see you anywhere! Lalya?"

"You're funny."

He chuckled. "Thank you. I mean, for helping Sarna escape. I can never repay you for that."

"But you are. You're letting me come with you to Burnya."

He resumed applying more leaves to her collar. "Having a female with us has been a good reminder about why we're doing this."

"Good." She stretched her arms and bent over. She collected more leaves from the ground, fallen from the surrounding hardwoods. "My Lord, there's something I've been wanting to tell you about Sarna."

He looked at her. "Is it bad?"

When she straightened, she kept her eyes on her hands, filled with dry leaves.

"Tell me," he said. "I can take it."

"When we were with those bandits, they came under attack from some Tartarian knights."

"Yes, I do believe I sent that battalion myself. What happened to them?"

Lalya shook her head. "It was Sarna. She killed them." Lalya mashed leaves with her hands. She pressed the leaves onto her body.

"Wait, Sarna? Killed who?"

"All of them. The entire battalion of knights. Sarna screamed, and her body lit up, and every knight dropped dead all at once." Lalya looked up into his face and must've seen the confusion there. "I wouldn't believe me either, but I was there. I saw it."

"So…what? You're telling me it was magic?"

"I have no idea what it was. All I know is that …everyone kind of became understandably terrified of her after that."

"Did she…," he trailed off, unable to find his train of thought. "My sister is a witch?"

"I didn't say that." Lalya looked back down at herself, her torso shingled with leaves and the single, thin vine drooping past her waist. "I've known Sarna since I was little, and I'd never seen her do something like that. Ever."

"Me either. You're telling me she killed her own people?"

"She didn't mean to." Lalya blew a speck of dirt from her lip. "I shouldn't have told you."

"Anything else you're not telling me?"

She lifted her eyes to meet his again. She shook her head slowly. "No."

He rubbed a hand over the top of his hair. He walked a few yards away and rested his foot atop a small rock. "In times such as these," he said, "the impossible becomes manifested."

"What do you mean?"

"Nothing." The rock rolled loose, and he played with it under his shoe. "You've just told me that my sister is a witch with the power to slay knights. I'm not as astonished as I should be."

"Because you don't believe me. I understand."

"Here." He walked back over to her. He reached inside the belt of his tunic and removed the tooth, still in its pouch. He handed her the tooth. When she gave him a questioning look, he told her, "It's a drakksuk tooth. A kid gave it to me. Said it kills whatever it stabs. Anything. Doesn't matter what it is."

"How is that possible? It's so small."

"Compared to a dagger, maybe. For a tooth, it's huge."

"Does it have magic poison?"

"I have no idea."

She weighed the tooth in her hand. "But you're the king. A weapon such as this…shouldn't it be in the hands of someone more important than me?"

"And why are you not important?"

Lalya shrugged and dropped the tooth into a pocket on her tunic. "A real drakksuk tooth. *Joppa.*"

Shayan turned at the sound of two men arguing.

They yelled in each other's faces until the taller of the pair ended the fight with a sharp bark, causing the other man to step back. He used his sleeve to swab the spittle from his nose. Shayan started to say something to them but decided against it. He didn't have the strength. He couldn't control absolutely everything.

"Getting kidnapped changed me." Lalya fiddled absently with a leaf clinging to her elbow. They watched it fall off. "But seeing how brave Sarna was. I wouldn't be alive if it weren't for her. As I said, I know it's hard to believe, but that really did happen."

Shayan nodded, frowned. "She always cared a lot about you."

There came a distant but distinct sound from the northeast, like a giant hammer pummeling the entire planet. The sound came so close, so swiftly, Shayan didn't have time to check if everyone else was reacting properly. He could only glimpse the men running, and he joined them, grabbing Lalya's hand and pulling her with him. He heard the now familiar bellow of yelkin behind them. He looked back and saw two of them closing the distance. When it became obvious they couldn't outrun the giants, Shayan and his men each hid behind the largest tree they could find. Others flattened themselves on the ground.

The two yelkin roared as they crashed into their surroundings, hulking masses of flesh, teeth, and horns. Shayan heard some of his men screaming. He heard bones crunching, and the screaming stopped.

Shayan clawed the debris from his face and tried to see who was being hurt. Four of his knights lay in pieces, eviscerated by the jaws of the yelkin who chewed them with focused intention. Their long, sharp teeth clamped down and tore.

He tried to get up but fell back onto his knees. Spotting their king down, several of his squad rushed over to him. Khilji was the first.

"My king, my king," he said. "Are you all right? Are you hurt?"

More gathered around, and Shayan slapped at their hands. "Stop it!" he yelled. He was surprised to hear how badly his voice broke. "Run, you idiots!"

He spotted Lalya lying beside a tree. She embraced her knees to her chest, clutching the five-inch tooth he'd just given her. Her hair hid her face, so he couldn't see exactly how her nerves were handling this event. She rocked herself. The remaining men ran for their lives through the trees. Shayan raced to Lalya and pulled her to her feet again.

They sprinted for what felt like hours. When Shayan slowed to a walk, his men fell in line behind him. He could always feel how their mood matched his, so he tried his best to remain brave and determined. But he no longer knew if it was worth it anymore. He kept leading good men to their ghastly deaths.

They stumbled their way through tunnels of tall trees. Bone-white rays of moonlight interwove through the branches. He held Lalya's hand as they walked.

OZYAN

General Amgelan entered the Queen-to-be's private quarters. He was dressed in a royal-blue tunic, black pants, leather shoes, and a light-blue cloak. He approached Ozyan, who stood in front of the mirror. She admired herself while a trio of maidens helped her into her dress. It was a silk burgundy garment trimmed with golden thread and pearl buttons. Beneath the floor-length hem were the newly-made calfskin boots she'd demanded.

Ozyan used the same mirror to watch Burnya's top military commander enter her quarters. She made a sideways smile. "There you are," she said.

Amgelan grinned. "You called for me, your Highness?"

She spoke to his reflection. "Burnya's fortification is three walls, reinforced with towers at regular distances. It runs from the abbey at the Golden Claw, near the modern Atatürk Bridge."

The general pursed his lips. "Indeed it does, yes."

"It runs southwest and passes east of the great open cisterns of Comius and Saspar, ending somewhere between the gates of Aemilianus and Psamathos." Two of the maids fastened brooches to the shoulders of Ozyan's dress while a third maid hemmed the bottom, pins held between clinched lips. Their faces remained neutral as masks.

Amgelan nodded at her. "Our great walls have remained impregnable throughout their entire history."

Ozyan turned one direction, then another, admiring the dress. "Not for long, it seems. You doubtlessly know of Chief Arlyn's threat to invade Burnya."

"It's more than a threat, I believe."

"That wall will be useless against what's coming, General Amgelan."

His warm smile drained slowly away. "How so?"

The maids stepped back and collectively folded their hands together, signaling they were done. They kept their eyes to the floor. Ozyan was taken aback by how attractive and sexy she looked. She became aware of how the dress showed off her slender torso. She knew this was something she would be forced to address soon should anyone doubt her pregnancy. She wondered if a strategically placed pillow might become necessary.

"I've made an important ally recently," she said to the general. "Someone I'd like to introduce you to. I believe he'll be of tremendous help to us."

As she'd done with him earlier, Amgelan addressed her image in the mirror. "Of help to whom, my lady? The military?"

"Everyone."

"Have I met this person? Is he from Burnya? If he's military, I would've heard of him."

"He's not military." Ozyan turned to face him. She grinned slyly. "Not exactly. By the way, I've just finished reading a book about you."

"Which one? There are five."

"Five! Oh, well!" She stepped over to him, her forehead nearly touching his chin. "Sounds like I have a lot more reading to do."

"What did the book say about me? I'm always curious to learn who I am."

"You lied about your age and joined the military at fourteen. You commanded Burnyan armies at twenty-five. You've made such a strong defense of this kingdom that no one would dare attack us. Until now."

"We are ready for any threat. I assure you. If that's what concerns—"

"The king says the Cathyrnee have made a deal with an evil spirit. That they are backed by an army of monsters and demons. Do you believe this?"

"Jyn does grow stranger by the day."

"General Amgelan, my new friend is waiting to meet you. He has some solid ideas on how we might save the world from a lot of nastiness." As she spoke, Ozyan wandered to the nearest window, where the sun spotlighted her lithe figure, its light sparkling off the expensive threading of her dress.

Amgelan cleared his throat. "I'm not...Does the king know about this?"

She sat on the windowsill, her gaze still fixed outside. "I want you to feel that you can always speak your mind to me. I might be the new Queen, but that doesn't mean I believe myself to always be right. All

I ask for is the truth, no matter how disastrous or painful. I can always accept it."

"I took an oath, Your Highness," he said, though he sounded unsure, off guard from so many elliptic statements and changes of subject.

"I'm sick of war," she said. "I hate it. It's always the poorest who suffer most in war. All I want is peace. Do you understand?"

"But the drakksuk," he said, unsure of how else to reply. "They are quite problematic. They do make for a type of warfare we've never faced before."

"Defeating them will be impossible."

"We have the best alchemists, priests, and engineers of this entire realm helping us. They've designed a new weapon that should be of considerable advantage."

"New weapons won't be necessary."

"But I have commissioned a type of fire lance using black powder. It's a weapon in the shape of a cylinder that fires projectiles. You should see it."

"I will do no such thing, General. Are you not listening to me?"

He wasn't. "This weapon uses the explosive pressure of the powder," he continued, "and it's quite effective. We're even developing several lighter, more maneuverable versions to use."

"Get rid of them all."

The general barked a laugh. He pressed his hand over his mouth, having apparently laughed louder than he meant to. "My lady?"

Ozyan crossed her arms. "I have my own plan. Given to me by our new ally. A plan that will guarantee peace." *And my Queenhood, despite not actually being pregnant.*

The general nodded, visibly unnerved. "My *experienced* plan was to have our army concentrate a superior force to encircle and wipe out the enemy from behind. The enemy is always weakest at the rear because there's less support there. We could then find the most favorable terrain for a crossfire of archers. Their arrows would be lit with oil and used to repel any man or beast until they run away. Our men will fight very bravely."

"And within seconds they'll be dead."

He held onto his military talk, undeterred, "We have also assembled an elite fighting force called 'The Alysee.' They are paid good salaries. Their sole reason for living is their complete loyalty to you and the king."

Ozyan walked over to him again, charmed by his need to keep explaining himself. She took his hand and placed it over her right breast. She watched his cheeks redden before bringing his hand to her mouth and kissing his fingertips. "You're exactly as the book said you were," she told him. "You are a hero to this kingdom, General Amgelan. Our gratitude will be eternal. Now come with me. It truly is time for the two of you to meet."

18

CHIEF ARLYN

After having the eastern wall repaired, Chief Arlyn hired two builders to construct a hut inside the royal bedroom. Despite already knowing that word about this would get out and that people would find this an odd and worrisome development, he couldn't bring himself to care. Months and months of making a home inside a hut with his wife, living in the wilderness with only two guards and a hide-thin wall to protect them, had made him more comfortable convalescing in one. He felt more insulated, cocooned. The size of the royal bedroom allowed for the space, so why not?

The homeless kid he'd adopted slept in the hut as well. Though he did so in his own cot, Arlyn knew of the salacious rumors this might spawn. While the boy never said anything, his attitude eased up after he was fed. Arlyn knew he and this child needed each other. The child needed him because he had no one else to take care of him. Arlyn supposed the same was true of himself.

Also, it was what Yarlaa would've wanted him to do.

He hoped the kid would tell him his name soon. For now, he settled for being with the child, letting him nod or shake his head as to whether he was hungry or thirsty. The boy slept soundly now while Arlyn sat on his own bed of felts and furs. He drank from a musty bottle of babsulisk. He'd discovered the narcotic in the former Queen's vanity, perhaps a guilty secret of hers to soothe those long nights when ruling the kingdom beside a demented king became too much. Once intoxicated, Arlyn grew transfixed with the impressive craftsmanship of this mostly unnecessary hut, how the lattice was divided into sections, each forming a collapsible series of crisscrossed bamboo poles, attached to each other with leather ropes. The walls were wooden-slat lattice supporting sapling beams, held together at the top by a wooden ring.

Arlyn recalled many nights being in a hut exactly like this one, out on the Narlan Plains, the warmth of his wife Yarlaa beside him, sleepless as he was now, fearing another attack from the yelkin. The giants would feed on the Cathyrnee at will, subsiding their attack only when their red bellies were full. It was a never-ending battle that had prompted Chief Arlyn to do the unthinkable and conjure that horrible spirit, to go along with that witch Corsika's plan, poisoning Yarlaa's mind so she went along with it, too.

Their plan had initiated so much destruction. So much distrust and anger from his own people. If he were truly a leader of no worth anymore, then he could at least be of some value to this child. He supposed this was as close as he would ever get to being a father for a while.

There came a quick, sharp knock at the door. The person entered without waiting for a reply. Arlyn relaxed when he recognized the heavy clank of Khuyag's plate boots. Arlyn had long ago learned from warrior training how to identify people by their steps alone, discerning the weight of their movements, the noise of their clothing, even the vibration of their essence. Khuyag's movements were always swift but heavy. His clothing was relatively unadorned but with enough metal and leather to announce himself from meters away.

Arlyn watched for the inevitable lifting of the hut's flap.

Khuyag's bearded visage peered in. "Chief Arlyn, forgive me for disturbing you, but you have a visitor."

"Tell him to leave me alone. I'm drunk."

"It's a woman."

"Tell her to leave me alone."

"I would've already, of course, except that she's…I don't know."

"You don't know?"

"She's a peculiar woman."

"In a good way?"

"You'll have to see for yourself, I believe."

"Do her eyes glow red?"

"No, but it wouldn't surprise me if they started to." Khuyag took a breath. He appeared nervous, which wasn't like him. "She says she's traveled all the way here from Burnya to see you."

"Was she sent by Seelskan?"

"Who?"

"Ask her if Seelskan sent her. The warlock! The one you're supposed to be on the lookout for at all times!"

"Yes, yes, yes, I already asked her. She claims not to know who that is."

"I still don't care. Tell her she's not welcome here." Arlyn stood and drew his sword. The sleeping boy stirred. "Tell her to leave, or I will kill her, then have breakfast."

Khuyag got nudged aside by a tall, slender woman, dressed in a red silk chiffon-paneled gown. The instant she power-strutted into the hut, Arlyn understood why Khuyag had been so lost for words to describe her. She was conventionally gorgeous with a high forehead, large eyes, and a slender nose. She possessed full, red lips, a defined chin, and fair skin smooth as marble. Her figure was dainty without frailty. Her dress' waist-high slits exposed her long legs.

"Get out of here, witch!" Chief Arlyn yelled at her. "I was defending myself from Seelskan!"

"Pull yourself together," she said, her voice a blunt note, as if to imply her removal would doubtlessly require a great deal of violence.

"You're not here because of Seelskan?"

"I am here for you," the woman said. "I am Ulaan, and I am merely here to offer my aid."

Arlyn turned on Khuyag. "How could you allow this woman to just walk in here?"

He started to respond, but Ulaan cut him off. "My powers prevented him from seeing me until I wanted him to."

Another two guards appeared in the hut behind him, idly observing.

"What are you standing there for?" Arlyn yelled at the three of them. "Kill her!"

They stared back at him without reacting, mesmerized. Arlyn wanted to scorn them again but realized they were under a spell. Or they were simply that scared of this woman. Possibly both.

Arlyn raised his sword to strike her, but when he tried bringing the blade down across her body, his arm turned impossibly heavy, and he dropped the weapon. It rattled across the floor, and the sound was unbearable. His head pulsed from the impact. He clutched his head and tried to keep from toppling, understanding he'd come under the same spell, or one similar.

"I am not here to harm you, Chief Arlyn." The odd, exquisitely arresting woman named Ulaan smiled, her right brow arching. "I am here to save your life."

SARNA

She allowed herself to enjoy the simple sensation of the tall grass against her ankles and knees. It tickled, a desperately welcome feeling, since she remained so incredibly tired. No matter how hard she walked, she lagged behind the others. If the Ghe-sui felt frustrated with her over this, they were too nice to show it, even though they had to stop numerous times to let her catch up.

After another couple of hours, Sarna felt a tremendous thud, like from an explosion. A bright light filled the night sky to the southeast. She squinted to see the light spreading across the entire horizon. Every shaman gasped, except Momaset, who stepped forward and shielded his eyes. When the brightness subsided, Sarna saw that the light source was indeed an explosion, bigger than she had ever seen or imagined. A tower of debris and dust pillared into the clouds before blossoming into a rosebud of flames. The tower of fire ascended until it seemed it would never stop.

She wondered if she was dreaming again but next came a roar growing louder. A great crescent of upheaved soil and vegetation peeled towards them. Sarna noticed a small pond nearby to her right. She had to reach the water and dive in, stay underwater until the approaching wall of fire and death finished passing over. There was no other way to survive. She ran but realized that she wasn't close enough. She wouldn't make it. She dove anyway as white-hot light carried her into the air, instantly incinerating her and the shamans. Their ashes became stars.

Her vision, blurred by water, came into focus until it formed Momaset's face. He was shaking her again. Sarna looked up at him, perplexed at learning the entire destruction of the world had only been another dream. She touched her cheek and, to her shame, felt a patch of dried drool there. Next to Momaset stood Corsika, who handed Sarna a sarong. She accepted it, though unsure at first over what to do with it. She assumed it was to wipe her face with, but she found the sarong too pretty, so she simply held it.

"Are you all right?" Momaset asked her. He helped her to her feet.

"I think maybe I'm going crazy. I'm having visions."

"You dream of great flames swallowing the world. Yes, we're all having the same dream. There is a great battle coming."

She blinked at him. She felt dazed and sore. The ground was softer than it had looked before she lay down, but that was not to say it was terribly soft at all. Small leaves and pine straw clung to her hair and tunic.

"Would you take a walk with me?" he asked her.

"I will," she said before she could think about it. It didn't feel right to refuse him. She walked by his side while he held her elbow. Corsika started to follow, but he stopped her with a gently raised hand.

Further down the hill, when Sarna almost lost her footing, Momaset caught her. She was impressed by how tender yet strong his grip was. It summarized nearly everything about him, as far as she could tell.

The rest of the shamans lay sleeping within shelves of granite and grass, tucked along the hill, some covered by blankets, others not, since the evening was strangely warm. She noticed two sentries perched in the branches of two different trees, watching over their group. She followed Momaset to the border of the woodline.

She stumbled again, still stupefied from finding herself awake, images from her apocalyptic dreams still fresh. He caught her by the waist this time. He kept his hand there as they walked.

"Are you going to make it?" he asked her. "You seem so weak. Are you sick?"

She wanted to say she was merely tired, but instead said, "I've been through a lot." She tried running a hand through her ragged hair. Finding her locks so tangled that she couldn't even comb her fingers through, she dropped her hand and unintentionally whimpered.

"I need what I'm about to tell you to stay between the two of us," Momaset told her. He gave her a look, searching for what effect these words had. "Princess

Sarna, there is great magic in you. I can see it. The Magshaa Bells ringing for you was clearly not an accident."

She tensed. "How can you know?"

"I know much, my princess."

Why was everyone always making that claim to her? She averted her eyes, her face flushing. "Look, I told you I've killed people. And they were Tartarian. Lots of them. I even killed someone I thought I might've at least cared about." There was a silence, and Sarna understood he was waiting for her to elaborate. "I don't know exactly how it happened. I was angry with him. And..." Her mouth remained open, but she had stopped talking. She shrugged. She was at a loss. "No, the Magshaa Bells rang for me by mistake. I don't deserve such importance."

Sarna became extra aware that his hand remained on her waist.

"I want you to know that you can tell me anything you need to," he said. "You never have to be afraid to tell me anything."

"Thank you."

"But something else is on your mind, no?"

She held her hands out, waved them around, exasperated. "I wish it were. These powers I have, I can't control them. I'm killing people. That's why I went to see the Magshaa. I was hoping he would train me."

"But I will train you!" He smiled at her. "Nothing would bring me greater pleasure. I promise."

The idea of someone's promise invigorated her. She

felt fortunate to even be accepted by their group. Grateful for the protection. "Sure, that would be amazing," she said. "I was even beginning to worry the Sünsü had left me. One moment I was flying—"

Momaset grasped her and pressed his mouth over hers. His tongue probed its way past her lips as he held her tight. She stood stiff, completely shocked. His tongue explored her mouth while his hand trailed to the small of her back, pressing there. She prayed the hand wouldn't venture lower. He pulled back and smiled down at her, pleased with himself, oblivious to her surprise. Or unconcerned by it.

"I've been wanting to do that since I first laid eyes on you." He took her hands in his and resumed walking.

Sarna was still so surprised that she followed without speaking. He had agreed to train her, but there was evidently a price, a contract that would've never come from the Magshaa. She had no idea what to do or say.

"We will make an unstoppable pair, you and I," he was saying. "Our powers together will be unmatched. This is divine destiny. Do you feel it?"

She kept walking with her hand in his. His behavior was unsettling, but she did need someone to teach her. Otherwise, she might kill someone she cared about again. Maybe others. Maybe hundreds.

"When do you think we will reach Burnya?" she asked. She hoped to change the subject.

"Midday tomorrow, maybe." He turned to her and

placed his hands on her shoulders. "I know you're frightened, but everything is going to be all right. Do as I say, and you will be protected. This is meant to be. You'll see."

He kissed her again, and this time she closed her eyes. She tried to enjoy it. When that didn't happen, she told herself that she would learn to. She would learn to enjoy it. She would have to try.

19

CHIEF ARLYN

Arlyn couldn't get over how spellbindingly beautiful this woman was, even in the dull light of this ragged hut, nestled within the wrecked bedroom of former royals. An undulating radiance came from within her, a flittering, ambient exposure.

"The Burnyan military has been preparing for your invasion," she told him. "You gave them plenty of warning."

"How would you know?"

"We have allies in common, Chief."

"Are you with Baal? I want nothing more to do with him."

"I know you don't mean that."

Chief Arlyn shifted his feet, surprised she would take such a conversational tone after he had just tried killing her. She acted genuinely nonplussed, probably having expected such a reaction. Khuyag, for his part, stood inside the hut's front flap. He stared at her with a dopey grin, as though drugged. The boy sat up on his cot and smiled at the woman. He appeared fully pleased by her arrival.

"So you weren't sent here by Seelskan?" Arlyn asked her.

"No." She smiled back at the boy.

"You are not here to avenge anyone?"

She lowered her face and smiled sideways. "Avenge for what?"

He considered how to best answer and decided he had nothing to lose. "I killed Seelskan."

The woman's smile dissipated. "I see." She took a breath. "You were raised a warrior, Chief Arlyn. Your first impulse is to defend your loved ones. To protect your own. I can perfectly understand that. I'm sure Baal forgives you."

"Yes? And where would he be?" Arlyn brushed by her, nudging her shoulder as he left the hut. He crossed the room. He turned, but Ulaan was already outside the hut. She faced him.

Her smile had returned, except larger now, revealing a front row of gleaming white teeth, her cheeks dented with deep dimples. "Trust does not come easily for you, does it?"

"No offense," he said, "but I don't see why this great and mighty spirit needs me. I kept asking Seelskan the same thing."

"And what did he say?"

"Something about me being a great leader of men and Baal needs men because we know how to rule and keep order."

"Baal does have a tremendous affection for humanity. It's true. And right now, he has no more important friend than you, Chief Arlyn. You are indeed a great leader."

"Many would disagree with you."

"Who else could have endured what you did and still conquer the greatest kingdom Jyn has ever known?"

"It was hardly a fair fight."

"All men of legend have their detractors. I don't have to tell this to you." The beautiful woman with the ugly name folded her arms. She cradled her own face thoughtfully. "I wouldn't have come all this way if we didn't believe in you, Chief Arlyn."

"If Baal believes in me so much, why didn't he come here to tell me all this?"

She ran her hands down her thighs. She smoothed her dress over her hips. "I believe Baal simply assumed I would be a more pleasing sight for you."

"He wasn't wrong."

Khuyag staggered out of the hut and saw the woman standing beside his chief. He belched a low, lurching guffaw like that of an idiot. A spindle of drool clung to his bottom lip. The two guards remained inside the hut. They stared at nothing.

Arlyn made his hands into fists. "So you want me

to lead my pissed-off, war-weary soldiers to attack Burnya with your demonic army and then what? What do my people get out of all this?"

"All war is profitable, is it not?" asked Ulaan. "You already know what you'll get out of it."

Khuyag picked his nose and looked at it.

Ulaan held her arms out expansively. "You and your people will be safe forever," she said. "It's all the Cathyrnee have ever wanted." She folded her arms under her crimson-clothed, barely contained breasts. "Ever since the Great Awakening advanced our civilization, these monarchs have been in charge. And they've shown themselves to be nothing more than lecherous, corrupted maniacs who live in luxury while their people starve. It is time for that to end. Immediately."

"And how do either of you know I won't do the same? "

Ulaan threw up her hands. She dimmed her eyes. "You've conquered the kingdom of Tartaria yet you're sleeping in a hut. A few of your people are upset with you, and you're moping around with your feelings hurt. Do you think King Khilji ever did that?" The smile seeped back into her face, creating those dimples again. He wished so much to touch them. See how much of his finger he could fit in there. "Because you are a good man, Chief Arlyn," she answered herself. "A strong warrior. Baal understands why you killed Seelskan. The warlock was self-serving and devious. He took things too far when you asked him to stop."

Arlyn went to take a step and winced from a tightness in his side. Despite the constant applications of healing ointments, his wounds throbbed from standing too long. He wanted to lie down but resisted. He came closer to her instead while holding his side. The proximity of her beauty and figure stirred something between his hips. When he met her eyes, a glint there told him she was already aware of this stirring.

She licked her lips, which appeared glossy, oiled. "We can lead the attack together, Chief Arlyn. I can be of tremendous service to you."

Arlyn recalled King Montrose on his knees, coated head-to-toe in dust, bleeding cuts on his belly. Dust in his mouth, coughing clouds. "I did promise that fat, worthless bastard I would do it, didn't I?"

"I wasn't there, but I heard. It's already legendary."

"Look, if Baal is so mighty, why can't he wave his hand around and kill every knight and soldier in Burnya? That way we could stroll in and take over without losing a single man."

"Baal is an exceptionally powerful spirit, but he has ethereal constraints. The longer he's here, the more power he will gain. But he needs the support and the belief of more and more people. People such as you, Chief Arlyn. He wouldn't even be here if it weren't for you."

"I'm thinking what might save my people is to stop waging war and focus on putting our lives back together."

"Except once you accomplish that, people will come from every corner of Jyn to take it away from you. Be it warfare or trading, these monarchs will succeed. Are you not familiar with your own history?"

"Don't insult me."

"Besides, we are liberating the citizens of Burnya, Chief Arlyn. Not conquering. They are suffering because their kingdom is broken. They will welcome you as heroes, I assure you."

"And you will ride by my side?" He could feel the increasing heat from her body, spreading over his. He put his face into hers and cupped her rear in his hands, digging his fingers into its softness.

Ulaan stepped back, unoffended but repelled by his touch. "I am not the one intended for you."

"I disagree."

"You will be offered another as your new wife."

"What if I don't want another?"

She went to the door and stopped there. The witch gave him a look over her shoulder, and he felt transfixed with those radiant-green eyes, that pale neck, slender as a deer's.

"Prepare your army," she told him. "We will attack in three days."

"*Three?* It'll take me that long to even organize a *strategy* for recruiting that many men."

"You are well-known for disliking drawn-out campaigns. Everyone knows that the great Chief Arlyn prefers to strike quickly. You will do it."

"Three days is far too quick." He looked to Khuyag for agreement, but the head of his military was preoccupied with the threading of his right sleeve. He grinned at his own arm, as though marveling at the length of it.

"Three days is plenty of time," Ulaan said, "if you start right this minute."

"What's the rush?"

"King Montrose is getting married in three days. The wedding will be the perfect time to attack. The kingdom will be distracted."

"He's getting married? Already?"

She ignored the question. "Baal appreciates the use of any advantage he can find," she said. "This keeps our casualties lower. Is this not what you prefer? Were your casualties not minimal when you took Tartaria?" Ulaan made that sideways smile again, and Arlyn contemplated how such a small contraction of facial muscles could have so much allure, such potency.

He noticed her attention switch to the boy who had just left the hut. He stood inside its flap, and the two of them stared at each other.

"I see you," Ulaan told the boy.

20

KING MONTROSE

After morning prayers, the king of Burnya left the chapel and was met by a crowd of commoners inside the courtyard. The people came from every walk of life: rich, poor, ladies, maidens, widows—anyone who had problems. They made their petitions to him as he patiently pretended to listen, only responding to those who behaved the most hysterically or despondently. He next turned them over to a "Master of Requests" for examination. Later, the king met with a council of his most high-ranking government men inside the Council Chamber with its coffered ceiling and marble statues of former kings.

The number of government ministers kept increasing over time, so Montrose had decided to expand the chamber. He'd removed the wall dividing it from the adjacent antechamber, combining both rooms. During the reign of King Olaag—Montrose's grandfather—the room had been painted blue with blue curtains and blue upholstered chairs. The effect of this had been intended to inspire peace, tranquility, security, and order. However, it made King Montrose feel moody and withdrawn, even morose. Standing beside a handmade dais desk, he poured himself a goblet of babsulisk from a green bottle. He sipped the narcotic nectar, its warmth and energy spreading through every artery.

Once the last meeting had finished, he retired alone to the chamber, seated at his throne, drinking straight from the bottle. Artemis returned, still dressed in his tunic of gold and silver brocades. A velvet coat hung from his shoulders, but his arms were free from its sleeves, free to gesture while he addressed the court.

"The meetings are over," Montrose said to Artemis. He belched. "Stop bothering me."

"I'll bet if I requested for you to recall a single word of today's meetings, you would be hard-pressed to do so, My Lord. Is everything all right?"

"Have you seen Ozyan?"

"Not recently. Why?"

"I awoke this morning to find her already gone. For the second morning in a row."

"And this is unusual, I take it?"

"Yes, Artemis. Completely. I don't know what's gotten into her. She's not the same woman."

"Your wedding is in two days, My Lord. I imagine

she has a lot to attend to. It's a huge day."

"Artemis, am I making a mistake?"

The Master of Gold walked closer. He twisted his mouth. "I'm afraid my counsel only relates to matters of finance. Matters of love are an entirely different science, My Lord."

"I fear that being married to this village girl is going to be far more of a challenge than I could've possibly bargained for."

"I recall your marriage to Queen Saraal as being fraught with worry, too. Such is the temperament of Queens, My Lord."

Hearing Saraal's name jolted the king. He'd done his best not to think much about her. It was the main reason he'd surrendered to Ozyan's demand of a lightning-quick wedding. It distracted from the pain of not only losing his Queen, but the horror of personally witnessing her violent and cruel death. He often saw that image of her when he closed his eyes, even to this minute, that look of confusion as she became sawed apart by a hot, forked bolt of drakksuk breath. Montrose felt convinced her death lay linked to her innumerable consultations with the wicked shaman woman Ulaan. Consistent proximity to such wickedness always attracted harm and danger. Why couldn't she have seen that?

Artemis cleared his throat. "Are you aware your bride-to-be has been making plans with General Amgelan?"

"They're arranging a stronger defense against the

invasion."

"With what money?"

"I don't know. Everything we have left."

"And you're confident about this?"

"The general came to me last night and told me. He needs more money for the military, so I gave it to him."

"I don't mean to step beyond my duties, My Lord, but I have information which would indicate your bride has far different plans."

"From your spies?" Montrose swung his fist at Artemis but missed. Unfazed, the Master of Gold stepped back as the king wiggled his sizeable girth down the court steps. He sauntered to the lone wooden cabinet against the western wall. He went to work, opening every cabinet door and drawer, searching for more babsulisk.

"You asked me if I thought you were making a mistake," said Artemis. "I wouldn't suggest such as that, but I would keep a more careful eye on her."

"You're telling me she's a liar?"

"She's made an important alliance with someone. Some mysterious man."

"Who are your spies anyway? Servants? Those girls make up stories just to spite her. She used to be one of them, and they hate her for it."

"Queen Saraal was from a high family, born for royalty. Ozyan is a village girl with no education."

Montrose paused from his feverish hunt for drink. He faced Artemis. "And that alone makes her a liar?"

"Could be that the issue, My Lord, is that it's time to give a speech and detail what happened at King Khilji's funeral. About the attack. You've given not one single public speech about it. Nothing. And now this extremely rushed wedding with a servant girl from a remote village? Yes, people are beginning to make up stories."

King Montrose found a bottle in the bottom cabinet. He nearly toppled from having to bend over, but stood up straight, holding the bottle and swaying. His lips made a smacking noise after finishing his swig. "And tell them what, Artemis? That there are giants and creatures and monsters? That these nightmares are real?" He looked at the bottle but dropped his arm again without drinking. "Ozyan and General Amgelan can go ahead and make their plans, but it's utterly pointless. They didn't see what I saw. If Chief Arlyn chooses to attack us, we'll be wiped out in minutes as Tartaria was. I can no longer deny it."

He could sense Artemis choosing his words carefully. "Public knowledge of impending doom can be a hazard, it's true. But at your wedding, you could at least offer a speech with some words of hope and enlightenment?"

"What hope? What enlightenment?" The king heard footsteps approaching the main door. "Enter!" he barked before the knock came.

A castle guard opened the door, his cherub face wedging in. Montrose recognized the boy from a recent orgy. "Your majesty, a young girl who claims to be Princess Sarna of Tartaria is here. She's requesting an audience with you."

"King Khilji's daughter? Are you sure? Here?"

"She's with a shaman. The Ghe-sui."

"Bring her to me," Montrose growled. "But tell the shaman to go die somewhere."

The guard closed the door. A moment later, a tall, lean man entered. He was bald except for a ponytail atop his head. His white tunic had turned gray at the bottom, soiled from travel. Behind him walked a petite young girl in a blue tunic that was even filthier but obviously woven from superior thread. Still, King Montrose had a difficult time believing this scrawny girl was of any importance whatsoever.

"I said only *she* can come in!" Montrose swung his hand for emphasis, but it held the babsulisk bottle. Slack-jawed with intoxication, King Montrose dropped the bottle, and it shattered.

SARNA

As Momaset had predicted, they reached Burnya by the next afternoon, though it required a full day of walking without a break. Upon reaching the kingdom gates, Sarna felt disheartened by their reception. Everyone was, except Momaset, who appeared endlessly optimistic by the accompaniment of royalty. He even bounced when he walked.

The gate guards allowed them entry, but only following a drawn-out, condescending interrogation about their intentions in visiting. Telling them she wished to see King Montrose made the guards laugh, but then it made them angry. After Momaset defiantly and continuously informed them of who Sarna was, the guards said they could enter, but there was no way they would ever be allowed within several leagues of his Highness.

Considering her decrepit appearance, Sarna could understand their skepticism, but she'd anticipated more respect towards the Ghe-sui. After all, they were the kingdom's official religion.

This was Sarna's fourth time visiting Burnya. The previous three visits had been royal delegational trips with her family. She owned happy memories of this kingdom. She remembered Burnya for its crowded streets filled with beautiful ladies wearing bright, colorful dresses. The men, for their part, were impressively fit and handsome. The entire kingdom felt like a huge open-air celebration. Merchants from all over Jyn gathered in stalls along the main streets to buy or sell products, ranging from spices and cheese to flour, babsulisk, and meat. There was the selling and trading of cattle, horses, and sheep. She recalled handicrafts, perfumes, intricate wood carvings, furs, and fruits. Row after row of stalls stood stocked with delicious candies and small pies. Musicians, dancers, and jugglers occupied nearly every intersection, often attracting crowds large enough to plug the way.

How everyone had gazed at her father in awe, and the shame she felt at his indifference towards them. Her father, King Khilji, had been a detached man, overly dismissive and avoidant of people he didn't know, repulsed by the emotional entanglements they created.

Luckily, Sarna would get caught up in her brother's enjoyment. Burnya brought out the best in Shayan. The newness of their environment kept him from being so influenced by his father. Coming to Burnya was the one time her brother was allowed to let loose and be a kid, instead of clay battered into whatever shape a future king was supposed to have.

Only a few yards beyond the main entrance, she could already see the Burnya she once knew was long gone. This Burnya had lost its color and exuberance. The fun, lightness, soul, and magic of this kingdom had been scooped out, left cratered and gloomy. As they wandered through grimy stone streets towards the castle, she wondered how much of what she now felt was from the kingdom changing or because *she* had changed. Sarna was certainly not that dumb little girl anymore.

While they walked, she saw numerous street beggars, whom she could never have imagined before. Most of them were women and children, which was nothing short of heartbreaking. They sat on the ground and held out cups for money, their faces coated in soot and soil. Their dingy clothing draped off their limbs like moss.

When Momaset realized that some of them were Ghe-sui, he approached them to ask how they had come to such a state. The invariable answer was that the Ghe-sui had lost favor ever since fleeing for the Kholm Mountains instead of helping. They were regarded as useless frauds. Misinformation spread that they were even involved with the attack on Tartaria. Employment and donations stopped.

A few times, Momaset had to halt a citizen and ask for directions to the castle. A couple of them helped, believing them tourists, but others ducked their heads and kept walking. Sarna felt further demoralized at having struggled so hard, having endured through so much to get here, only to be treated as just another unwanted immigrant.

When she spotted a one-eyed man receiving oral pleasure from a prostitute in broad daylight, Sarna watched it happening the entire time they passed by, astonished that no one else reacted. As the castle came into view, she became aware of Momaset's hand on her shoulder, as if steering her. It made her uncomfortable until she convinced herself that the gesture was meant more as fatherly than romantic. Still, she wished he would stop touching her. The shaman carried an easiness with her that he hadn't earned yet.

The castle appeared mostly as she remembered it—an impossibly tall, majestic structure closely resembling their own castle. A stone curtain wall surrounded a main building with watch towers at the corners and crenelated battlements across the top. Rows of square windows perforated the main building's base. Cylindrical turrets flew the blue Burnyan flag on which a long-bodied lion was imposed over the sun, its rays depicted by triangles circling the edges.

After reaching the guardhouse, Momaset once again informed the guards she was Princess Sarna and that she required an audience with King Montrose. The castle guards didn't wear plate armor since they weren't knights, but a combination of hardened leather connected by cloth. Sarna knew these were likely farmers working as guards in exchange for land. At least, this was the arrangement in the days of her own kingdom.

To her surprise, one of the guards ordered a constable within the castle to relay their information. She'd expected to be insulted and turned away, but these guards didn't care much.

When the constable returned, he told them they would allow the girl entry, but no one else. Before she could respond, Momaset said, "I go with her, or she doesn't go."

The guard rolled his eyes. "Fine, but if you even blink in a way that annoys me, you're losing your head." He motioned for them to follow.

Momaset turned to the rest of the shamans and gave them a small nod, a signal for them to obey and wait there. Everything was fine.

They followed the guard into the courtyard, the

beauty of which was in astounding contrast to the kingdom outside. The shrubbery had been freshly cut and gave off a minty fragrance. The sun shone brighter here.

Upon reaching the inner gate, she and Momaset were interrogated by a second pair of guards, who greeted them with far greater suspicion. They drilled Momaset with questions, giving his every answer a rapid-fire follow-up. He told them everything straight, never blinking or hesitating. Sarna admired the strength and trustworthiness in his voice. He was a master at using certain words and a tone that made people do what he wanted.

Though it took much more convincing than with previous guards, leading Sarna to believe at one point they were most certainly going to be turned away, they were led by the two inner guards closer towards the castle. They passed through a network of concentric courtyards, following a sloping trough filled with running water. They walked by stables populated with horses and other livestock before ar-riving at a set of narrow stone stairs. These led them along a secondary internal wall. One of the guards used all his strength to drag open one final large wooden door.

Sarna and Momaset were led into the castle down two torch-lit halls. After these halls followed more halls. Next came stairs which led to yet more halls.

When the guard reached a door that spanned the entire floor, ceiling, and side walls, he told them both to wait there. He opened the door and poked his head inside. "Your majesty, a young girl who claims to be Princess Sarna of Tartaria is here. She's requesting an audience with you."

"King Khilji's daughter?" she heard a slurred voice shout from inside the chamber. "Are you sure? Here?"

"She's with some shaman. A Ghe-sui."

"Bring her to me," Montrose growled. "But tell the shaman to go die somewhere."

There came the sound of broken glass, and Momaset brushed by the guard. He marched into the Great Hall. Sarna wasn't sure what else to do, so she followed him. They stood before King Montrose, who had just dropped a bottle. Light spilled in through the windows in colorful parallelograms. The room vibrated with a strange and translucent holiness.

The king steadied himself against the table. "What do you want from me?" he asked, though he addressed everyone.

Momaset went to speak, but Sarna interrupted. "I didn't know where else to go," she blurted.

"And now what? You're my responsibility?" The question from King Montrose didn't sound rhetorical. He actually didn't appear to know. He turned to the other man in the room, obviously a noble, judging from his shiny tunic and ruby-encrusted sandals. "Why is she here?"

The nobleman turned to Sarna. "How do we know you're truly Princess Sarna?" he asked, but with a level of warmth, in case he offended.

"No, that's her," the king said, sounding dejected. "I remember her. She hasn't changed so much."

Sarna lifted the tattered hem of her tunic and bowed. "I am flattered by your remembrance." She straightened. "You knew my father. We used to visit Burnya throughout my childhood. You were always so welcoming to us, My Lord."

"I lost my wife because I went to your stupid father's stupid funeral. Dumb whore! I'm lucky to be alive!"

Sarna flinched. "I am sorry to learn of this. If it makes you feel better, I wish it were me in her place."

The king scoffed. "It's your family's fault that our Queen was killed! You couldn't rest with defeating the Cathyrnee, could you? No, you had to drive them to complete destruction and leave the refugees to flood our streets."

She tried to speak, but the rush of too many words stuck in her throat. How could he think she had anything to do with such decisions? She'd been as appalled as anyone at her father's cruelty. Nonetheless, her father wasn't here for King Montrose to punish. Sarna shuddered at the sudden, deep realization that coming here had been a grave mistake.

"We've come to ask for your mercy." Momaset stepped up. He held his hands out, a gesture of calm and confident diplomacy. "I wish to repair relations between royalty and the Ghe-sui. To restore that honor and trust. We have fortunately separated from the old ways of passivity. The Ghe-sui are powerful mystics, and we can fight for you."

"Last time I saw one of your shamans, he was taking a shit by the side of the street. Right in front of me. Me! His king."

Momaset bowed his head, waited a beat. "The Ghe-sui have performed many beneficial functions for your kingdom in the past. We heal. We sacrifice. And the Ghe-sui will no longer sit idly by and do nothing. Your Highness—" Momaset stepped closer, his chest out. "You will have no greater ally than me. My power is unmatched."

The nearest guard took two steps towards Momaset and punched him across the jaw. His proximity helped the blow land especially hard. Momaset toppled and tried catching the wall, but not before smacking his head there. The impact made a hollow clomp. Momaset slid to the floor, where he lay on his side, unconscious. A bleeding knot on his temple turned purple.

"Looks like you just got matched!" yelled the guard while rubbing his hurt knuckles. Still, he smiled, pleased with himself.

"I'm going to piss in his mouth," the king announced.

Sarna watched in horror as Montrose worked at unbinding his trousers.

The fancy nobleman grabbed the king around his stomach and held onto him. "My Lord, no!"

"Let go of me!"

"You cannot do it. You mustn't. Not unless you plan on killing everyone in this room. People will hear about this."

King Montrose twisted out of the man's grasp. He advanced on Sarna.

She held her hands up and retreated. "We meant you no ill will, My Lord."

"What should I do with her?" The same guard asked the king, still grinning, emboldened by the easiness with which he had knocked Momaset out.

King Montrose pointed into the bridge of Sarna's nose. "Have this bitch taken to the stables, collect all the fresh horse dung you can find, and smear her in it. Head-to-toe. Then throw her in the dungeons. Both of them."

"My Lord, please," the nobleman said. Sarna understood this man—whoever he was—was possibly the closest thing to a friend she might ever have in this world again.

The guard laughed and roughly grabbed her by the arm. His hand was big enough that his fingers enclosed her entire limb. She shut her eyes and concentrated on using her magic to save her. Like it had always done before. Right when she needed it.

The guard tightened his grip, as though he meant to squeeze her arm off. Her knees folded from the pain, and she tried yanking her arm back, but his hold was vice-like.

Sarna tried to speak, to defend herself, but could only stammer incoherently. Where were her powers?

Why was nothing happening? She looked at each man pleadingly. "I don't understand. Quit it!"

"So sad that someone born as well off as you would succumb to a cult." King Montrose said, smiling widely, humored by her helplessness. "Believing in their stupid bullshit." To the guard, he yelled: "Get her out of here! Make damn sure she suffers."

The guard pulled her out of the chamber within seconds. Halfway down the hall, another guard joined the first in dragging her, grabbing her other arm. Sarna lost her new sandals, and the two men just didn't care. They were enjoying this. She screamed as the stone floor raked the skin from her ankles.

21

SHAYAN

They circled back to the sight of the yelkin attack and buried the four who had been killed. The king ordered what was as close to a proper burial as they could manage. Shayan also took it upon himself to personally cut out their hearts. He placed the organs into a sack to be sent back to their families in place of a body.

They were forced to bury the men together, one of them appearing barely seventeen. Faced now with a shortage of time and supplies, the king also had to abandon the normal rites of death. Instead, the surviving men took turns digging a large opening. They stabbed the ground with the only shovel they'd brought. They did so repeatedly until the hole became deep enough to ensure their bodies wouldn't be dug up by animals. Afterward, the bodies—some missing limbs or heads—were dragged and dumped inside, then covered.

Shayan and his men made a circle around the patch of disturbed soil. He took out his longsword and planted the tip into the ground. He paused there, but no words came to him. He heard Lalya sniffling by his side, and he decided that was enough. The longer they took to reach the safe walls of Burnya, the likelier they were to join these men in the ground. Heartfelt speeches could wait.

The squad spent the day traveling, mostly in silence. Lalya did her best to keep up but was beginning to fall behind. Everyone had to stop twice to allow her to rest. After a third time, he ordered her to be carried, which he appointed two soldiers for. Their own exhaustion and annoyance fell across their faces, even in front of their king. He sensed the men's building anger at him for allowing a woman to come. She was going to get them killed.

The soldiers picked her up anyway and carried her between them, one in front of the other, as though she were a sack of flour. Meanwhile, everyone darted between the trees, collectively hunkering down at the slightest, unidentified noise. Each time, Shayan felt the pulse of his heart inside his throat, his breathing inside his ears. He checked the sweaty, grimy faces of his men as they waited for his signal to resume. He saw only terror, fatigue, and desperation.

Before nightfall, a scout spotted a drakksuk gliding

silently through the chestnut-shaded sky. The creature scanned the ground, smelling them but unable to see them through so much foliage. The drakksuk made several passes at varying heights. The squad held completely still, taking only the shallowest breaths possible.

The creature flew higher, then higher still, and vanished. Nonetheless, the drakksuk's appearance was so unsettling that everyone remained still, fearful the creature had faked its disappearance. They didn't dare relax.

When night fell, Shayan ordered everyone to set camp and eat. They refrained from building a fire, and no one spoke except to whisper. As always, Lalya chose a sleeping spot closest to him. She hadn't spoken much that day, ashamed at becoming a burden. He watched her sleep and felt bad for her. He moved a wisp of her hair out of her face. After looking to make sure no one was watching, Shayan touched his knuckles against her cheek. He yanked his hand away when she blinked. He turned away and used his bag for a pillow. He drifted into sleep as well.

Hours later, Shayan awoke from the sharp prick of ants biting his neck and ears. He sat up and slapped his head, doing his best to wipe them off. He felt something crawling inside his pant leg, though this could've been leg hairs coming unglued from his skin. He smushed the spot, shook his leg, and a worm-like insect with a million furry legs spilled from the bottom of his tunic. The insect rolled into a circle.

Shayan blanched. He looked around to see if anyone had witnessed his silly, convulsive reaction. He saw only Lalya peering at him. She lifted her face from the ground where she had been sleeping on her stomach. Her cheek was smudged, a tiny section of spiderweb dangling there. They met eyes, locked in silent discussion until she shut her eyes and slowly lowered her head again. He tried returning to sleep also, but the ants had evidently organized a counter-attack. This sent the king in search of a new sleeping spot, and he chose one on the other side of Lalya. He spooned her without touching her. The king slipped into a restless sleep filled with monsters and insects and dead people with rotting faces. Asking him for their hearts back.

SARNA

She surrendered. The guards were too strong. One held her by the back of her neck while forcing her along. Some of her hair lay bunched under his palm, which kept causing her hair to get pulled. She yelped, unable to catch her breath long enough to even plead with him, beg him to at least allow her to get her hair free.

In a memory magnified from pain and terror, Sarna recalled being a little girl again, remembering how impressed she'd been with the handsome, fresh-shaven Burnyan soldiers. Even their guards fascinated her. This guard, now, the one handling her like a disobedient dog, looked like he'd been picked from the dungeon he was charged with taking her to. He smelled as though he hadn't bathed for days yet believed that rubbing cheap spices over his skin and clothing would replace soap. His fleshy, whiskered jowls were a field of moles and pimples, swaying grotesquely from his face. He treated her with the lumbering brutality of an ape. She felt certain he might kill her before reaching the dungeons, just from sheer carelessness.

She shut her eyes and tried once more to conjure her powers and put an immediate stop to what was happening. But nothing. Her abilities had evidently renounced her for what she'd done, stripped from her by whatever cosmic hand had given them to her in the first place. Because she was killing people. Thirteen men, if she counted Luca. She was a murderer, and this was her judgment: To die in a dungeon.

As they traveled deeper into the castle, she struggled to find her feet, but the guard refused to slow down. She became aware of people halting in the hallways, knowing likely it was to gawk at the sight of four guards rough-handling two shaman prisoners, one of them a young girl. Behind her, another pair of guards carried Momaset between them, one holding his feet while the other grasped him beneath his arms. Momaset lay limp as cloth, his closed eyes and open mouth making him appear as though he were merely sleeping.

She yelled for Momaset to wake up. She figured if she could get him to regain consciousness, he would use his own powers to free them. However, her words were useless. Momaset didn't stir, at least not from what she could glance, getting her head around when she could. At times, he appeared quite dead, but the notion of that was too hopeless to even allow inside her mind.

"Are we really going to take them to the stables and cover them in horseshit?" asked a guard carrying Momaset.

"You can if you want," said a guard holding her. He gave Sarna's hair a vicious yank, for no other reason than his attention had landed on her. "Not sure how we're supposed to do that without getting it on us, too."

"So we're not doing it? Great."

"Let's take them to the dungeons. The king will never know."

"I almost feel bad about this. She's a girl."

"Why?" The guard paused before deciding on the right direction. He pulled Sarna along. He moved his grip on her, so she stayed doubled over, her arms dangling.

"They'll both be killed in there. You realize that, right?"

"I don't give a shit. Fuck these people."

"Better them than us. I'm just doing what I'm told."

"The Ghe-sui supposedly possess all these magic powers but only use them to stare at their navels instead of helping people. Doing this makes me laugh."

Sarna couldn't help but note that the man had not once laughed.

She sensed they were in a room now, or right outside one. She heard people chirping, confused. She could only pray that whoever was being spoken to was not interested in who Sarna was or what was happening. Through wet, blurred eyes, she could barely make out people at a table, in the midst of an early dinner, bewildered by the interruption.

Please, she thought, *stop staring at me. Ignore this. This isn't interesting.*

Please, Momaset, please, please, wake up.

A clump of gruel smacked her square against the cheek. The hot juice entered her eye, and she squirmed from the pain. Everyone laughed. Something harder collided with her hip, and Sarna shut down, deciding to let whatever was going to happen to her just go ahead and happen. She didn't care anymore. She became lathered in the semi-liquid food being hurled at her. She opened her eyes enough to see that Momaset was also covered in food but was finally moving a little. His lips pursed, and his brows clenched. Was he waking up, or was this her imagination?

Sarna became pushed, and she fell. The guard cursed as he jerked her back up. He grabbed a handful of her tunic and ripped it. She shouted Momaset's name again until the guard struck her across the back of her head. They left the room. The guards carrying Momaset complained that he was getting heavy. They wanted to hurry. Overcome with fear, Sarna's knees went out from under her, and she collapsed. She couldn't help it. She expected this to spark a full-on beating, but a guard only lifted her and tossed her over his shoulder.

They went down darker and danker halls, sloping towards the dungeons. Of course, her own castle had held dungeons. She knew about them from her tutoring. It was always a curious thing to know of criminals and miscreants residing beneath her feet. Many childhood nightmares involved men with heavy iron collars and cuffs around their hands and ankles. Throughout Jyn's history, soldiers preferred death before dishonor, so captured men were viewed with special disdain. These were not honorable people. Understanding this was to know she would conclude this day being raped, tortured, then killed, not necessarily in that order.

Shadows wavered from torches hung on the walls. Light became sparser the further down they traveled. Even the quality of the cement work deteriorated. The atmosphere developed an increasingly muggy smell. The amount of mossy water puddled on the floor became more frequent. A few times, she heard feet splashing through these puddles as people passed, going the other way. Before long, her stomach hurt from the guard's shoulder bone poking her stomach.

She heard voices. They grew louder. They surrounded her. They walked by cages filled with exuberantly bouncing shadows. Disconnected hands reached out for her, fingertips brushing her thigh, the bridge of her nose. She felt clumps of mud hitting her again. Next came the smell. It wasn't mud.

The guard flinched. "Knock it off, you disgusting ...*Aye!*" He ran ahead, and the pain from being jostled, where she was already sore, caused her to cry out.

"Which cell should we put them in?" asked a guard from further ahead somewhere.

"Anywhere."

"No, come on. We can't put this girl in with these animals. They'll destroy her. King didn't say to have her killed."

"Pretty sure he doesn't care, one way or the other. I don't either."

She could hardly hear them over the roar of prisoners, roused to the point of hysteria by the sight of a girl, helpless and ragdolled. All the blood was rushing to her head. With any luck, she might join Momaset among the unconscious.

"Put her in here with me," said a voice, sounding vaguely female. "I'll look after her."

"I'll bet you will," said the guard holding Sarna.

"No harm will come to her," said the husky female voice. "Not with me."

Sarna turned her head enough to see a pair of large,

fleshy arms folded outside a wall of iron bars.

"Don't give her over to these men," said the woman. "Just don't do it."

The guards carrying Momaset dropped him, and he went to the damp floor with a quick, dull splash. One of the guards worked with a glob of keys at opening the cell door. Sarna's head became too heavy, and she dropped it.

"Whatever. I'm tired of carrying her." The guard deposited her as well, and she fell to her hands and knees. Before she could even shake the stupor of a new position, she was shoved into the cell. The door slammed behind her and struck the balls of her feet. She gagged from the overwhelming stench of excrement, some of which she assumed she was wearing.

"He's waking up," said one of the guards.

"I see him," said another. "Got it."

The roar and excitement of other prisoners subsided as their attention shifted to the sight of Momaset stirring more. He lay on his back inside the same cell. He touched his forehead and blinked until a guard plopped his full weight astride Momaset's chest. The guard used his fists to pummel the shaman's face, which soon leaked copious amounts of blood from his nose and mouth. His entire face turned red and wet, a broken tooth resting on his lower lip, glued there with bloody spittle.

"Stop," Sarna whispered. She whispered it until her voice left her, and it was only the movement of her lips forming the words: "Stop. Please, stop…stop."

22

CHIEF ARLYN

The chief stood amazed. There were thousands upon thousands of people before him. More than he was even aware had survived the siege, though he supposed many could've been former Tartarians. He'd chosen a drum tower from which to give his speech. The tower made for an adequate pulpit, though the chief would've much preferred standing lower.

The tower was Khuyag's idea. A precaution. The general had urged him against giving the speech in the first place, feeling strongly that Arlyn would be far too exposed. Too many Cathyrnee remained agitated by the atrocities they had witnessed. The temptation for vengeance on an open target leader would be too great.

Arlyn placed his hands on the turret and leaned forward. Khuyag stood behind him.

The crowd stretched into the distance, endless, filling the courtyards and streets. They lined the horizon. Their excited, collected voices created a hum that Arlyn could feel in his chest, right down to his balls. How could he possibly be expected to carry his voice so far?

He noticed every face in the crowd was human. Not one single Chotgor. He wondered if their absence was due to fear. The chief had heard more tales of his people discriminating against the same tribesmen who had helped them. Sadly, their fiendish appearance made them easy scapegoats for the Cathyrnee's existential grievances. Evidently, the Chotgor had decided to stay away and avoid any harassment. Either that, or it was their sheer indifference. Who cared what this foolish human had to say anymore?

In any case, the reason for his speech stood to his right—Ulaan, dressed in a figure-hugging, silken black dress that pooled over her feet. Her long curls tumbled over her shoulders in thick strands, so black they shone. Her rouged cheeks supported large, hypnotic eyes and blood-red lips blooming above her dimpled chin. Her appearance remained mesmerizing and foreboding to Chief Arlyn. If she'd asked him, he might've suggested a different dress and hairstyle. Something sunnier that conveyed calm or comfort. Put the crowd at ease. She had evidently elected to do none of those things.

Chief Arlyn had initially insisted on delivering his speech before a committee of parliamentarians. They would deliver the chief's message throughout the kingdom individually, but Ulaan wouldn't hear of it. The witch insisted this showed cowardice. Evasiveness. No, Arlyn needed to face his people. Speak to them directly. Let them hear his own words from his own mouth. Look them in the eye.

So here he stood before a sea of heads. The chief lifted his chin, spoke in a voice strained from using his entire throat: "I am honored by the presence of so many of you coming here today. This must be genuinely everyone!" He paused, awaiting confirmation of this. The crowd continued to buzz. "As with many of you, I learned the full story of our people as part of my schooling. We have suffered like no others in these lands. And for doing what? What did any of us ever do to deserve such cruelty?" He paused, awaiting a response again. "The arrival of the Sünsü into our realm has touched everyone. There is no escaping that. When those gifted felt the need to break away into two different kingdoms, develop their own government, and set about robbing us, I was the one who stood up for us. I led us during the war. I have never stopped leading, never letting go of my one true wish—that the Cathyrnee return to prominence. And that those who took advantage of us pay the price for what they did."

He took a moment to assess how his words were going over. It became apparent that only those directly beneath could even hear him. Chief Arlyn began to feel stupid. "After the Great War, the Tartarian government declared these remaining lands as its own. They left the Cathyrnee homeless and wandering the Narlaan Plains. Together, brothers and sisters, we faced disease and starvation! Ceaseless attacks from yelkin!" He didn't care anymore who could hear him. He shouted for himself now more than anyone. "Our helplessness was exploited! We, the Cathyrnee, were a regular part of another being's diet! As your leader, I did the one thing I felt I had left to do!

"I understand you want answers. You want to know why and how we were aided in our conquest by creatures that aren't supposed to exist." He noticed a pile of people getting pressed against the castle wall beneath him. A line of warriors made a perimeter at the wall's base. They did their best to shove back against the crowd but were losing momentum. The people yelling reached a level that Chief Arlyn found impossible to overshout. At first, he assumed they wanted to be closer to hear him better, but soon the looks of anger and hatred were unmistakable. They intended to enter the castle and reach Arlyn for a more aggressive discussion.

A meager group of warriors encircled the chief, their swords already drawn, nervous. Ulaan stepped forward until she stood next to him, showing a brave face for whoever cared to notice. She raised her arms and searched the surrounding windows. She wanted attention from the protective archers Khuyag had positioned there and inside the surrounding drum towers. The archers were instead fixated on the oscillating crowd below, growing more agitated by the second. Arlyn could see the ferocity and rage move through them like a wave, all the way back to the furthest man.

He jumped at the touch of Khuyag's chest against his elbow. "We need to get you out of here, *ha'wiih*," the general told him.

"And go where?"

"Out of the castle. They're going to swarm it, and there's not enough of us to protect you."

"Why didn't you call for more men?"

"I did, but most of them chose to join the people out there."

Chief Arlyn's heart plunged. The sun was too bright. He felt dizzy.

Ulaan grabbed his elbow. "Why did you stop talking?" she hissed. "Talk to them!"

He stepped forward again. He held his right hand up. Before long, incredibly, a stillness came over the crowd, a silence pierced only by a dog's barking. Arlyn could hear the breeze. Someone coughed.

He allowed the quiet to linger before saying, "When we stood against the former owners of this kingdom, they had no such resources as we have now! We have nothing standing in our way but one more kingdom! One more hell hole of oppression."

There came a few shouts for him to speak louder.

The chief tried, but his voice already felt rubbed raw. He kept on as best he could: "We must resist our enemies in any and every way. Our work is not done. I am now calling for an army to help us move forward. Take advantage of the steady aid of the Shulam and their mighty beasts! Yes, their appearance might not be what we're used to, but this doesn't change the fact that they are on our side. A combatant must always use every weapon at their disposal! He felt himself settling into the role of orator. His vigorous, repetitive gestures imposed his mood. "Our lands are enclosed by the Ayal Sea. There is only so much territory to be safe from. The last boundary that remains a threat is the kingdom of Burnya!"

A murmur became a rumble. The people shouted and shook their fists.

Not knowing whether this was in agreement, Chief Arlyn resumed. "Should they choose to attack us first, which they most certainly will eventually, we don't have a single means of escape. We must ride out to meet our final enemy. We must conquer Burnya or be conquered by it. Those who gave their lives for us to reach such a victory, those who gave their lives for you today, now demand yours in return. This will be a battle worthy of each of you, whoever joins me. Join me in glory and carry forward the dreams of your ancestors!" He swallowed. Another wave of outrage rippled towards the crowd's rear. Some of the commotion belonged to those repeating the chief's words to the people behind them. Arlyn cringed to think what his message might warp into once reaching the furthest rows.

"I am amongst you at this time," he shouted, "to live or die amongst you all, to lay down, for my wife's memory, who gave her life as many Cathyrnee have. I have made sacrifices with you and for my kingdom and for my people, my honor and my blood. We will never allow our enemies to violate our new territory! Will you not march with me to meet them? Tear from King Montrose's brows the laurels he has won from sucking off the teat of the Cathyrnee! We should teach the Realm of Jyn that a malediction attends those who violate the territory of our Great People!"

He stopped once more because people were pointing. It took him a few moments to understand they were pointing at Ulaan. The strange woman next to him was becoming the object of their scorn and wrath. The entire crowd seemed to draw the instantaneous conclusion that she was behind everything he was saying. This was *her* message, not his.

Sensing this herself, Ulaan stepped in front of the chief, where she basked in their insults. A large grin creased her face, and yet another hush came over the people. Many stood on tiptoes to better see her.

"The results of your efforts will be nothing less than eternal glory and a durable peace!" she yelled.

The crowd went berserk. As people in the back and middle pushed forward, the guards did their best to hold them back. They held their spears horizontally as a barrier, but were forced back, slowly crushed.

Ulaan's face faltered, puzzled. "The path we have chosen for the present is full of hazards," she said anyway, "as all paths are, but…but.." She looked down as Arlyn did. The guards lost their formation, and people raced by them towards the castle. They hacked at the large entrance door with daggers and hatchets. Some pounded with nothing more than their fists.

Ulaan kept shouting but was heard by no one. "The cost of freedom is always high, but…"

The doors crumbled inwards. This allowed the mob to enter the castle vestibule.

Arlyn drew his sword and ordered the closest warriors to make a protective circle around both Ulaan and himself. The people below rushed forward like a torrent of water released from a mountain. They grunted and yelled like savages.

Arlyn turned to Ulaan to plead with her not to use her magic, to let him handle this. But he was too late. Her eyes rolled white, and she chanted in a language he'd never heard before.

An ear-stabbing screech split the air. An immense shadow swallowed the drum tower and the entire area around it. Arlyn felt an intense heat overhead, the atmosphere filling with screaming, then ashes.

SHAYAN

Rivulets of sweat dripped from his nose and brows. Shayan felt himself turning careless with exhaustion.

The sun bore down without mercy. He led his men through the deeper forest, where swords were needed as hacking tools to get through. Low-hanging branches lashed at their skin and hair while coagulated soil sucked at their feet. Occasionally, he would check behind and recognize the same level of fatigue in everyone else, especially Lalya. He saw how impossibly hard he was pushing these people. And he just didn't care. He even took small pleasure in Lalya's struggling to feverishly keep up, to witness her regret at coming. They were the ones foolish enough to have followed him. *They'd* wanted this.

When he stepped out from the forest, leaving the shelter of the trees, he trounced through the high grass of the plains, daring anyone to object. But none did. They followed him like the suicidal fools they were. A couple of times, he stopped to face them. He regarded them with open disgust. They stared back, confused, before falling in behind him when he turned and kept walking.

A few meters across the field, he could hear the noise of someone's legs swishing through the pampas grass. He expected to see Khilji, astounded if not furious at where his king was leading them. To his surprise, it was Lalya.

"Your Highness," she said.

"Don't call me that," he snapped.

Her gait faltered a beat, but she regained it, her arms swinging. The girl was certainly tenacious. She may have been sweaty and caked with dirt, yet here she was, no longer lagging, matching his every stride. Shayan often wondered what her kidnapping must have done to her. Whatever she'd gone through had unquestionably toughened her. Perhaps she wasn't as regretful as he'd supposed. There were at least two hundred Tartarian women in their refugee camp. Out of all of them, how else could Lalya have been the one to talk her way into coming?

"We should return beneath the trees, no?" asked Lalya. "We're quite visible out here."

"I'm leading us to those trees over there." He pointed to a wood line of towering, vociferous trees to the northeast. He hadn't been leading them there at all, but the trees had simply shown themselves when he needed them to. "We'll cross over," he added.

"I see," she said. She said nothing else for a few steps. "We should stop and rest, no?"

"So rest."

The men are awaiting your word, your Hi—King Shayan. I doubt they're willing to stop if you keep walking."

Shayan stomped to a halt. "Fine!"

"Only for a little while."

"I can't do this," he said quietly. "I'm not my father."

"No one expects you to be, Your Highness." She froze from her mistake in using the phrase again. "But you are our king," she added. "We would follow you anywhere."

"I can see that. It's driving me crazy." He swatted at an insect buzzing near his face.

"You led the search to find Sarna," she said.

"And I failed."

"And you've led knights into battle. I've known you to be nothing but a great leader. Everyone has."

"That was against Cathyrnee warriors with swords and spears. Not flying creatures of death and giants and...whatever else exists now. This is beyond me, Lalya."

He noticed the men getting closer. Many of them staggered. The few in front had likely heard at least part of his conversation with Lalya. He held his arm out and motioned for the men to stop. A few in back went to their knees, and Shayan felt overcome with guilt. His wish to torture had been too successful. He should've been washing their feet for having such trust in him. What was he doing anymore? And where was Burnya? They should've been there by now.

The rest of the men dropped their equipment. He spotted Khilji towards the back. It took a few times shouting his name for Shayan to get the scout's attention. When Khilji heard, he came jogging. The scout stumbled and made an embarrassing tumble before landing on his face. He hopped back up and trotted forward, only to fall again. Shayan rushed over, but two men got there first. They helped Khilji regain his feet.

Feeling sure the scout had reestablished his composure, Shayan placed a hand on his shoulder to steady him. "You all right?"

The scout nodded. He placed his forearm over the king's and blinked, still trying to catch his breath.

Shayan looked around at everyone. He shook his head. "Rest, rest. All of you, rest. I'm sorry I've pushed you so hard. But the faster we get to Burnya, the faster we get to safety." He placed his hand against the side of the Khilji's face. "Get yourself fed. We need to scout the territory ahead before going much further."

Khilji nodded. He gained strength and energy from the notion of being needed again. He straightened his back and wiped his mouth. The scout darted away, likely to round up the other scouts. Shayan grabbed his arm, nearly getting carried along.

"Whoa, whoa, whoa," he told Khilji. "Rest and eat first. Eat!"

"But you said it yourself, Your Highness. We need to reach Burnya. And I agree. We're dead meat out here."

"I order you to eat first. And drink. At least a little."

The other men were already sitting, many with their heads bowed. They did not share Khilji's enthusiasm. Shayan decided to approach each man individually. He urged them to eat and drink, though some appeared too spent to even satiate themselves. One of the younger men began weeping, and Shayan went to him.

"It's all right," the king told him. "We should almost be there. Have strength."

The men ate a meager amount of pickled vegetables and dried, salted lamb before retaking their feet and trudging forward. They dragged their equipment rather than lifting it again. None would look him in the face. Shayan supposed he wouldn't have loved himself in that moment either. Thankfully, once everyone had made it back into the shelter of the trees, their spirits lightened a bit.

"How are you?" Lalya asked him.

"I'll be better when we have shelter and protection."

"Why do you seem angry with us?"

He glanced at her, not losing a step. "I'm doing my best, Lalya, but all I seem to do is get people killed."

"Those were soldiers. Soldiers die."

He raised his hand but dropped it. "What about those people I took on that reconnaissance expedition? Those weren't soldiers. They weren't even experienced. And I led them straight to their death."

"To die for you is to die honorably, no?"

"Honorably? I sacrificed those people. Because they weren't so important. Where was the honor in that? Who am I to decide something like that?"

She shook her head, dismayed. "You're the king. If not you, then who? Someone must decide such things."

"But...gods. I don't know. Why me?"

She finally looked back at him sideways, grinning. She laughed, playful. "Because it is."

Shayan returned her look, also askance. He'd taken note of an adorable but quirky quality to her demeanor. She was pixie-like and far from unappealing. "Can I hold your hand?" he asked her.

Before she could answer, he spotted Khilji and two of his scouts trotting towards them, appearing first as quick shadows between tree trunks. He hadn't even realized they'd left on their scouting assignment already.

"We're there," Khilji said, exhilarated. "Burnya! It's right beyond there. Beyond that—" He gestured with his right hand, unable to decide on what he wanted to call it—"thing of trees. You can see the outer walls and turrets. Only half a kilometer away." He grinned the widest that King Shayan had ever seen him, or any man, grin. "We're there, Your Highness!"

Shayan opened his mouth to correct him for calling him "Highness," but he changed his mind. He realized the entire crew, even Lalya, were looking at him.

"Onwards to Burnya," he said. He had to clear a lump in his throat. "We've made it."

23

KING MONTROSE

He searched the entirety of the castle for his bride-to-be. When he came across Artemis in a hallway, before the Master of Gold could utter a word, Montrose demanded to know if he had seen Ozyan.

Artemis was taken aback by his king's abruptness. Everything the king did either astonished or perplexed him, which Montrose found the pinnacle of irritation. He was even irked by the way Artemis' tunic was lined with fur and garnished with silver and lavish ring brooches, which Montrose knew were imported. Though they stood indoors, Artemis had covered his head with a hat of close-fitted, linen coifs, fastened under his chin like a bonnet. He looked utterly ridiculous. And well-deserving of a hard punch to the throat. But the king refrained. He needed him right now.

Artemis had been his top advisor since he'd taken the throne, his preeminence being every bit as hereditary as the king's. The status of "advisor" was derived exclusively from the descendants of noblemen. Montrose resented his influence every bit as much as he required it. Artemis was, in effect, his other bride.

"I'm afraid I still have not seen her," Artemis informed him.

"She's hiding from me."

"How are the wedding arrangements coming, My Lord?"

"Precisely what I would like to know." The king looked around for something to fix his gaze on besides the cretinous, questioning face of his advisor. He realized the head swinging made him appear dazed or drunk, which he was. The effects of the babsulisk he had imbibed the previous evening, and this morning frayed his attention span. He felt depressed and anxious.

Montrose spotted none other than Ozyan walking towards them, her gait hurried as if she'd been searching high and low for him as well. Her petite frame was enfolded by an immaculately tailored dress with a coat falling below her knees. She accessorized with a three-strand golden necklace, an heirloom brooch, and white cotton gloves. The shimmering fabric of her dress complemented her tan complexion, her light-blue eyes, and her black tresses.

"And here she comes!" bellowed the king.

His frustration with her evasiveness evaporated the instant he laid eyes on her. Such elegance in her, such serpentine grace. Despite the brunt force of her personality, Ozyan possessed a smoothness of movement and singleness of mind. She was a gazelle, her poise coming more from her body and spirit than character or intellect. King Montrose never ceased to be amazed by her. While he knew people such as Artemis saw him as pushing the bounds of corruption and authoritarianism—a king unbound by the rule of law, or a sense of shame, or even the care for others—Ozyan made no such judgments. The king did not trust many people, but he trusted her.

Once close enough, he took her by the arm and led her into the nearest side room. Montrose performed this act with such urgency that he failed to even notice which room they entered. He noticed only that Ozyan smiled, amused by his forcefulness. As he was about to speak, Montrose realized he'd led her into a servant's hall. Two servants—a boy and a girl—sat at a long table together, caught in mid-conversation, now stupefied to discover their space suddenly occupied by their king and new Queen. A high, wide window cast a thick bar of light across the space between them.

"What is the matter, My Lord?" Ozyan asked him.

Montrose joined his hands around her lower back and pulled her to him. He touched his waist to her stomach, and he kissed her neck. "I've missed you. Ever since this wedding business started, I don't see you anymore!"

"I've been busy, My Lord. Arranging for our kingdom's future safety is not easy."

He resumed kissing her neck. "We have people for that! The Queen doesn't do such work."

"This one does."

He laughed. He lifted his head to look at her. "You're in charge now? Is that it? And what is this I'm hearing about some important alliance you've made?"

"Amgelan, My Lord. I was referring only to Amgelan."

"Swear to me?"

"Who else could it be? How else would I have time?"

"I thought you said the Lord Chamberlain would do everything."

"Yet somehow I still have two entire councils to invite to our wedding. Officers of state, court magnates, tenants-in-chief, officers, and landowners. The list is endless, and I'm not even sure who these people are or why they're supposed to be so important."

"They're not." He hooked a finger beneath the collar of her dress and slid it down, exposing her shoulder. "Nobody matters but me and you."

She tickled his beard with her long nails. "That is my goal. I will be satisfied by nothing less."

"You realize that ruling will mean showing cruelty at times. Cruelty is a tool, my dove."

"I'm willing to do whatever it takes, My Lord."

He'd wanted to brag about it later, but he suddenly found he couldn't wait. "I was visited today by Princess Sarna of Tartaria. Guess what I did with her."

Ozyan squinted, perplexed. She shook her head. "Princess who?"

"Sarna," he said. "I threw her in the dungeons."

Ozyan's flirtatious smirk melted. "You did what?"

"She had the nerve to show her face here with one of those Ghe-sui frauds. I sent them both to rot. Do you want to know why?"

She stepped back and held her arms stiff beside her body. A trench appeared between her brows. "Are you sure it was actually her?"

The king felt pleased with the effect this news was having on her. She was gobsmacked. She would certainly respect him now. "It was her without question. *The* Princess Sarna. Who could forget that face? Her father used to visit here at least twice a year, invited or not."

Ozyan kept shaking her head. She couldn't close her mouth. "But why would you lock her in the dungeons?"

"I recognize a threat when I see one. That family has always been a threat."

"You felt threatened by a young girl?"

"And a Ghe-sui shaman. Yes, they threatened me."

"So she's in the dungeons right now? This moment? How long ago?"

He flushed, taken aback by her anger. "Her family was always against us and always have been," he said. "Why do you care about her?"

"My Lord, you're not making any sense. How could a young girl threaten you?" Ozyan slapped her forehead and closed her eyes. He tried touching her shoulder, but she jerked away. She turned on the two servants, likely a housekeeper and butler, still sitting there. "Do either of you know how to get to the dungeons?"

The butler nodded slowly, though Montrose doubted the man knew the exact way. Everyone knew the dungeons were beneath the castle...somewhere. "You must take me," she told him. "Do it now."

The butler got up, but the king waved for him to sit back down.

"I cannot allow that," he told Ozyan. "The dungeons are not a place for you."

"Have you ever been there yourself?"

"Of course not."

"That explains a lot." She grabbed the butler by his shirt and pulled him back up. She stormed with him past the king and out of the servant's hall. The butler followed. He walked without bending his knees or elbows, as if fearful the king might assault him.

Montrose watched them leave but didn't stop them. Second-guessing this, he turned to leave the room. Bring her back if possible. He was instead startled to find Artemis in the doorway. He held his hands behind his back, his face carved into that stolid, phlegmatic smirk he always carried.

"Get out of my way!" the king yelled at him.

"Prince Shayan is downstairs, My Lord. He awaits you in one of the solars."

"What does he want? Is he here about his sister?"

"Not exactly sure. I assume he wants what everyone wants these days. He wants our help."

The king looked at the housekeeper, still sitting at the long table, frightened she might be called on to participate in these events unfolding before her. Montrose ordered her to undress. The housekeeper held motionless until realizing the king was serious. She began to unbutton, her small face caving with grief.

"Naturally, the great Prince Shayan wants our help now," said the king. "I'll meet him when I'm done here. Have him sent to the Great Hall to wait for me. I'll take care of him, too."

SHAYAN

Burnya had changed. Walking with his small squad of soldiers, knights, and Lalya through the congested stone streets, Shayan became struck by how strange the kingdom felt. Like Sarna, he'd last been here as a child with his family. He'd loved the kingdom back then, its newness filling him with wonderment and a childish notion of adventure. Now the place felt like a disorganized event. The citizens of Burnya were busy with so many activities at once that he could easily imagine getting carried along in the bedlam, losing sight of himself and everyone else.

A feral look haunted the eyes of those around them, as if sizing them up for how much of a fight they might offer. After reaching Burnya's Lower East Side, they passed a canal, which Shayan recalled was the main source of fresh water for the entire kingdom. However, an assemblage of breweries and slaughter-houses had sprung up along the canal's banks, pol-luting it with spent grain and rotten pig carcasses. He saw an obese, shirtless local relieving himself into the water. The reek of sewage was nauseating. The air sang with mosquitoes.

Shayan and his group made their way without speaking except for the occasional bark of directions from whoever happened to know. As they came upon the castle of Burnya, he noticed that the struc-ture appeared to be in disrepair. The flags carrying the Burnyan banner were sun-faded and shredded at the corners. Having lost the splendor and comfort of his own kingdom, to take such grandeur for granted felt absurd. It was apparent that the tragedy of losing their Queen had unfurled a blanket of gloom over the kingdom in general. How could the current royals of this once great kingdom allow for such carelessness?

They made it to the castle's front gates, where they were greeted with heavy suspicion by the guards. Shayan had become so familiar with his men's rag-ged appearance that he hadn't considered how off-putting they might appear with their bloodied skin and filthy clothing. It hadn't crossed his mind that the royal guards wouldn't believe he was the former prince of Tartaria. One of the guards disappeared within the courtyard. He returned to tell them they were permitted to enter. Shayan supposed their clothing might have given them credibility. Most tunics worn by Jyn nobility shared a basic pattern with those worn by the working classes but were made of finer fabric. His men were dressed in piecemeal armored plates and kettle hats with gauntlets and arm harnesses, none of which were found in these regions.

Shayan and his men passed through the outer wall, through a courtyard, and on to a second wall. They were met by another set of castle guards who halted them. They were informed that only Shayan would be allowed to enter beyond that point. He was not particularly surprised by this but still felt annoyed that they were not offered food or water.

He instructed Khilji to watch after the rest in his absence. Barter for food and water with whatever possessions they had left. The scout nodded, but with worried eyes. He bowed anyway. Shayan gave each man a reassuring handshake and thanked them in earnest. He arrived at Lalya last.

"You're saying good-bye to us like you don't expect to ever see us again," she noted.

"Absolutely not true."

"Can't I go with you?"

"Doesn't seem so, no."

"I don't like this." She looked around at the guards,

at the stone walls surrounding them. "I don't feel safe here."

"You worry too much." He wasn't sure why he did it—possibly an impulse—but he touched her nose a second, coquettishly. He was indeed glad she had come. Lalya was, after all, his last connection to the sister he missed so dearly.

They held eyes until it became uncomfortable. Shayan became aware of the castle guards waiting behind him, shifting their feet impatiently. Five additional guards chaperoned the new king of the former kingdom of Tartaria. They encircled him as they walked. Shayan felt affronted until recalling that flying creatures and monsters had joined their world. Jyn had become a far less welcoming and trustworthy realm to live in.

As he entered the castle's main building, Shayan felt increasingly tense and vulnerable. This became especially so after having his weapons taken away, though he'd certainly expected this as well. He would've done the same himself. He also expected to endure a veritable army of officials before ever reaching the throne room to meet the king.

The interior of the castle retained much of its splendor, abounding with large, gold-trimmed furniture, rich tapestries, and intricate chandeliers. It was a style that evoked power and grandeur. Enormous mirrors with gilt frames hung carved into ornate designs. The opulence of his surroundings reminded Shayan of his former home, accentuating the lowliness of his situation. Humiliation and rage swept through his veins, and he clenched up. He made a point to welcome the wariness and concern in the eyes of everyone he passed.

As he was led further, Shayan could easily recognize who was a cook, a groom, a carpenter, or a mason. He even recognized the managers and servants.

Before long, they arrived at a large door. The lead guard opened it and, with no fanfare or fuss whatsoever, they ushered Shayan into what he assumed was the castle's Great Hall. Tapestries, shields, and banners accessorized the walls. Wooden paneling lined the corners.

There sat none other than King Montrose at an extensive trestle table. Also incredible was the king sitting at the table's side. Shayan took this to be another insult. He wasn't worthy enough of being greeted from the head of the table, as was custom when greeting a foreign royal.

King Montrose had even thrown on a casual tunic, his enormous belly swallowing his waist. He had gained considerable weight since Shayan had last seen him at his father's funeral.

"Prince Shayan," Montrose said flatly.

"'It's 'King Shayan' now, actually."

"Oh, right, right, your father threw himself out of a window." Montrose grinned. "Why would he do that? I've often wondered."

"He was sick, My Lord."

"No argument here. And how about your dear

mother? Did she survive?"

Shayan looked at the floor. He felt his rage returning. The condescending tone of the king was unmistakable. Montrose was enjoying this. "I don't know what became of her," Shayan said.

Montrose leaned forward. "My wife was obliterated into dust. Were you aware of that?"

"Queen Saraal was a remarkable woman. I regret to learn of her passing."

"Her 'passing' happened right in front of me." Montrose sucked on the side of his cheek. "Just like that, and she was dead. All because I was dumb enough to attend that madman's funeral. Tell me, please: What do you and your family want from me anymore?"

Shayan hesitated, unsure of what Montrose had meant. "I have come here alone, My Lord. I don't know what's become of my family."

"So you're not aware your sister was just here?"

His heart shrank. "Sarna?"

"You have another sister?"

"She was here right now? She left?"

Shayan became aware that there was another man in the room with them. Judging from his clothing, he was a nobleman of some type. He gave Shayan a bizarre look, like he truly pitied him.

Montrose touched the table with a single finger. "I'm getting married tomorrow," he said. "Wouldn't you like to congratulate me?"

"Are you sure it was Sarna?"

"Did you not hear what I just said?"

Shayan snickered, incredulous. "I congratulate you on your betrothal, My Lord, I truly do, but I wasn't even sure if my sister was still alive until this very moment. Do you know where she went?"

Montrose stuck his bottom lip out and shrugged, shoulders rising to his ears. "She didn't say."

"Was she alone?"

"She was with a whole group of men. I think they were her boyfriends."

"Boyfriends?"

"I was shocked, too. Such a wanton little thing. Your sister said much that I found...shocking."

Shayan shook his head. "She...Like what?"

"Didn't have a lot of nice things to say about you. That's for sure. What did you do to that poor child? What kind of brother are you?"

"What kind?" Shayan couldn't shake his head clear. "What are you talking about?"

King Montrose laughed. He settled back in his chair and crossed his arms. "You and your entire kingdom fully deserved what happened to it."

"To be slaughtered by monsters?" Shayan took a step forward but was halted by the lead guard drawing his sword. The other guards did the same, still standing behind him. Shayan turned back, having forgotten they were even there.

Montrose scowled. "Your father sure knew a lot about slaughter, didn't he? He slaughtered thousands of people."

"War is an ugly business, My Lord. My father did what he had to for his people."

Montrose barked over him: "And now you want me to take you in and what's left of your people into my kingdom? Is that it? Simply allow all of you to march in as if I haven't taken in enough immigrants from your incessant warmongering? Immigrants who live according to their own culture rather than ours? Who cause overcrowding? Eat our food, spread diseases, rob and steal? This was once a great kingdom that has fallen to shit. And all because I opened my doors—"

Shayan held a hand up for quiet. "We wouldn't be a burden. Neither would any of these people if you would give them a chance."

"I doubt that!"

"Fine, fine." He closed his eyes and shook his head, dejected. "I can see coming here was a mistake. I will take my men and leave."

The other king struggled to his feet, his enormous paunch and short legs truly making this a spectator-worthy event. "I'll have someone find some lodging for your men downstairs," Montrose told him. "Right near the castle. Get them cleaned up and fed. And you, Prince Shayan—forgive me—*King* Shayan will stay here as my special wedding guest."

"What about the rest of my people? They're being killed off by the drakksuk as we speak. They have nowhere to go."

"And, so, yeah, I don't give a fuck." King Montrose

lifted a bottle of what Shayan assumed was bab-sulisk. He poured it into a golden, ruby-ringed gob-let. He spilled some of the narcotic nectar onto the ta-ble and floor. No one reacted, so Shayan assumed this was a normal occurrence. "A toast to my special guest!" Montrose raised the goblet. "To King Sha-yan!" He appeared to think for a moment. "That title with that name sounds rather comical. You should change it." King Montrose refilled the goblet, again missing half of his aim. A puddle formed on the floor. Once the goblet was filled to its brim, he aimed it at Shayan. "Would you care for some of this delicious juice?"

"Does it matter what I want?"

Montrose croaked a throaty laugh. "No, your High-ness, it certainly does not. Not anymore. Ha!"

Shayan met eyes with the nobleman standing on the other side of the table. The nobleman smiled and gave a quick nod, as if micro-sharing a message of sympathy. Outside, the sun brightened and lit up the rows of stained-glass windows along the far wall, separated by tall, trunk-like pillars. The play of the light through the stained glass created a shaded gar-den of multicolored patches across the floor. The Great Hall offered no other signs of hope.

24

SARNA

She lay with the shaven-headed, brawny woman, embraced inside her meaty arms while lying on the filthy floor. To her relief, the woman didn't seem to desire anything sexual, only the inherent, powerful need to hold another human being. Someone soft. A half-dozen men occupied the cell with them. They hovered nearby and stared. Sarna guessed the guards must have shown mercy with this woman, too, when deciding which cell to toss her in. The men in their cell appeared slimmer than others, even sickly.

Sarna could not comprehend how this woman, or anyone, would want to be anywhere near her after having bodily waste thrown at her. This freakish, but kind person was so desperate for affection that she wasn't bothered by it, at least not yet. Sarna allowed herself to fall asleep, despite knowing they were the center of attention for every prisoner, many of them masturbating.

Her lids shut, and she enjoyed the sensation of having someone protectively hold her. She felt warm, precious sleep overcome her, and she slipped into the abyss of a dreamless rest. A short time later, she was awakened by an uproar. She felt herself being pulled to her feet. Disoriented, she groaned and resisted. Everyone bellowed. She checked where the large woman was and discovered she was the one forcing her to stand.

Her eyes puffy, Sarna stayed fastened on the woman's face. "Were you sent to me by the Magshaa?" she asked her.

The woman looked at her. "The what?"

A group of people stood at the entrance to her cell. In the center of them was a petite woman with clean, intricately braided hair. Her dress appeared to be made from obscenely expensive material. Four armored guards stood with her. Sarna recognized them as royal guards from their golden armor and the bright-blue plumes sprouting from their helmets. The princess did her best to clear her head. Despite the fog, she understood that whatever was happening now, she needed to be alert for it.

"Open the door!" the petite woman snapped at her guards.

The guard closest to the door produced a set of keys. To Sarna's amazement, he opened the door with the first key, and the cell door swung open. Everyone gaped at Sarna as though expecting her to do something incredible.

"They're letting you out, honey," the large woman said. Sarna felt sure this woman had been sent by the Magshaa from beyond death. There was no other explanation for such an unexpected yet vital angel. "I think it's pretty easy to figure out that you're in here by mistake," the woman added.

She gave Sarna a gentle nudge towards the cell door. As Sarna walked by the male prisoners, she expected at least one of them to make a grab for her, but they each stood back, hands folded obediently in front of them.

In a few steps, Sarna left the cell and entered the cramped hallway between cages. Before Sarna could react, the petite woman in fancy clothes hugged her tight. Once more, Sarna felt astonished anyone would come even remotely close to touching her, much less embracing her.

"I'm so incredibly sorry this happened to you," the petite woman said. She broke the embrace and stood back but held onto her arms. "I was told you were coming, but not so soon. You must forgive me, Princess Sarna. I'm getting married tomorrow, and my mind was elsewhere."

"You were expecting me?" Sarna asked.

"I am Ozyan. I am to be the new Queen of Burnya." The woman beamed and waited, expecting the princess to congratulate her.

"Oh," Sarna said, "that's great."

"We'll talk about that later, though. Let's get you out of here." The woman named Ozyan held onto Sarna's arm and led her back up the hallway. The guards followed.

Sarna stopped. "Wait, no, we have to get Momaset."

"My dear, who?"

"The man who arrived with me. I can't leave him behind. He saved my life."

"Aren't you sweet." Ozyan cocked her head, still leading the princess away. "Don't worry about the shaman. He's already coming with us, too."

Sarna checked over her shoulder. Two of the other royal guards lifted Momaset from the floor. Ozyan rounded a corner with her, and she could no longer see them. After a few more turns and countless sets of stairs, Sarna realized she was going in a different direction than the one she'd arrived from. At the end of a long, dim-lit hall, Ozyan guided her into a large room, built around a fireplace. It was the middle of summer, so it was strange to have a fire going. It provided the room's only light, a halo of dancing orange. To either side of the fireplace stood four towering velvet curtains, sheathing the windows and preventing any sunlight from entering. Gray sandstone made up the walls and floor.

Two royal guards entered the room behind them. They stood against the back wall with their heads bowed. She figured this was in response to her smell.

As if reading her thoughts, Ozyan said, "My dearest princess, tomorrow, for my wedding, you will be my special guest. I cannot apologize enough for what has been done to you. The king is…he's not himself. Please, understand. He's been through a lot."

Sarna was spinning. She felt nauseous. It took another moment to understand that the source of her sickness was another presence in the room.

Before the fireplace stood a looming, black-robed figure. As she looked longer, she grasped that there was no one inside the robe. The other two guards entered, dragging Momaset through the door. He appeared conscious, but his eyes were only half-open. His face was engorged with bruises. His cheeks were striped with bleeding lacerations of various lengths and depths. Even the area of his chest exposed above his tunic was spotted with discolorations.

"I know he's scary-looking, but you don't have to be afraid of him," Ozyan told her. She nodded her chin at the robed figure. "This is Seelskan, and he's going to save Burnya from war."

"What is he?"

"He's a warlock ghost. Or something. I'm not sure."

Sarna stared in astonishment at the robed figure. She tried to piece together exactly what she was looking at. The figure gave off a pungent vapor that filled the room, making it impossible to look at it for more than a few seconds. Sharp fumes stung her eyes and filled her nose. She shielded her face and turned away.

"You'll get used to him," Ozyan said. She patted

Sarna's back in a consoling manner. "He's Dark Shulam. His allegiance to Baal has helped him return from the dead while gaining powers from a higher realm. He's going to barter a peace deal with the Cathyrnee army that's coming to invade. Isn't that wonderful?"

It was impossible for Sarna to imagine that anything whatsoever about this being could be wonderful. "How did you...you found him?"

"He found me. He appeared in my bedroom late the other evening, and I was scared witless as you are now. But Seelskan and I came to an understanding. He's not as villainous as he looks." Ozyan took both of her hands in hers and kissed them. "Join us," Ozyan said. "Be my new sister. Let us help you become the symbol for salvation you were always meant to be."

Sarna's mouth moved to make words, but it took several tries for any to come out. "But I-I don't have...powers," she stammered. She coughed. "They're gone."

Ozyan looked confused. "Powers? Who told you that you had powers?" She looked at the robed figure in the room, floating there off the ground. The prolonged exposure to this being gave Sarna a headache. She fought the urge to flee the room. She wanted to be outside of this room more than anything in her entire life. She would've preferred the dungeons.

Ozyan smiled and pointed at Momaset, who rubbed his eyes, coming around, trying to make sense of where he was. "Let me guess," she said to Sarna, "this man here told you that you have powers." She laughed heartily. "The Ghe-sui have no powers!"

"But, no, I did once."

She placed her hand to the side of Sarna's face. "Sweetie, no, that was all in your head. You never had powers. These shamans have deluded you. Drugged you with special herbs." Ozyan walked over to Momaset. She paused there a moment before slapping him across his face. The impact was hard enough to roll his head. His jaw impacted his collar. He dropped his head, letting it hang there as though disconnected. She looked back at Sarna. "Does this man look like he has powers to you?"

"Momaset?" Sarna asked him, her voice unsteady. He didn't react. "Please, wake up."

Ozyan went to speak but was interrupted by something only she could hear. She spoke to the noxious being called Seelskan. "Yes, my love," she said to it, "I'll tell her." She turned back to Sarna. "We've arranged for the gates to be opened upon the arrival of Chief Arlyn's army. It'll be the most important event of our age. Oh, I'm so glad you're here! We're going to be such close friends."

"But..." Sarna touched her forehead. "I don't understand what you're saying. You really believe the Ghe-sui have no powers?"

"Because they're frauds, sweetie. I know these cult leaders can be extremely convincing sometimes, but

I assure you that you never had any powers, and neither did they."

"That-that's not true. How can you do this? Look at that thing! You see that and honestly believe it wants the best for you?"

"All I want is to live without war and have my family comfortable after everything they've endured. After losing our father to that stupid fucking war." Her expression darkened. "I shall become the Queen. Even if no one respects me, I no longer care. At least I can do the one thing worth doing. I can keep my loved ones alive."

The woman returned to Momaset, still held upright by the two guards on either side of him. "Time for you to kneel," she said to the shaman. "Kneel before Seelskan, your master."

Momaset lifted his eyes slowly from the floor but said nothing.

"Make him kneel," she said to the guards. They let go of him, and Momaset collapsed to the floor, barely catching himself from face-planting. To Sarna's profound dismay, he scooted his knees beneath him, then used them to lift while keeping his head against the floor. He was bowing. When he returned to the floor, a royal guard grabbed his ponytail and jerked him back onto his knees.

Sarna shook her head. The last thing left to happen was for the rest of the Dark Shulam to enter the room in formation. "Where are the rest of the Dark Shulam?" she asked without realizing she'd spoken aloud.

"The Dark Shulam and Ghe-sui are nothing more than pointless countercultures. They're worthless tools indoctrinating generations with anger and idiocy. But Seelskan has matured into something more."

"And you share his opinion about the Ghe-sui?"

"You don't have to bow if you don't want." Ozyan took her shoulders in her hands. Sarna noticed that some of the filth on her had come off onto Ozyan's fine dress, yet she behaved as if owning no awareness of this at all. "We have important plans for you," she said to Sarna. "You've been through a lot yourself, but I promise you that nothing bad is going to happen to you ever again. You're safe now. You're with friends."

"But the Ghe-sui—"

"They drugged you, sweetie. Seelskan told me everything. They filled your head with lies." Ozyan shook her own head sadly. "I wish I had powers, too. Trust me. How much easier my life would be."

CHIEF ARLYN

It rained black ash, and Chief Arlyn couldn't stop screaming. The ash was debris from the smoldering remains of his people. They had been so crammed into the streets around the castle that multitudes became scorched alive before even realizing what had happened to them. In-between patches of random survivors stood human-shaped mounds of charcoaled flesh. The single drakksuk—an especially large specimen with a black bulbous body and reptilian head balanced atop a rope-like neck—made several passes overhead. The creature showered the entire area with trapezoids of static energy. Ropes of blue light crackled as it uprooted and exploded everything it touched. Multi-pronged explosions of dirt and stone blossomed upwards, crumbling buildings and incinerating lives by the dozens.

Arlyn went to his knees and stared catatonic at the aftermath. A single flying creature had been all it took to nearly annihilate the Cathyrnee.

Archers did their best to counterattack by launching continuously ferocious volleys of fire arrows. But most bounced off the drakksuk's hard, scaly underbelly. Those arrows that did stick appeared to have no effect. Before long, any building containing an archer in its windows became obliterated by vast sprays of bright death. Structures collapsed in a cascading mass of lumber and sandstone. The landscape became a garden of black smoke plumes. People ran in every direction, and they screamed.

Arlyn checked behind himself. He saw Khuyag and the other warriors still there, still in formation, yet also aghast by what they had witnessed. The chief's jaw ached from holding his mouth open too long. Black smoke smothered the sun. The mordant perfume of burnt flesh made its way to his nostrils.

He caught movement in his periphery and saw the small boy walking onto the drum tower's platform, as calmly as if he'd been strutting around such scenes the entirety of his short life.

"How sad," the boy said.

Chief Arlyn stared at him, dumbstruck. His ears rang.

"When these people calm down," the child continued, "I need you to assemble the army. I do believe they'll obey you now."

The chief cleared his throat and tried to stay calm. "What are you?"

"I am the one who has ended your poverty and hunger, Chief Arlyn. The better question is: Who are you?"

Arlyn made it back to his feet, though his knees remained shaky. "What?"

"You know who I am," the child said. He smiled at Ulaan.

The boy stepped to the nearest turret and looked out over the carnage. The sun appeared as a crimson lesion breaking through a cauldron-black sky. Men and women blubbered and choked. They wandered a field of slaughter made oily with the remains of their neighbors and loved ones. The effluvium of death surrounded their world.

"You've murdered almost half my people," Arlyn croaked. His throat burned from the hot air and smoke. He could taste the ash. "Why would you do this?"

"Do you think I wanted to do that? Those people were about to kill you."

The chief of the Cathyrnee buried his face in his hands, and he sobbed.

"We have a war to win," said the child. "But you'll be happy to know I've taken measures to subdue the enemy without fighting. This will be the easiest victory in the history of battle. Do not despair."

Arlyn watched Ulaan, the witch, descend the stairs against the inner wall. She held her dress up by its hem to keep from tripping on it. She reached an open space encircled by the curtain walls of the castle. A rigorous belt of hot wind caused her drooping sleeves to flap behind her.

The boy placed a hand on Arlyn's neck. He grew into a man before the chief's eyes. He was a boy, then he was a man. Fast as that. His nose was cat-like, his hair black and shiny. His face held a blend of feminine, boyish, and masculine features. "I'm your friend," he told the chief. "I swear by it. You and your lovely wife were smart to invite me here. I will help you to correct what's gone wrong. Everyone deserves an equal chance at life, Chief Arlyn. And they will have it. Thanks to you."

"Kill me," Chief Arlyn said. "Go ahead. Right here. You don't have to torture me."

Baal shook his head. "No great man has ever been defeated because bad things happened, Chief. He's only defeated when he doesn't persevere after those bad things happen."

Through his tears, Arlyn noticed a nearby bronze statue that had melted. He could see roof tiles fused together from the intense infrared energy. More fires started closer to the castle. Turbulent crests of smoke bubbled like magma.

He spotted Ulaan below, outside the castle. She passed unharmed through several, flaming patches. When she approached a crouching heap of survivors, stunned senseless at still being alive, they cowered together in a tighter mass. She held her hands out as if to comfort them. She spoke, but she was too far away for Arlyn to hear her.

"Here they come," said Baal. He pointed at the horizon. "I do believe we're ready."

25

SHAYAN

He ate a meal of freshly caught river fish with raw fruits and vegetables heavily flavored with cardamom, ginger, and pepper. Afterward, he rested on the bed of his privately assigned room. It was the pinnacle of flair and solace, and he felt horrible about it, especially knowing the people he had traveled and suffered with were provided no such comfort.

Wearing only his loincloth, Shayan blew out the bedside candle and contemplated the dark. Soon he could make out various gray shapes in the room—tapestries on the wall, a bookshelf filled with uniformly-colored books, a few jeweled chalices on a desk. He could make out a trestle table stacked against the far wall next to a sitting stool.

Despite his exhaustion, sleep failed to find him. He kept replaying their journey inside his mind, still hearing the screams of his men as they were killed. He also couldn't sleep because he simply didn't trust King Montrose. He found Montrose's earlier behavior to be incredibly unstable. He could easily imagine the king sending an assassin to his room, though he'd had plenty of opportunities to have Shayan killed already.

He recalled how little respect his father, King Khilji, once held for King Montrose. For him, the king of Burnya was a laughingstock. A hedonistic child whose goal was attention and nothing more. This might've been fine if Montrose used the attention for the betterment of his kingdom, but he didn't. His rule was nothing more than abusive buffoonery. He was a coward with no morals or compassion for anyone, even for those who supported him.

He thought of Sarna. His long-lost sister. There was no telling if Montrose had been telling the truth about her having been there. Or if the story were just another platform for insulting and belittling Shayan.

His thoughts dispersed from a light knock at the door. He considered telling the person to go away, but common courtesy prevailed, and he called for the knocker to enter. The door opened so slowly that Shayan nearly yelled for the person to please come in already. A naked leg appeared, followed by a naked thigh. It was Lalya dressed in transparent cloth, scant enough to have been knitted from a handkerchief. He understood right away that her measured pace in entering was caused by her shame.

Shayan got out of bed and rushed to her, bringing the blanket with him to cover her. He embraced her and guided her to the bed, where he sat with her.

"What happened?" he asked.

"They told me that you had sent for me. They made me bathe, then they put me into this outfit."

"They assumed…," he trailed off. He didn't want to say it because it was too embarrassing.

She let out a small laugh and shrugged. "This is how women are treated here, I think."

"I'm sorry."

"But you did send for me?"

"I did."

"Thank you." Lalya remained focused on her lap. She brushed something unseen from her knee. "At least the clothes are clean. At least I was able to wash myself."

"How are the men?"

"We were led to a tavern. Not terribly far away." She gestured over her shoulder, as though the tavern lay right on the other side of the wall. She looked at him and squinted. "There is something I have to tell you. Your sister is here."

"King Montrose already told me."

"Do you know where she is?"

"I do not. He claims she left here with a group of mysterious men."

Lalya looked away, releasing a heavy sigh. "At the tavern, we met some people around the hearth. They told us there's a story going around the kingdom that the princess was thrown into the dungeons."

"You mean she's still here?"

Lalya frowned. She shrugged.

"I don't believe it," he said, though he most certainly did. He stood and made for the door. He opened it and searched both ways down the hall, trying to determine the quickest route. He decided the direction didn't matter. He simply needed someone to pulverize or scream at. He exploded with the need to punish someone. Instead, Shayan went back inside the room and retook his seat on the bed next to Lalya.

"Are you sure what you heard is the truth?" he asked. He kept his voice low.

"No, of course not. Your high—Shayan, I'm not sure of anything anymore."

Rushing to the dungeons would certainly accomplish nothing more than him joining Sarna there. Or getting them both killed. He needed a plan. He needed to see the king again. One way or the other. He needed clothing, armor, and weaponry.

He took Lalya's hand and held it. He trembled. "Lalya, would you accompany me to a wedding?"

Before she could answer, a heavily booted foot kicked in the door, which crashed open against the wall. The impact swung the door halfway closed again but couldn't stop the hordes of soldiers from charging inside. Shayan and Lalya were swarmed by a mass of armored bodies pinning them down. The King of Tartaria struggled with all his strength, but it wasn't nearly enough.

SARNA

They took her to a stone washroom. Inside lay a wooden tub within a light linen canopy. Ozyan and the guards thankfully waited outside the room while she washed herself. Sarna hoped Momaset would be taken to a similar washroom, but when she reentered the hallway in a fresh, ankle-length dress, her hair flattened into wet shards, she saw Momaset there, still held from blacking out between his guards, bleeding and grimy as before. However, seeing her again seemed to return some strength to him, and he managed to stand on his own. His loopiness made him half-grin like a drunkard.

For Sarna, every moment played out like a slow dream. She could only process what was happening by detaching. It was all happening to someone else. It didn't matter.

They next escorted her from that place to another. She remained fearful of which corner might reveal another robed figure emanating toxic vapors. Ozyan and the guards led Sarna and Momaset up the longest set of stairs yet. At the top came another hallway, followed by more stairs and more hallways. The higher they ascended, the better the condition of the walls and flooring. Their lighting source changed from hanging torches to brass chandeliers, super-ficially lifting her spirits. Ozyan remained silent but kept smiling anytime their eyes met.

Momaset also improved. He walked on his own now. Whenever Sarna found his swollen and bruised eyes, he would offer her a small smile and nod. It confounded her that he acted completely fine with what was occurring. If he felt much pain anymore from his multitude of injuries, he did an outstanding job of hiding it.

"Why are you being so nice to me?" Sarna asked Ozyan.

Ozyan looked at her, that smile returning. "Princess Sarna," she said, "I have to confess I've been hearing about you since you were born. Everyone around me did. You were looked up to by every girl I knew. Burnya hasn't had its own princess in almost thirty years, so we had no other role model."

"Queen Saraal was quite loved, I thought." She instantly regretted saying this. She recalled how Ozyan was taking the dead Queen's place. There could have been hurt feelings at the comparison.

But Ozyan took the statement in stride. "Queen Saraal was extremely loved, but she was older. We loved her, but we didn't identify with her. Not girls my age anyway."

"You looked up to me," Sarna said. She turned the phrase over in her mind, switching it between statement and question. She'd always understood the amount of special treatment she received that most other girls didn't. Having more money. More fame. Still, she felt stunned to learn that she could be idolized. Her childhood had been so sheltered and lonely. What was there to idolize about that? A part of her even detested being different, of being unable to separate genuine friends from those who required her friendship for personal gain.

Their group arrived at a door that the front guard opened. He held it ajar while the rest walked inside. Sarna looked up when she noticed everyone had stopped walking. What she saw before her was difficult to understand because of its resemblance to a nightmarish painting, the subject far too horrific to assess. There was the robed figure again, but the toxic fumes had lessened, and she was able to look at it more directly this time. Or it could've been a different entity altogether. That didn't concern her right now. What did concern her was the image of a young, nude man hanging from chains hooked through his flesh, his body slick and shiny with sweat and blood. It was impossible to understand how human flesh could hold its own body's weight, but here it was right in front of her.

She noticed Ozyan grinning at her, expecting a reaction, hands clapped together with delight. Sarna saw that one of the guards had caught the scene over his shoulder and was staring at it, agape, in disbelief. One of the other guards nudged him to stop looking, and he turned around, breathing heavily, like he might be sick. It was indeed hard to take in.

When Sarna involuntarily glanced back at her brother hanging from hooks, she caught a glancing familiarity there. In the young man's face.

Ozyan giggled. Sarna realized the robed figure stared at her as well. They all were. Her pulse accelerated as she conceded who this young man was. It was only that she had never seen her brother in such a context before. She certainly hadn't expected to discover Shayan in this particular scenario. Through the sweat-wet tangle of his front hair, Shayan looked up at her, barely conscious. His teeth gritted with the agony of having his flesh impaled and stretched in a way it was never meant to be. Her mind flashed with the hope that this was sorcery. It wasn't real. That wasn't Shayan here in this castle, stripped naked, impaled in mid-air, a robed figure staring at her from between them.

Glimmering orange light covered the backdrop in a mossy, demonic light, as though the scene had been arranged this way, just for its effect on her. It even occurred to her that she'd been rushed away to get a bath merely because they'd required more time to get her brother prepared. Now they were ready for her. And here it was. What they wanted her to see. Look at it. Eat it.

Ozyan leaned in, bent over. "It brings me no pleasure to do this, Princess, and I will let your brother down from there as soon as possible. But first, you're going to have to agree to wed Chief Arlyn of the Cathyrnee. He needs a new wife. He's been very bereaved since losing his last one. We owe him a new wife for what he's done. And you're going to be that new wife. Do you understand?"

"Let him down!" Sarna screamed, also sobbing: "What are you waiting for? How could you even do that to my brother?"

Ozyan glanced up at the king. Sarna unwittingly glanced with her. Shayan's face was a mess of spittle and blood. A pinkish fluid dripped in a thread from his toes and splatted into a puddle on the stone floor. His exposed tummy was striped with red and purple.

"Seelskan commanded it," Ozyan said. "It's the only way to suspend hostilities for the sake of humanity. Our only hope is to show mercy where we can and avoid war."

There was a commotion, and Sarna turned to see Momaset struggling with the guards. One of them struck him over the back of the head, and he folded.

Sarna spoke to Ozyan through teeth clenched with fury. "Let him down!"

"So you will wed Chief Arlyn? You will help to bring peace the way we want it?"

"Yes! Anything! I don't care! Let him down!"

As he was lowered to the floor, Shayan lay on his side. Handmaidens appeared from the shadows and went to him. Sarna ran to her brother as well. The maidens washed his wounds with water, then covered them lightly with honey. Seeing Shayan up close, she could tell how badly beaten up he was. He had been tortured. Sarna became worried her brother might not even be alive. He was so limp and swollen. His head rolled atop his neck like that of a dead bird.

Ozyan walked over, hands still joined. "I know this

seems cruel, but I had to do it, Princess. My wedding will take place tomorrow, and once I'm crowned Queen, I will allow the Cathyrnee army to enter Burnya without resistance. Our kingdoms will then join in an alliance that prevents war for all eternity."

She took Sarna's weeping face in her hands. Sarna sat cross-legged with her brother's head in her lap. He lay covered with an herb-soaked cloth. Shayan, for his part, could only blink at the ceiling.

"You're going to be fine, Princess Sarna," Ozyan was saying. "Your suffering is finished. Even if Chief Arlyn rejects you as his new wife, I will still provide another use for you."

The rage of her powers disappearing, the rage of seeing the person she cared about most in this world being treated with such barbarism—Sarna placed all of her energy of this maltreatment into a single sentence of wrath: "I will kill you!"

For the first time, she saw Ozyan frown. "Naturally, I understand why you would hate me. I can only pray you'll forgive me one day."

Ozyan kept talking, but Sarna stopped listening. She did her best to give her brother what comfort she could. She remained only half-aware anymore of Ozyan standing nearby, watching her.

At some point, the robed figure had left.

26

CHIEF ARLYN

While riding his horse, Chief Arlyn turned to survey the landscape behind him. The sight of so many marching men with their carts and animals, shields and weaponry, he had to admit that it was an impressive sight. Columns of warriors stretched over distant, lurching hills.

He'd been concerned that the size of his forces might have been greatly diminished from such a massive attack as the one suffered three days ago, but this wasn't the case. The number of fighters wasn't the problem. It was how the logistics of organizing and supplying this amount of manpower had left them thinner than he would've preferred. He doubted they even had enough firewood to cook their food. Weaponry would be useless without

Arlyn's ability to feed men and animals in the field.

He'd begged the witch for more time, but she insisted they be there for the wedding. This way, the Burnyan military would have its back turned, as Tartaria had with King Khilji's funeral. Also, there were apparently allies within Burnya poised to help them, but the attack had to be now.

The jostling of his body from riding a horse for hours took its toll on his wounds. The places where he'd been stabbed throbbed with a steady ache. His ability to withstand pain had worn down with age. Many times, he resisted the urge to selfishly stop, but this simply wasn't possible. Moving an army over eighty leagues would take two entire days. There was little time for stopping.

The chief and Ulaan hadn't spoken much since marching out from Tartaria. Arlyn cocooned himself inside the noise of carts and animals mixed with the idle chatter and songs of men who sounded more nervous than brave. Violently coercing soldiers into battle was never good for morale. Meanwhile, he and Ulaan rode together at the head, astride the healthiest steeds his handlers could find. White-skinned, brown-maned Jyn horses, muscular and remarkably swift.

After a beat, Ulaan asked, "Where are the Chotgor?"

"My hunch is that they didn't feel welcomed. Or they found our people offensive."

"I dare say it was the other way around."

"Could be. Their displacement was minuscule,

though. They increased demand on our economy, but they also expanded it. I thought we were getting along."

"You thought wrong. I hope someday you will reflect on why."

"Your boyfriend killed about a thousand people in front of my eyes. I do trust the two of you will reflect on that someday as well."

"It was your fault! You spent too much time cooped up in that royal bedroom, feeling sorry for yourself. Drastic measures were needed."

"Killing your own people will never make them love you."

"Love us? You saw those people, Chief Arlyn. They were climbing the stones to get at us. To rip us to pieces! Baal saved you."

"We'll certainly see about that part." Chief Arlyn sat back on his saddle and winced in agony. The pain made him think of tiny gremlins digging into his flesh with dull forks. Only his flask of babsulisk kept him upright and remotely focused.

Arlyn kept looking back, checking the ranks for deserters, but he had yet to spot any. He did spot Khuyag riding a few meters to the north. His top military leader kept his distance, distrustful and fearful of the witch. This was entirely understandable since she'd placed him under a spell. For all Arlyn knew, he was still under it. He was also likely distrustful of his own chief for lodging them into compliance with evil once more. No, he didn't blame Khuyag for keeping his distance. Not one bit. Arlyn wouldn't have minded some distance from himself as well.

Despite the pain, he still understood that he was the thermometer of his army. He had to remain level-headed and positive, no matter what. Do whatever he wanted his men to do. Remain mission-ready.

"Ever been married?" he asked the witch, more needing to escape his worries than an actual answer from her.

"I was," she said. Following a few beats, she added, "Long time ago."

"He was killed in the Great War, I assume?"

"Strange, but I can barely recall his face. It's as if…that wasn't me who knew him. That was a different woman." She looked at the sky, a blue-grey brindle with white accents, its flanks bordered with jagged mountains. Swollen hills elongated in the west, running parallel.

"Wish I could say the same," Arlyn said. "I remember my wife's face quite clearly. I see it all the time, especially when I try sleeping."

"I assume it's hard for you to grasp the idea that she's no longer living."

"I keep wondering where she is now. Can you tell me, witch? Does anything happen after we die?"

"*Everything* happens after we die, Chief. This life is only today's story. Your soul will find its next house."

He chuckled. "So it's a riddle. Figures."

He wanted to ask her more questions about life and

death, but the effort felt woeful. The grief from losing his wife was so deep that it often rose from his toes. Although Yarlaa's death offered a finality to what their people had gone through, he still wondered how he would ever get through his loss. Arlyn faced an emptiness swimming with memories. His grief never left him.

It was also what made it so difficult to look at Ulaan when he spoke to her. Those ocean-green eyes. The chiseled face and sharp chin. The plush flesh of her hips jiggling against her colored linen, the embroidered bands, her legs covered with tight-fitting hose.

"Where are the drakksuk?" he asked her instead. "Where is Baal?"

"They're waiting for us to get there."

"Why doesn't that make me feel better?"

They met eyes, and she grinned. "Because you fear the unknown, Chief. You distrust new ways."

"Ever since I watched a young girl puke a giant maggot, so large it choked her to death, yes. Your boyfriend thinks the people of Jyn need to be largely exterminated. Where's the heroism in this?" He winced from the pain of his horse high-stepping a rock. "Those were good people he killed."

Ulaan chortled. "Birth is never easy, Chief, nor is it pretty."

"He wants peace, so we're marching to war. That makes sense to you?"

"There will be no war. You'll see."

They rode a ways in silence, filled only by the wind

whispering through their ranks. Less than an hour later, they made camp. Slept and ate. Before dawn, they resumed their march.

SARNA

For the first time in months, she awoke in a fully made bed. She stared at the ceiling as the sunrise brightened the room. She gazed around at the dusty tapestries hanging crooked on the right wall. A bookshelf filled with uniformly-colored books stood by a desk of jeweled chalices. A trestle table had been shoved against the far wall next to a sitting stool. All these items, as well as herself, were here because they had been disregarded for the moment.

A deep nap concluded from the entrance of two handmaidens, who arrived to help her dress for the wedding. They coaxed her out of bed and wrapped Sarna in an outfit with a tunic, surcoat, and mantle. The tunic had narrow sleeves fastened with several silver buttons, while a silver rose brooch held together the neck. Despite having been a princess in a former life, this tunic was the nicest piece of clothing she had ever seen, much less worn. It felt monumentally refreshing to be free from the tunic she'd been wearing ever since her kidnapping. She wanted to shout from the elementally pleasing sensation of just fresh clothing.

She asked questions of the handmaidens, but neither knew much. Their only orders were to dress her, perfume her, fix her hair—make sure she looked breedworthy for the arriving Cathyrnee chief. From what she already understood, the plan was for her to help welcome their new allies during the ceremonies. At some point, she would be offered up as his new bride—a gift. Beyond this, Sarna wasn't sure what exactly was supposed to happen or what was expected of her. She only knew she had no choice about it. Any semblance of magic power she might've once possessed had completely abandoned her. She even considered that Ozyan was right: There were never any powers in the first place. She'd been brainwashed by mind-altering herbs with delusions created by suggestion and fantasy.

Once dressed and desirable, the maidens led her to an area on the abbey's left side. There, she stood with groups of commoners who made a point of ignoring her. After eavesdropping on their conversations, Sarna understood these were Ozyan's relatives mixed with some of her fellow villagers.

Sarna turned to find Momaset politely excusing his way towards her. His head was wrapped in a tight, gleaming-white bandage. His face appeared to have healed, though his jawline and cheeks remained misshapen. He was clothed in a clean, light-blue robe with a hood that was off his head, bunched instead around his shoulders.

Momaset smiled, which made him stand out since so few people were smiling. She noticed his missing teeth from getting beaten and inwardly cringed for him. Without a word, he approached and embraced her. Warmed by the sight of someone, anyone familiar, she hugged him back hard. He had to stand back and peel her arms from around his back. He held her elbows and spoke into her face.

"When I give you the signal," he whispered, "you need to unleash your powers." The wide spacing between his broken teeth caused him to lisp, so his words came out as "unleasssh your powerths," and she felt bad for him.

"What are you talking about?" she asked him anyway.

"Sarna, you need to give it everything you'th got and not hold back. You'll know when."

"Are you serious?"

"Your Highness, look, your powers went away because you told them to."

She squinted at him, trying to comprehend the sense in anything he was saying. "I don't have any powers. Stop telling me that."

Momaset sighed heavily. "People lost their lives, and you couldn't handle the guilt. I get it. We all do. But the time has come to stop holding back." He touched her cheeks with his fingertips. "Tell the Sünsü to come back to you."

She bristled. "If I could do that, don't you think I would've already?"

"You are imbalanced and untrained, but you're going to come through when it counts. I know you will."

"What if I don't?"

"You have to."

"What about *your* powers? Where have they been?" She swiped his fingers off her face. "Last time I saw you, you were getting dragged around the castle like a sack of bones. And what did you do to save us?" Her voice raised enough that other wedding attendees around them stopped talking and stared at them. Sarna didn't care. "You even bowed to that thing! How can you call yourself Ghe-sui and bow to evil?"

Momaset noticed the people staring and smiled back at them. He kept his voice low and even as he told her: "We were trapped in a large castle with an evil spirit and thousands of soldiers and guards, and we had no idea how to get out. I bowed to get us out of there, Sarna. We wouldn't be alive otherwise."

She turned away. "Enjoy the wedding."

"This journey here," he said to her back, "it has been a lesson to me as well. A humbling one, I confess. I was so high on myself. So incredibly convinced of my messiahhood. But I'm not above anyone."

"Because you have no real powers."

He shook his head. "You're the last hope we have. That outlaw kidnapped you, abused you, and kept you from getting to where you needed to be. Think about the harm he caused to you. You did what you had to, Sarna. Forgive yourself. Please. For the sake of our world, forgive yourself."

"It's not that simple."

"It is precisely that simple." He stepped closer and quieted his voice even more. "You'll know when it's time to act. No more pretending. It's going to come out of you."

"Nothing is going to happen!"

He cut her off by moving past her and to the other side of the street. He joined the other Ghe-sui there, only a little further away from the abbey. Sarna felt pleased, at least, to see that there was still enough local support for their religion. Enough so, they were allowed their own section, though not as close as she might've thought. She watched as Momaset moved among them, bowing to and embracing several other shamans. Sarna recognized many of the shamans from their journey together, even Corsika. Sarna couldn't help but feel a small pang of guilt, remembering how she'd been unable to feign interest in this lonely woman and her planet-sized woes. She recognized still others as those she'd seen on the street, on their walk to the castle. The dispossessed and supposedly holy.

Momaset faced the street. He awaited the wedding procession with everyone else. When he found her eyes, he smiled at her once more. He placed a finger against his lips, a conspiratorial plea for secrecy, though she had no clue who she might possibly tell.

27

CHIEF ARLYN

Arlyn stared at the back of his horse's head, the ears directed forward, toward their point of focus. He wondered if the animal had any idea of the events to come, its wider hearing range and superior scent detection giving it some clue as to the danger. Or was it as ignorant as his own men, simply doing what was expected and accepting the free food this task gave them?

"Tell me about your parents," Ulaan said. She rode beside him. Always beside him. "Are they still living?"

He threw her a sharp look. "Get away from me."

"Just trying to get to know you better, *ha'wiih*."

"Yeah? Don't mess with my head."

"I'm not—"

He pulled his horse to the left and doubled back. He trotted back along the ranks. He followed the long supply train moving just off the main trail.

Arlyn decided he would choose a healthy, clean place to camp soon, once they reached the stream he knew was coming up. They couldn't rest long, though. With so many living things together, it was easy for disease to spread, especially whenever sanitation became compromised. He would wash the horses downstream again, so their trampling and droppings didn't turn the water useless.

He heard a clear shout and turned his horse back around. Everyone watched as Ulaan galloped ahead. She turned her horse upon reaching a rocky ledge and paused there to gaze below.

She turned back and searched for him. When she found the chief, not far away, she waved at him, excited. "I can see it!" she called. "Burnya! We'll make the wedding. We might even be early!"

A throaty screech split the sky, causing everyone to cower, even the horses. Arlyn couldn't see the drakksuk entirely, but he could make out its eyes blazing like twin lanterns pushing through curtains of clouds. Behind those eyes came dozens of others, then even more behind those. They filled the northern sky, a sea of fireflies growing larger.

A fight broke out between two factions of warriors, spurred on by one trying to run away and another stopping them. They slashed their swords at one another in broad sweeps, some falling, already bleeding and dying.

OZYAN

It was the morning of the wedding, and Ozyan stood in her private chambers. She argued with the Lord Chamberlain while simultaneously being knitted into her wedding dress. The wedding would take place within the abbey at the end of the kingdom's main street, which led in from the eastern gate. This street was chosen because it could accommodate the largest number of attendees.

It was the Lord Chamberlain's duty to organize the wedding, which was why he and Ozyan argued. He was responsible for helping to draft a guest list of over two thousand invitees, as well as arranging the seating plan, complicated by the fact that only eight hundred people would be able to see the entire procession because pillars blocked the view. Even fewer would glimpse the wedding ceremony itself since it would take place inside. The worse the view, naturally, the less important the guests were.

Ozyan insisted on defying this royal tradition. She demanded that the Lord Chamberlain keep political and religious leaders entirely off the guest list. While previous Burnyan royals had been obligated to invite hundreds of guests they'd never met before, in the interests of diplomacy, Ozyan insisted commoners be given the best seats. Politicians and shamans would sit with everyone else.

She'd even insisted that the four seamstresses stitching her into her wedding dress ignore all protocol surrounding it. Tradition called for no short hemlines, no low necklines, and no naked shoulders. Instead, she insisted on all of the above. Her dress featured an ivory lace bodice with long sleeves and a satin skirt, also never seen on a royal wedding dress. Furthermore, she decided against wearing a veil, fully aware that this would be an even bigger controversy. Instead, she chose a diadem of braided jewelry. Her dress was body-skimming with a low-cut rear, allowing everyone to admire her backside. She expected and welcomed the outrage. She remained confident she would set the bridal fashion stage for decades to come.

Although tradition called for a royal Burnyan bride to wear blue, Ozyan chose white instead. She wanted to be as visible as possible to the huge crowds thronging the processional route. More importantly, white was the color of peace, which she would need to emphasize once the Cathyrnee arrived.

Exasperated with his objections, she dismissed the Lord Chamberlain, furious that he would dare argue with her, even up to the last minute, like this. If she could get through this difficult day, the rest of her days would be daisies and daffodils. So many moving pieces at once made her nervous, though. Whenever there was the slightest break in sewing, she would go to the window to check how many people had gathered already. She felt alarmed that there weren't more people, though her aides repeatedly assured her the people would show. Love her or hate her, they would pack the streets. Royal weddings were historic.

She felt acutely aware that the general populace was not thrilled with the wedding. One reason was the cost of the after-wedding meal, extravagant and sumptuous enough to require an enormous tax levy. She chose food that she believed would excite lust. (Chestnuts and pine nuts had long been used in Burnyan medicine to stimulate the libido.) Meats included large quantities of venison and fish, all served to the joyous singing of hired minstrels.

What people didn't know was that the meal was ordered to be so large because it would also be offered to the Cathyrnee army. They were due to make their appearance right after the nuptials. She'd been assured by the warlock ghost that Chief Arlyn and his men would arrive precisely on time. Burnyans would be initially fearful, even panicked, but they would celebrate with joyous relief once realizing the Cathyrnee wanted nothing more than to make friends. Shake hands, embrace, harmonize.

The biggest variable was the king himself. Though his power was absolute, she knew he was a coward. At the sight of those flying creatures again, she felt certain he would shrink into a state of utter helplessness.

When the seamstresses were nearly done, Ozyan

heard screaming from outside the window. She ran to see what was going on and became mortified. No, it couldn't be! Not now. Not yet.

Off to the east, cascading down the distant hills, roared the Cathyrnee army. There were so many men, they blanketed the topography like a spreading shadow. Horns blew from every watchtower, sounding the alarm and sending the crowds below into fits of yelling and confused scrambling.

Lifting the hem of her dress, Ozyan fled the chamber. She headed for the street to stop what was happening or at least bring it under control as best she could.

The hollowed-out ram horns kept blowing with long, deep notes, primal beacons for battle.

SHAYAN

His flesh still throbbing with soreness, Shayan sat with dignitaries in the South Transept, positioned off to the side. He counted forty-six noblemen in attendance, occupying the south side of the abbey behind the choir. On the north side sat Ghe-sui representatives in their blue-and-white robes. He noticed they appeared disquieted, restless. Even those who bowed their heads in meditation appeared to do so with their eyes only half-closed, their muttered prayers halted by deep frowning and suffering.

He'd only just discovered what true suffering was himself. The wounds on Shayan's back made movement difficult, despite the herbal sedatives given to him by a female medicine shaman. The bandages on his back felt wet, which meant they were bleeding again. He held as still as he could. Luckily, no one knew who he was, though he imagined that would change at some point. Ozyan had mentioned to him that she would be calling him out during the ceremony.

There was to be a public congregation of kingdoms. It wasn't only a wedding of two people in love, but of three kingdoms seeking a life together. It was to be the best day in the known history of their realm. Of course, Shayan felt sure this was nonsense. His suspicion was that Chief Arlyn would show up to use fire and death to annihilate everyone in sight and take the kingdom, exactly as he had Tartaria.

It was a late-arriving crowd, but the streets did begin to fill. Shayan looked for Sarna and Lalya in the crowd. He hadn't seen Lalya since the two of them had been assaulted and roughly removed from the bedroom. He'd still hoped to be seated with her and Sarna, but there was no sign of either girl. He flinched to consider what atrocities might've befallen them.

There was no denying that it had been Sarna who held his head in her lap, weeping for him. He supposed it could've been hallucinations from the intense pain, but that was her. He knew. Didn't matter that no one would tell him anything. He knew. Inquiries into the fate of his men were also laughed off.

He clamped a hand over his mouth to keep from

vomiting. The spoiled food he'd been offered, added with the excessive trauma of what his body had endured, kept his bowels in knots. He'd spent the entire night in the latrine but was thankfully accustomed to not sleeping by now. Sleeping was painful, especially at the joint of his right shoulder, where the arrow had pierced, a wound reawakened by the other injuries.

More and more citizens crowded in, as though arriving from the same place at once. When a few climbed up and joined Shayan in the stands around him, he realized he was not seated in a special section. These were not dignitaries. While Shayan had expected to still be an emissary of sorts, his insignificance couldn't have been stressed more to him. These royals were insane, and Shayan took note that King Montrose despised Shayan's entire family. Many people hated his father, which surprised Shayan to his core. He would never assume otherwise again.

Someone dropped a hand on his shoulder, which caused Shayan to nearly wilt to the floor. The man stood back, surprised, then rushed to help him stand.

"Are you still injured?" he asked. He held Shayan's elbow.

This was the man he'd seen inside the Great Hall with King Montrose. "Who are you?" he asked him.

"My name is Artemis, Your Highness. I've been wanting to find you, so I could tell you how incredibly regretful I am over what our future Queen did to you. That was unthinkable."

"Not unthinkable enough apparently."

Artemis turned so that he stood shoulder-to-shoulder with Shayan. He surveyed the crowd with him. "Look at them," Artemis said. "These people work jobs that nearly kill them, all so they can hand over half their money in taxes to people like King Montrose. Then they line the streets to gawk and wave at them, worshipping the wealthy whose only genuine achievement is being born into the right family."

Shayan gave him a sharp look and frowned. "I assume you're referring to me as well?"

Artemis nodded sagely and shrugged. "I always admired your father, actually."

"You would be in the minority around here. What do you do, Artemis? Who needs you?"

"I am the Gold Master, though it appears lately I've also been drafted to serve as the king's advisor. Or his fool. Depending on his mood, of course."

"If you're his advisor, then why did he hate my father so much? Why is he treating us like this?"

"Unfortunately, your father always believed it was safer to be feared than loved. Like me, he finds the common man to be ungrateful and fickle. They're deceivers and greedy for profit. This philosophy keeps you safe, but it doesn't make you popular, not even with other kings."

"What game are you playing at, Artemis?"

"I don't understand."

"If you're so smart, then why work for someone so awful?"

"Because he's powerful. It's only through my help

that he's served the people's welfare, Your Highness. That's how they become entirely loyal. They'll offer you their blood, their possessions, their children, whatever you ask. Stop being of use, though, and they will get rid of you."

Shayan held a clever retort on his tongue, but there came a disturbance from the east. Castle guards blew their shofars. It was a noise that built until it echoed from every wall. A large group of slender, undulating shadows appeared on the horizon, each one with its own pair of glowing eyes. The morning sun glinted off their long, scaly backs.

28

KING MONTROSE

He entered the Great Hall to find it empty. Since this was his very own wedding day, he assumed there would be people around to tell him what to do. Where to go. What to wear. It was the way for his last marriage. Saraal had arranged everything.

Ozyan, on the other hand, had forgotten about him entirely. He reminded himself that this wasn't her fault. She was a village girl. She needed to be trained.

First, he had to find her. He left the Great Hall and went in and out of each chamber. He went from the solars to the lavatories to the garderobes. He visited the kitchens, pantries, larders, and butteries, each a swirling stream of workers preparing food. No one had seen her. He went to the chapels and oratories, the cabinets and boudoirs, and still no sign of her. Mumbling unintelligibly, his aggravation building, the king came across one last random room. Inside, he saw a balcony and went there to scan the castle grounds. Below him, the streets were getting crowded. The ceremony was less than an hour away.

Within the courtyard, the grounds were landscaped with fishponds and lush with orchards and vineyards. On the outskirts, cattle, sheep, and pigs wandered sporadic farmland, grazing, wholly uninterested in anything the king might want or need.

In a moment of rage and humiliation, Montrose decided to protest this offensive lack of attention publicly. He would not dress up at all. He would show up to the wedding wearing his night clothes, the ones with the widest sleeves and shortest hem. Meanwhile, any individuals responsible for his offense would be made to regret their own birth. This way, he could set a precedent for Ozyan, lest she fail to understand her lesson.

He decided to unleash his frustrations on Artemis first. When he arrived at his office, he didn't find him there. On his way out of the room, he heard screaming from outside the window. King Montrose recrossed the office and looked outside.

An immense stream of men and horses covered the far hills, dripping downwards, a sloppy-tentacled oil flow. Three black drakksuk swooped ahead of the mass of Cathyrnee warriors, throwing long shadows across the kingdom below. Even from that distance, the king could feel blasts of wind from their giant wings. Wedding attendees and citizens ran for their lives in every direction, already bottlenecking at the intersections.

Montrose stood frozen. His blood pumped through his chest and arms. Within minutes, the front of the army disappeared behind the eastern gate.

This was it. The end times had come. Chief Arlyn was making good on his promise to annex Burnya. It was happening. And on his wedding day! He should've expected this. This made the indignity worse. He was a fool not to have expected it.

How had Chief Arlyn known about his wedding day?

He heard an argument in the hallway, followed by the pounding of footsteps. The arrival of this huge army had not gone unnoticed by others inside the castle. Heavier panic set in for the king. His heart galloped, and he couldn't catch his breath. He felt dizzy, and he trembled. He resisted the urge to hide beneath his bed.

He couldn't decide what to do. He didn't want to die, except that the day of reckoning had arrived. He would pay for the slothful, lustful lifestyle he had participated in. Montrose became transfixed with the intricate craftwork of Artemis's desk. He considered the advantages of potentially hiding under there as well. He bent over to get on his knees, but someone shouted at him.

It was a young boy Montrose had never seen before. "Your majesty!" the boy yelled. "The Queen is looking for you!"

Montrose huffed his way back into standing. He approached the young servant boy and balanced a hand on his shoulder. He thought he'd known what he meant to say to him, but now he had nothing. He felt he might be dying from fear. A numbness spread from his left arm to the side of his chest. An upper back pain traveled upwards into his jaw.

"Take me to her," he whimpered.

The servant boy hesitated because Ozyan now stood there in her wedding dress, trailed by seamstresses who sewed at her dress regardless, as though the end of the world didn't matter just yet. Ozyan's hair had come undone from an abundance of missing clips and pins.

She began speaking but was interrupted by a drakksuk passing the window, so close Montrose could see the soil and mold between its scales, the thick tufts of razor-sharp hair dividing its tail. The seamstresses fled the room, sprinting, nearly pushing the king and his bride to the floor.

"I don't understand what's going on," Ozyan said, dazed. "He promised me they would be here after the ceremony. What is he doing?"

"Who are you talking about?"

A battle horn sounded, followed by several more coming from different directions. Montrose returned to the window once more. This time, he saw a battalion of Burnyan knights charging towards the eastern gate. Amgelan led the advance from his horse, doing his best to retain control of his men. His main force managed to gather at the base of the inner gate. They set up positions to repel the initial assault through close combat.

"I have to get down there," Ozyan said. "I must take authority over this. They weren't supposed to be here yet!"

"But who are you—?"

Ozyan was already out of the room and down the hall, her gown's train bouncing behind her. She looked quite insane.

Montrose watched as the outermost eastern gate mysteriously opened. He could see Amgelan's face drop with dismay right along with his own. Who could be opening the gates at a time like this? He caught himself yelling, "No!" Over and over.

Each gate opened until the way was clear for the Cathyrnee army. There he was—Chief Arlyn. He rode a horse at the head of the army. He trotted his horse next to a woman in black, obviously a Dark Shulam. The chief stopped his horse, and the moment became locked in time. Some of the citizenry even ceased trying to flee and watched.

From the other end of the street, a black-robed figure glided towards the gate, hovering just over the ground. A gelatinous haze percolated from each orifice in the robe, refracting light into the shape of what should've been a human being but wasn't. Its appearance renewed the screaming and panic. People fled in such hysteria that many were trampled.

"Oh my God…," whispered someone behind the king, startling him. It was the servant boy. "What is that?" the boy asked.

The robed figure approached Chief Arlyn and the Dark Shulam. They bowed to each other.

"That's death," said King Montrose. "He's here."

LALYA

After Shayan had been roughly removed from the room, Lalya remained there on the bed. She stared at the open doorway where he and the men had just disappeared, feeling completely stunned. Frozen.

The events of that entire day defied belief. First, she'd been awakened at the inn and told she was needed at the castle. Afterward, she got ushered into a dressing room and told to put on this humiliating outfit. She was then led to the room where Shayan rested.

She'd always felt a natural attraction to Shayan, even back when she and Sarna were childhood friends. The simple familiarity of him was a steady comfort for her. His calm but sturdy demeanor. His delicate handsomeness. The future importance. It was the reason why she'd followed him on this journey: To be with him and offer what protection she could, laughable as that notion seemed now. He was still Sarna's older brother.

Lalya always felt that, because of their positions, both siblings sorely lacked positive human interactions. Many of the relationships with others their age were antagonistic. Lalya felt proud to be an exception to this, her friendship with them having nothing to do with beauty or power. She even found it a sad fact that most people in their society were set up as competitors to Sarna and Shayan rather than as allies. It was abusive.

After getting separated from Sarna all of those months ago, Lalya had wandered the forest until she was found by a passing band of ethnic people known as the Qomani. They lived in every kingdom of Jyn, speaking their own language, which included many dialects, all deriving from Xhenkhel. Rampant prejudice made it difficult for the Qomani to establish settlements. With the kingdoms adhering to strict purity codes, the Qomani were also barred from owning land or joining guilds, leaving them with no choice but to keep moving.

Though Lalya and the Qomani couldn't understand one another, they were still more or less accommodating to her. They allowed her to travel with them. They offered her water and fruit. They delivered her safely back to Tartaria, where her mother paid them handsomely for the kindness they'd shown her daughter.

She'd planned the entire hike to explain to Shayan about why she needed to come along, which was to make up for her cowardice. If she'd been stronger,

Sarna could've gotten away and wouldn't still be missing. There was no telling what had become of the princess because Lalya had failed her friend. It filled Lalya with a shame deep enough that it followed her like a shadow. There was no way she could've stayed in the camp while Shayan and that pitiful group of leftover men set out on their trip to Burnya. She was ultimately of no use to anyone any longer and wanted to prove otherwise.

When the time came to confess, however, there were other, far more serious worries etched into his face. She couldn't bring herself to trouble him further. Her confession wouldn't have done any good anyway.

She lay back on the bed, propped on her elbows, still covered by the blanket. She watched the open doorway, expecting someone to come in and get her or tell her where to go. After several moments of ringing silence, she went to the door and softly shut it. She returned to the bed for what felt like hours, not knowing what else to do. Exhaustion overtook her, and she curled up on the bed and cried, truly letting it go. She had never felt so alone in her life.

Lalya fell asleep and awoke to a racket in the hallway. It was morning. She got up and went out of the room, where she saw handmaidens filing past. Clutching her blanket around her, she fell in with them. Her hope was to follow inside the group, only until she could find an exit. She tightened the blanket around her, noticing the odd looks she received from the other girls or people they passed. Thankfully, no one stopped to bother her about who she was.

As she walked, she felt the drakksuk tooth against her thigh. She had hidden the tooth there because it was so easy to do so. She had also brought it along because she simply didn't trust a single living soul inside this castle.

She'd been thoroughly searched before entering, of course, but the guard had failed to find the tooth on her, being far more interested in feeling other, more private parts of her. Lalya wasn't sure if she even believed what the tooth could supposedly do, killing anyone it stabbed. From what she'd seen of their new world, there was no reason to doubt the supernatural abilities of anything anymore, no matter how paramount.

Following the maidens for a while, she realized they were headed nowhere near the outside, at least not yet. If anything, they were going deeper into the castle. She soon found herself in a dressing room, much larger than the one she'd been pushed into earlier. The ruckus was dizzying. Surrounded by the shrill clamor of girls becoming wrapped in frilly, flower-embroidered dresses, Lalya stood and watched them. Nearby, a middle-aged, frumpy woman squatted on a low stool while doing her best to control the chaos. Lalya understood these girls were part of the wedding ceremony.

The woman's eyes landed on Lalya standing there with her blanket. She looked her up and down, then snapped at her to put a dress on already. She handed her a basket of flowers and, like that, Lalya was made part of whatever elaborate lineup of flower girls had been arranged. It wasn't long before a bout of shouting and arguing commenced since they were now a dress short. Lalya reminded herself to stay calm and to keep busy fitting into her outfit, doing her best to appear as though she absolutely belonged here.

After a short time, the girls were led outside the room, down a few hallways, and they reached the outside world far faster than she would've expected. Unfortunately, the streets were mobbed, so she had nowhere to escape. She clutched onto her basket and decided to go along with whatever was expected of her for now.

Across the street and down the block, she spotted Shayan, visible from his elevated position in a dignitary box. Her heart vaulted. There he was! Right there! And he was alive. And dressed up, though he did move funny. She thought maybe she was imagining it, but no—she saw it again. The way he moved. He was hurt. Anyone could see it. They had hurt him.

And something else was wrong. The crowd became highly agitated. Though the sun was a bright and powerful presence in the sky, the entire area dimmed. She looked up and couldn't believe her eyes. The entire heavens were layered in flying creatures, the same ones who had destroyed her home, except now there were hundreds of them. More than she could count. Lightning shot from their mouths and detonated buildings, walls, and people, all of it somersaulting. The throats of the creatures lit up and revealed networks of thick neck veins.

The rest of what happened was a blur. A rush of people pushed by her. The panicked crowd closed in, and the pressure built around her entire body. She couldn't even raise her arms, and she struggled to breathe. An extreme heat filled her lungs, and she felt as though she might faint standing up. If this happened, she knew she would get trampled. Her small bones would crack under the weight of so many people.

She tried moving towards Shayan, but she was trapped; the movement of the crowd like a fluid mass, she was helplessly bonded to. More buildings exploded, sending spears of wood and balls of brick in every direction, some of it striking those around her. She saw people bleeding and crying out. It rained pebbles. A shock wave rippled through the masses, and Lalya was lifted off her feet, then propelled down the block, carried along by an undertow of human beings. The insulation of surrounding bodies made breathing increasingly difficult. She suffocated.

She turned, searched for Shayan again, and there he was still. He was out of the box and on the street. She shouted his name, but there was no way he could hear her. Not from that distance. She focused on finding escape, but her vision faded as she started passing out.

As a last hope, Lalya turned her body sideways and used the slimness of her figure to squirm away from the crowd's center, to find some break, just any break—instead, she fell. She scrambled to find her feet again, but the rushing mob was already over her, a single beast with a thousand legs and feet who didn't know the difference between her and the ground. All they cared about was saving themselves. Lalya tried again to find her breath but coughed. She tasted soil. She caught a knee against her temple and rolled underneath the crowd.

29

SHAYAN

He watched what was happening with a kind of bemused neutrality. The babsulisk, combined with whatever medicine they'd given him, made his head cloudy. When a shiny-black drakksuk glided low over the wedding crowd, the wind and debris sent the masses diving for the ground. The area became alive with screaming. Those closest to the narrow, clogged side streets leaped frantically over those ahead of them. Those stuck out in the open made themselves as flat against the stone ground as possible.

The deposed King of Tartaria felt numb. This wasn't his people nor his kingdom. Not this time. He didn't feel as involved as he had during his father's funeral. Events played out as if from a stage, solely for his entertainment.

This lasted until he saw the eastern gates opening wide. The Cathyrnee army marched in, unimpeded. The ground trembled from the jostling of so many men and horses. Shayan was in awe. This had to be the entire Cathyrnee military. Every single last man. He realized he would be better off running away with everyone else, but he felt rooted, flabbergasted. Why did Burnya open its gates to an invading force?

He spotted a girl who resembled Sarna next to the royal bride. The bride argued with a knight, his neck, head, and chin hidden by a metal helmet with only eye holes and vertical slits for breathing. From what Shayan could discern, the knight wanted to get the two women to safety, but the bride resisted. She kept pulling herself free of him. The girl who looked like Sarna bit her nails and gazed around, anxious, except for the way her brows tightened. The way her lips puckered around her finger as she gnawed on her nail. No, that was Sarna. That was her. Not a looka-like. Only her braided hair had made her hard to rec-ognize. Still, she stood so close that it puzzled him over how he hadn't seen her earlier, then he recalled that he was intoxicated. Too many details coming too fast.

Another flying creature sailed over their heads. People cried out, and Shayan could see entire waves of people getting pushed forward and falling, those behind running over them, desperate for any chance at survival.

The surprises kept coming: He recognized Chief

Arlyn at the front of the army. He rode horseback next to a slender, dark-haired woman. Both rode slowly, their chins up, daring anyone to strike them.

Shayan couldn't believe what he was witnessing. Leaders of Tartarian and Burnyan armies always led from the rear. Riding at the front was suicide. You didn't waste leaders like that. Also, strategizing abstract issues of battle was impossible when dodging swords and arrows.

He supposed Chief Arlyn's sense of invincibility came from the creatures flying overhead, but curiously, the drakksuk weren't attacking. Not like during his father's funeral. The absurd idea entered his head that they were merely here for the wedding. Uninvited spectators.

This notion became muted when the Burnyan knights let loose with a charge, led by a battalion dressed in long, dark-blue tunics and tall bork hats. They launched themselves fearlessly into the fray, swinging their swords with the grace and swiftness of trained assassins. The battle line was noticeably dented by their attack. Soon, the eastern entrance became a battlefield of soldiers, knights, and warriors.

A thunderous explosion undulated through the ground, followed by two more. A trio of blasts appeared within the ranks of Cathyrnee warriors, launching several warriors through the air, some of them in pieces. Long, thick metal tubes on wheels had been rolled out of different barns. One soldier inserted a large ball inside the tube, while a second man used a torch to light a fuse atop the device. A third man steered the tube in the direction they wanted it to fire.

Soon, another volley of explosions sent more Cathyrnee flying if not vanishing on the spot. This sent the warriors into a confused, frightened retreat, stunned by the sight of such a weapon.

A fast-moving storm darkened the horizon. Before long, the clouds separated into winged shapes. The chill of fear spread through Shayan's veins as he realized what he had witnessed—an approaching, extra-heavy swarm of drakksuk, more than he could have ever thought existed. Hundreds of them, enough to eclipse the sun. One flew from behind, and Shayan reflexively went to his knees when it shrieked. His ears rang as he watched windows shattering around him. Pellets of glass exploded in every direction, some scratching his cheeks and neck. He pivoted and crouched. He shielded his face.

Sarna. He had to reach her. He needed to do that much at least. He could figure out what to do next from there. But when he looked back, she was gone. He felt alarmed, convinced she'd been hurt. She'd been even closer than he to the rupturing windows.

The woman riding next to Chief Arlyn pointed at Shayan. Arlyn leaned in to follow her finger. His face brightened warmly when he recognized Shayan. He kicked his horse and galloped towards him. The woman called out to him from behind but seemed to think better of it. She kicked her own horse to follow, riding harder. When the chief reached a spot right below the dignitary's box, he pulled his horse's reins to halt it.

"Your Highness!" Chief Arlyn called up to him. An arrow zinged in front of his face, but he didn't flinch. "I didn't expect you to be at this wedding. I guess I should've."

"What are you doing?" Shayan asked him, surprised at how much strength he had left in his voice.

"The oppression of monarchies is over, Your Highness. I couldn't stop what's coming if I wanted to."

The woman in black brought her horse to a stop beside Chief Arlyn. She smiled up at Shayan, breathless, as though she were the one running instead of the horse. A white spear of lightning sizzled from the mouth of a passing drakksuk, connecting with a row of buildings. The structures detonated with huge sprays of dust and rock. Torrents of lumber and stone spilled over fleeing citizens and even some of the Cathyrnee warriors. Drakksuk commenced lighting up the streets, the sky, the trees. They spread bright, hot rays in every direction, killing indiscriminately. Towers of fire flowered out from each side of every street. Body parts launched across the air and showered the ground, now throbbing with orange craters.

"We're here to bring a new age," Arlyn shouted, not even turning around at the carnage behind him. Shayan could barely hear him. "The time of the rich ruling the poor is over!"

"This is better?"

Arlyn slid down from his horse while holding onto its reins. "You owe me a swordfight." The chief unsheathed his longsword. "Are you up for it this time?"

"I don't have a weapon."

Arlyn turned to the strange woman beside him. He motioned for her to give Shayan her sword. She delayed but took it out.

Shayan went to the edge of the dignitary's box. He stepped over the side and held on to the box's edge behind him while slowly lowering himself. He didn't feel the pain until he landed. He twisted his waist and halted there, agony straining his tendons. He straightened himself, but it took work.

"You're hurt," Chief Arlyn said. "I'd kill you in seconds, exactly like last time. This is disappointing."

Shayan brought his sword up and bounced on his knees, ready to engage. "I'm in the best shape of my life."

"Wish I could say the same."

Shayan lunged, but the chief easily blocked him. He kicked Shayan in the sternum, which caused him to stumble backward.

A tremendous collision noise from the south. A boulder had landed in the middle of the street. Another boulder, large enough to make a shadow, came hurling over the wall after it. The boulder smashed into the turrets alongside the castle, opening them up. An avalanche of stones tumbled over the streets in a violent cascade. Shayan had only to see their horns as they appeared over the kingdom walls. The yelkin pulled themselves up and over. The giants mimicked the cries of those dying as they tossed whatever piece of building or wall would come off in their hands.

Arlyn appeared dismayed, as though not expecting to see the giants either. He lowered his sword, an open target if Shayan wanted to take advantage. Except Shayan didn't. A burning ribbon, a former piece of wedding decoration, floated by just over the chief's head. It snowed ash.

The entire area around the abbey flashed with energy, incinerating anything in its path, even dissecting some of the yelkin. Red, fleshy portions of the giants spurted fluid as they separated. Regardless, an ever-growing group of giants barreled through the streets as more crawled over the walls.

Chief Arlyn turned his attention back to Shayan and lunged at him. He stabbed down recklessly, and Shayan rolled out of the way. He rolled several times while Arlyn's blade stabbed the ground where he'd just been. Shayan kept rolling, with no other defense. Sooner or later, he knew Arlyn's sword would catch up, so he changed direction and rolled forward. He stood and shoved Arlyn back. He didn't have much strength, though, and he failed to topple the chief. He was about to counterattack, but the ground shook, and he fell to a knee.

Both men were forced to pause in their swordfight again as the drakksuk began detonating in the sky.

Numerous beams of blinding light punctured them until they came apart. Shayan followed the lights down to their source and saw they emitted from a ring of Ghe-sui shamans, encircling the entire neighborhood. The shamans joined hands, creating a sphere of combined brightness that shot upward into a united band of energy. The drakksuk burst into pieces and fell. They created a shower of bleeding meat. Their carcasses expanded on the ground until hot gases further ruptured through skin and blubber, reducing them to sloshy pools.

Shayan looked on, dazed, as more blasts of energy rippled over the area. It became a sizzling spectrum, and he could feel the intense heat from where he stood. The ionization made his hair stand up. Even Chief Arlyn's own locks stood out from his head in a fright-wig.

The force of the proceeding blasts shoved Arlyn into Shayan, and both men tumbled together against the front walls of the abbey. Shayan fought through his excruciating pain to get back onto his feet. Luckily, he had held onto his sword. He stood over Arlyn.

The chief was feigning. Arlyn brought his sword up, but Shayan dodged, barely preventing the chief's sword from running through his chest. He staggered away, but something was wrong. His flesh felt changed on his left side. Arlyn's blade had still cut him, though he didn't know how deep. No time to assess. Arlyn advanced and swung his sword. It was a wild swing. Shayan avoided it easily but lost his footing.

Arlyn jumped, sword raised. Shayan lifted his own sword but already knew he was too late. His arm was too heavy. He held his blade at the wrong angle. He opened his eyes and knew his last hope was to meet eyes with his executioner, halt him a second with a pleading gaze. Instead, he saw Arlyn standing still, held upright by a beam of blue light through his stomach. The sparkling light resembled a large icicle, which pulsed with white-hot energy. Shayan raised onto his elbows and saw Sarna shining within a light-blue nimbus of glistening static. She held her hands out. She aimed them like weapons.

Behind her rose a spreading patch of darkness, flame-shaped eyes swirling within. The darkness so-lidified into a robed figure, the same one he'd seen before. The figure floated over the ground as it ad-vanced on his sister. Sarna didn't see it yet. She had no idea. He had to warn her, but it approached too fast.

A triangle of bright light traveled through the shad-owy figure, and it screamed before turning formless again. Behind it, a bald shaman held his arms straight out and pressed the palms of his hands together while keeping them parallel. The shadow figure dis-sipated like steam. The robe blew away, also dis-carded by the wind.

The cannon fire persisted, though concentrated on the yelkin now. Many fell from the launched ball, contacting their torso, removing chunks from their thin bodies. Before long, other yelkin reached the cannons and eviscerated those operating them.

"Momaset!" Shayan heard his sister shout.

"Are you with us?" he shouted at her. "Can you do this?"

"Yes, I think so. Yes!"

"Good. Because he's coming."

"Who is?"

Above a landscape of dueling armies, dead monsters, and marauding giants, an impossibly tall, dark being stepped over the wall. The Fiend was giant-sized, taller than the yelkin even, with a black, humanoid body that fluttered as though made from millions of ravens. The head was a cow skull with two pairs of wavering red eyes burning from a nest of black wrinkles. His head was crowned by seven horns, big as the head itself. On his back unfurled a pair of seven-fingered bat wings, identical to those used by the drakksuk.

"What is that?" Sarna screamed. "Momaset? What is that?"

Shayan heard a gasp. He turned to see Chief Arlyn on his knees with a large, smoking opening in his chest. He touched his hand to the wound, and Shayan cringed to see some of his fingers disappear inside. Arlyn looked up at him with teary eyes. His mouth quivered with the words he wanted to say. Shayan dropped his sword and went to him. He held the Cathyrnee chief from collapsing.

"Finally," Chief Arlyn said. "Finally."

"Chief,…I'm sorry."

He reached out and held Shayan's arm in a death grip. "Thank you," he wheezed.

"By the gods, don't thank me," he said, but Arlyn's eyes had gone empty, the light of his living soul extinguished.

Arlyn went limp. When Shayan released him, the chief fell and landed forward. The top of his head touched Shayan's feet.

The woman in black cried out and got down from her horse. She ran to him.

The Ghe-sui focused their collective powers on the giant, winged being. At first, their forks of lightning merely sparked off his skin. They hit the yelkin instead and occasionally blew them apart. Here and there, headless giants stumbled around, trying to determine a direction. Without their forebrains, the yelkin retained basic motor functions enough to keep attacking, although blindly.

The woman in black became lifted by a dark, amorphous energy, illuminated by a blast of blue power from Sarna's fingers. The woman cried out as she spun in the air before striking the ground. Shayan heard her leg bone crack. Strangely, she didn't make a sound but merely reached back and held the shattered limb. The woman moved it around, perplexed by its malleability but without any sign of pain. She looked up.

"Sarna, it's me," she said to Shayan's sister. "Don't you remember me? It's Ulaan!"

Sarna's eyes blazed blue. A crown of static surrounded her head, and she gritted her teeth.

"I took you to meet the Magshaa!" the woman yelled. She held a hand out. "Remember me? I'm your friend."

"Why do you look so different?"

"Baal has returned my youth to me."

"He put a spell on you."

"Not a spell. A miracle! Sweetest princess, he's only here to help us. I don't know why Burnya is fighting him."

"Because no one with a sane mind wants his type of help."

"But that's so narrow-minded! What are you afraid of?"

"I never paid you."

The woman went to respond to Sarna but halted. "Paid?"

"That day on your farm. When you saved me. I promised I'd pay you if you took me to see the Magshaa. But I never paid you."

Ulaan shook her head, aghast. "I don't care about *payment*. Money means nothing to me anymore. I'm free! Look at me."

"I am, and I keep seeing myself. I could've been you so easily."

Ulaan smiled shakily, then winced. She raised her chin. "I'm very happy for you that you didn't."

"You know what I must do, right?"

The witch named Ulaan choked up, tearing.

"Please, don't."

A shock wave blasted from the entirety of Sarna's body. The wave struck Ulaan, who writhed on the ground. She flickered between this body and another, much older one. Her veins glowed. Her hair swam around her head, as if underwater. Her form kept changing until losing its shape. Shayan watched as his sister reduced the woman to a puddle of gray matter, which percolated like spilled sludge.

He felt an immense warmth as his body became enveloped in blue light. Sarna stood next to him. She bent down to embrace him. From the instant of contact, Shayan recalled his sister having once hugged him this way, when they were much younger. She cried because she didn't want him to leave for sword training. She was too young to understand what training even was. She felt convinced he was going off somewhere to get mortally wounded. He'd had to pry her fingers off to leave. He felt certain he would have to do the same now.

The Fiend spotted them and walked towards them, his feet crunching any man or beast in his way, their skeletons crumbling like sticks. By now, even the giants had paused in their mayhem to gawk at his size and appearance. As he approached, many of the Ghesui turned black and wilted, their robes and headdresses bursting aflame. They evaporated into ash, which joined with the ashes of burning buildings.

Shayan held his arm up to shield them from the smoke, building to a thickness that choked him. He felt Sarna being pulled away from him by an unseen force. Though he couldn't see her, he could sense her legs dangling above her body as she was sucked into the sky. He held onto her hand as tight as he could, but she was slipping. Soon, he held her by only one finger, hooked together. Then she was gone.

ULAAN

In her last moments, she saw Baal watching her, smiling, that beautiful face beaming at her. He laughed, amused by her defeat. He had no concern for her whatsoever. Her predicament was hilarious. Her excruciating plight in life tickled him. She'd been fooled. She saw that now. What she'd told him that morning in her bedroom was the truth after all: She was nothing. A toy. Useful but peripherally so.

She saw him fully as well, the stark reality of why he'd entered her life. Not as a comforting ally, but a blunt, cruel punishment for the choices she'd made. He was unfiltered evil. He was her brother. Her real father. Baal was hate and death, and she'd surrendered to him long ago, before ever laying eyes on him. He'd come to her because she'd invited him. Same as everyone. She had no one else to blame, and this hurt worst of all.

Her essence dissolving, her heartbeat became nothing more than a hollow tap inside her throat. Each tick came more slowly until Ulaan felt sure it was the last one. But there was one more. And another. She slipped deeper into the dark, vanishing between each diminishing beat. She felt what had to be the last pulse, but—no, there was one more. Then—yes, that was it. Done. She was out of time. The shaman watched the clouds come closer as she rose. She passed through them and into the stars above, where a pink-red spectrum of galactic gases stretched into the eternal distance. It was beautiful.

SARNA

The dissected bodies of drakksuk tumbled from the sky. Rays of white energy poured from a regrouped circle of shamans, joined once more at the hands. Javelins of lightning struck the Fiend but with no effect. However, the distraction was enough for The Fiend to drop Sarna. She fell roughly onto her elbows. The pain shot through her shoulders, and she turned onto her stomach, squirming. Cheek pressing the ground, she watched in horror as the large being picked up one Burnyan citizen or soldier after another, squeezing them in his hands until their skeletons collapsed, their bodies popping open and gushing. She noticed some of those killed were children, and she had to look away, screaming inside.

Momaset must have heard her, because he rushed over and stood only yards away from her. After getting her attention, he did his best to snatch the attention of the other Ghe-sui as well. He waved his arms wide, but their shock left them immobile, unfocused. Losing so many other shamans at once had turned them defensive and frightened. Some even went to their hands and knees. They cowered as the ground periodically shook.

Sarna got to her feet and went to her brother. She placed her arms around him. Over his shoulder, she watched helplessly as many of the yelkin reached those shamans closer to the gate. They lifted them and pulled them apart, slurping their innards like sappy fruit. She heard buzzing to her right. She turned to see Momaset. Having given up hope of re-assembling an energy circle, he shot what must have been every ounce of Sünsü he had left in his soul—aiming all of it at the Fiend. Baal winced at the attack but appeared to do so more from its illumination than from its strength. He threw his left hand, and a crescent of distorted air spread out towards Sarna.

Momaset dove to place himself in the way and suc-ceeded. He absorbed the blast. Gulping, burping noises came from him as he shook. Within seconds, he dissolved into a mound of charred flesh and fat.

Sarna yelled. The halo above her head morphed into a blob that surrounded her. She felt her feet leave the ground. Both her sandals slipped off, yet re-mained inside the blob, elevating with her.

A blast of violet fire shot from the Fiend's chest and hit her dead-on.

She thrashed inside a pit of centipedes that crawled and squirmed within every crevice and orifice of her body. Spiders crawled among the hordes of other insects, and she thrashed to get away from them. She felt her skin melting. The scenery itself melted, lavalike.

She saw her mother, who cowered before a crowd of men. Crawling on her side, using her legs to kick away from them. They surrounded her in broad daylight, her face a mask of abject horror. Her cheeks felt sunburnt, dirty, her dress brown and slick with clay. One of them sat on top of her, and the rest of the men cheered. Sarna saw her father falling, his already frail body combusting against the stone pavement of the courtyard. She saw Shayan on his knees, being held while metal hooks opened the flesh of his back shoulders, his entire body slick with blood.

Stop it! Her mind kept shouting—*Stop! This is not happening!*

"Stand straight," she once heard Luca tell her. She felt the warmth of his body, his big arms around her, showing her how to shoot a bow and arrow. "Keep your feet apart," Luca had said, "even with your shoulders."

An enormous pair of hands closed around her throat. The air left her lungs. The muscles of her neck collapsed under the strength of those hands, her neck snapping, her face stretching into a clownish mask, eyes popping from their sockets.

"You can do this," Luca whispered.

"Give up," said a different, soothing voice inside her ear, so calm that it sedated her. "It's all right."

She stood atop a high, black hill that peaked beneath her feet, forming a dress of volcanic rock around her nude body. Below her, the hill was covered with people bowing to her, their foreheads against the ground, in complete obedience to her. They wept at her greatness. She felt gleeful from the power this gave her. She wanted to embrace each of them and help them understand how much she loved them. To let them know that everything was all right. She was in control now. Nothing would ever hurt them again. She wouldn't allow it.

"Kneel!" commanded a booming voice. She understood that it wasn't talking to her, but the people on their knees. "Kneel before her dark majesty!"

She was being shown a potential future. One in which she was the most important. The most powerful. The safest. If she would only give up.

Shayan in hooks again, except he was a child now, crying. Her older brother shrieked.

Luca was showing her how to spear a fish. "Extend your arm halfway out," he said. They stood together in the shadows of the Magoi River, the slow current, black water curling around their waists. "You'll need that room, so you can thrust forward, as far as possible. Attack in one smooth movement."

Sarna exploded into a tentacled cone of blue light, shining forward through the flames.

Another circle of energy formed from the remaining Ghe-sui. The resulting beam joined with Sarna's and struck the Fiend, who staggered, nearly toppling sideways. He swept his right arm out, and the Ghe-sui were collectively sent to the ground, most of them in pieces. Sarna was only spared because she was too far away and partially shielded by a fallen section of wall.

From what she could tell, there couldn't have been more than a few dozen Ghe-sui left. Meanwhile, the Cathyrnee army retreated in chaos. They ran out of the kingdom gates and back up the hill. The reality of so much supernatural activity happening before their eyes had become too much. They wanted no part of it. They fled.

The Fiend kept his eyes on her and appeared to know who she was. He made his way towards her, stepping over a churning field of carcasses and burning wood. The glimmer of flames shone orange off the Fiend's inky, flittering skin.

He held his hands together with the palms flat but left a small space between them. In the space, a ball of flames grew outside the hands until it filled the entire area. Sarna raised her arms. She created a blue shield that surrounded her and her brother. The blue nimbus held the flames off them, but Sarna could feel the heat getting closer. She could only hold it off for so long. The protective orb around them shrank. Sarna screamed in agony as she felt the flames reaching her skin.

30

SHAYAN

He ran forward to save his sister without hesitating. As he reached the Fiend, Shayan raised his sword to stab down into the being's foot. In a blink, his world became fire, and he was tossed backward. The heat went instantly cool, and he found himself skidding over the rocky ground. He did his best to wrap his arms around his chest and not flail as he went end over end. He was only halfway successful with one arm while his other flopped wildly, getting caught between the ground and his shoulder, so it bent backward. He felt a snap, numbness. Once he stopped rolling, he lay on his back with his injured arm across his stomach. For a moment, he could do nothing more than stare up at the sky, a haze of orange light and black smoke filling his vision. Higher above, the stars stared back, a million tiny, bright eyes watching the spectacle unfold.

With painful effort, he sat up and realized his clothes smoked. His tunic was filled with singed, open patches exposing the pink, burnt skin beneath. He smelled burnt hair and realized much of his was missing. He heard howling, which he first thought belonged to a yelkin. Looking up, however, he saw it was the Fiend holding his leg. A small guthook-shaped object stuck out from the top of his left foot.

Lalya stood behind Baal. She looked up at him, her eyes wide. She had stabbed him with the drakksuk tooth of all things. The bulbous root of the tooth was the only part showing. Lalya had managed to sneak up and nearly insert the entire tooth into the Fiend's foot. Baal turned and glowered at her as his body dissipated into a red mist. The mist briefly resolidified into the shape of a man. Phosphorescent sparks flickered within his form before losing his shape and returning to mist. It formed into a billowing red fog that pulsated before evaporating.

Shayan yelled with exuberance, even raising a fist in the air, triumphant. The Fiend was dead! That damn little tooth worked after all. The myth was true!

Baal elasticized back into his giant shape from a single point in mid-air. He appeared rejuvenated and furious, his upper teeth having become fangs. Lalya cowered, her arms over her head, ready for the evil spirit to do whatever it wanted. At once, Shayan went from feeling immensely relieved that the Fiend had disappeared and that Lalya was still alive to being terrified for her. The Fiend towered over her. Before Shayan could move another muscle, the Fiend inflated his chest, his skull head reared back. He opened his mouth to emit a cone of swarming flames that poured down over Lalya. One second, she flinched from the oncoming fire; the next, she vanished within a blazing fountain that spread over the ground where she'd just stood.

Shayan heard his sister scream. She made fists of her hands and roared at a volume which shouldn't have been possible for someone her size. An amorphous jet of blue ectoplasm sprouted from her chest and struck the Fiend in the back. He turned to face her, appearing mostly annoyed. He clawed his fingers by his side, opened his mouth, and another enormous spray of fire shot towards her, enveloping her.

Despite the agony in his arm, his shoulders, his head, Shayan crawled to his feet and prepared to yell at the Fiend, distract him. As the fire doused her relentlessly, to the extent he could no longer see her, he ran towards the Fiend to stop it. The flames seemed to have no end as they sprayed over her in a continuous cascade of hot death. However, when the fire receded, to Shayan's amazement, Sarna remained there, unharmed.

The Fiend took a step towards her, prepared to grab her up in its claws. Baal went to take the next step and was met straight-on in the chest by a wide ray of blinding light. He roared and stepped back, off guard. Shayan saw that the ray came from what was left of the Ghe-sui, banded together nearby. They joined hands, the blast coming collectively from an aura of changing colors around their bodies.

Baal clapped his hands together, and a shockwave of steam and fire sent half of the shamans flying. The rest went to their knees. As before, the Fiend inflated his chest in preparation to emit more flames but was halted by a second ectoplasmic blast from Sarna. The blast found its way into his open mouth before the fire could come out. Seeing how this dazed him, Sarna appeared to focus on sending more energy down his throat. Those Ghe-sui who hadn't been blown away noticed this as well and rejoined their hands. The aura reunited around their bodies until another ray of light shot forth, combining with the energy coming from Sarna. The Fiend staggered back. He tried to turn his head away and remove the collection of power choking him.

His arms swung in front of him to obstruct their energies, but he couldn't. The power coming from Sarna and the shamans had already entered his throat and stomach. The phosphorescence began to show through his skin and spread throughout his limbs. The point where the tooth had entered his foot sparked and sent a branched stream of light up his leg and through his torso. Light filled his body until his flesh could no longer contain it, and the Fiend burst apart like a melon. His flesh turned to flames that doused when touching the stone around them.

Now able to ease their efforts, Sarna and the shamans fell to their faces. Many of the shamans appeared unconscious. Smoke trailed from their robes in lazy wisps.

Sarna lay on her stomach and raised her head, her face wilted with anguish, cheeks wet with tears for her dead friend.

Clutching his dislocated arm, Shayan ran to his sister.

OZYAN

Surrounded by smoky ruins, Ozyan watched King Montrose crawling on his hands and knees. He reached the abbey minister, who appeared to lie there dead. However, when the king grabbed the man's ankles, his eyes popped open, and he reflexively squirmed to escape. The king held on and pulled at him. His hands were climbing the length of the minister's body. Ozyan stared, unsure of what the king thought he was doing.

She held still, dismayed at everything happening around her. Her plans had unraveled so quickly and thoroughly. She felt like an idiot.

She watched as her future husband used the material of the minister's double-breasted cassock to pull him closer. The minister's white hair sprouted from his head in comical, wispy ribbons, having come loose from under his cap. His saggy cheeks puffed when he coughed. King Montrose appeared to assault the man for no other reason than sheer hysteria, needing an outlet for his fear. He sobbed like a child, simply needing a stuffed animal to punch.

A large confetti of ash stirred in the wind. Public wedding decorations, singed and shrinking, swirled within shrouds of black smoke. Long broken tables, rose petals spilled from wicker baskets, seating markers, and even the altar arch were misplaced and ablaze. The minister attempted to stand but was brought back down by Montrose pulling hard on his sleeve.

Still mesmerized by this absurd scene, Ozyan ruminated. She'd never wished to conquer the world, only to improve the lives of those she loved. She didn't want them to suffer anymore. Instead, she had acted without empathy or consideration for anyone's needs. She'd allowed a dark wizard's ghost to fool her into believing she would come out ahead from his help. He'd claimed to know the exact moment of Chief Arlyn's arrival, but that had been a lie. Her allegiance's only value had been her ability to get the eastern gates open. Nothing more. All that manipulation. That scheming. All that torture, death, and destruction, simply to get some gates open. She'd been suckered for the sake of a simple military advantage, and now her world lay torched to the ground. The bodies of beasts and men lay in soft, smelly piles, and her life no longer meant anything to anyone. Yes, she saw it at last. How moronic she'd been.

Ozyan marched over and grabbed the minister on

his other side. She lifted him to his feet, despite the king's grappling to oppose this. When Montrose could no longer hold on, he flipped onto his side and hugged himself, whimpering.

"Get up!" Ozyan snapped at him, then to the minister: "You, too. Let's go."

After also pulling the king to his feet, she held the inside elbows of both men. She herded them inside the abbey, which was surprisingly easy. Both men shuffled ahead, urged on by the anger in her voice. After they entered, a semicircular recess above them cracked and gave way. It crashed over the entrance and missed them by only a few yards—yet close enough for Ozyan to leap back. She caught a hard rock against her shin and lost her grip on the two men.

She regretted coming into the abbey. She'd never imagined such an important building could be so collapsible. She supposed they could've done the ceremony outside, but it was too late. They were in here. Ozyan relocked their elbows and led them towards the altar.

She pushed and shoved both men until the king tripped and fell. He brought Ozyan and the minister with him. They went to the debris-covered floor where the king lay on his side again, this time with his arms over his head, as if expecting the rest of the ceiling to fall on them at any moment. The ground shook, sending a small shower of pebbles from the faltering ceiling. Debris cascaded over the pews. A stained-glass window imploded, sending a violent spray of sharp shards in their direction. Ozyan decided the altar was too far away. They would marry halfway up the aisle. Good enough.

Another smaller earthquake shook the abbey. The minister tried running away, and Ozyan barely managed to grab his coat sleeve in time to stop him.

"You are going to marry us, dammit!" she yelled at him. "Do it now! I command it."

The minister blinked at her. He dug inside his front pocket, arching his back to do so. He removed a small book as a band of dust sailed across his eyes. He flinched, but thankfully recovered and opened the book, despite a new, horrendous commotion outside.

He began reading, but she couldn't hear him, so she slapped him.

"Louder!" she yelled.

"Will you take Ozyan to be your wife?" he asked the king, who was not paying attention. His gaze was fixed on the newly shattered window, at the shadows and sounds coming from outside.

"Will you love her?" the minister asked. "Will you comfort her? Honor and protect her, and, forsaking all others, be faithful to her as long as you both shall live?"

She went to scold the king for his flimsy participation, but he surprised her by snapping his head around. "I will," he said.

"Ozyan, will you take King Montrose to be your husband? Will you love him, comfort him, honor, and protect him, and, forsaking all others, be faithful to him as long as you both shall live?"

"I will," she said.

"Repeat after me," the minister told the king. "Ozyan, I give you this ring as a sign of our marriage. With my body, I honor you, all that I am I give to you, and all that I have I share with you, within the love for the Highest Spirit."

King Montrose wiped his eyes. The meaning of what was happening began to sink in. He repeated what the minister had told him to.

"Montrose, I give you this ring as a sign of our marriage," Ozyan said, repeating the minister's next words. "With my body, I honor you, all that I am I give to you, and all that I have I share with you, within our—"

Behind them came a tremendous rupture of stone and glass. Ozyan turned to see a yelkin charging through the front entrance. Seeing them, the giant paused but resumed stomping ahead, exhilarated by the idea of killing them. The yelkin crossed the abbey in four strides but was halted by a vibrating spray of bright light. The light penetrated its body until it burned apart, shredded into complete nonexistence. Another giant behind it, which Ozyan had incredibly not noticed, fell face forward, collapsing into a smoky, bubbling heap. Tendrils of black smoke trailed from its shoulders.

Four men and two women walked through the giant opening the yelkin had created in the front wall.

As they came closer, Ozyan recognized them from their robes and progressive hairstyles. They were shamans.

This was it. It was all over. Ozyan's punishment had already arrived. They would execute her on the spot because they knew what she had done. She spun back to the minister. "Skip to the part where we're married. Do it now!"

"What do these people want?" The king had noticed the shamans. He struggled to his feet to face them.

She took his hand and spread it open, lacing her fingers with his. "We're getting married," she reminded him.

He squinted at her, calming. "You have the rings?"

"I have the rings," said the minister.

The Ghe-sui reached them and stopped. Ozyan tensed her body, steeling it against whatever spell or death ray they might kill her with. After a few moments, she realized the shamans were looking at her and smiling. She considered they were demented. What was there to smile about on a day like this?

She didn't say anything. She awaited questions about Seelskan and why she had made allies with him.

"May we still attend your wedding?" asked one of the female shamans. She was older but pretty, Ozyan thought. It was difficult to imagine her killing anything with eyes that blue. "I am Corsika," she said before introducing the other shamans. Ozyan forgot their names instantly.

King Montrose grabbed Ozyan in his arms and kissed her firmly. Caught by surprise, she squealed but was muffled by him. Afterward, he faced the shamans again. He waved his hand, dismissive. "Who even invited you?"

Ozyan clutched onto his robe, getting her hands full. "My dearest, they saved our lives. They deserve our eternal gratitude."

"Yes, you do," said another shaman, a young male, the youngest of the group.

"They're dangerous people," the king said to the new Queen, easily regressing into his spoiled royal tantrum manner. "I don't want them around any-more."

The male shaman stepped forward, his head crowned with a cropped top of hair and a long yet sparse mustache. His robe was yellow with red threading. "We are not the Ghe-sui you once knew, My Lord. We lost our leader today, but he still led us here. See, he wanted us to play a more vital role in shaping this world. We wish to be a part of it now, not defend from it. The old ways are dead, and we're here to help you both. It's the whole reason we came here with our dear leader Momaset."

"I know that name," Ozyan said. It was the shaman the king had thrown into prison. She felt more certain than ever that they intended to vaporize them at any moment. Surely their psychic powers showed them who she was. She even anticipated having her body blown apart as they had done to the drakksuk and yelkin and anything else they'd cared to.

"Yes," said the shaman named Corsika, "he was the one who came to you to save you, and thus you imprisoned him."

Ozyan went to speak, but she cut her off. "He will forever be remembered for his sacrifice. Promise us you will never forget it either."

"I promise!" Ozyan surprised everyone by shouting.

"I hope you will accept our demonstration of power," she said, "as a wish to form an alliance. To make Burnya the kingdom of the future. We wish to live in this kingdom with you, but not as the poor, forgotten beggars we once were."

"Which means what?" the king blurted. "You want money."

"Monetary donations would be a great beginning, My Lord, yes."

Montrose tucked his chin, incredulous. "Are you blind? My kingdom is not only destroyed, but it's also broke! The royal banks are empty."

"I have no doubt they are." Corsika kept her voice even: "Donations will be given to us by every level of Burnyan society. We will collect a ten percent tax on all sales in the kingdom."

"Sales of what? When?"

"Of everything. Once Burnya is put back together. Which it will be. Thanks to us."

"You believe I'm no longer the ruler here?"

She ignored the question. "We will use the taxes to build Ghe-sui temples constructed by the finest craftsmen. It will be filled with precious objects to reflect our new high status within the kingdom."

Montrose went to object, but Queen Ozyan silenced him with a soft hand against his chest. "We will give you whatever you need," she said to the Ghe-sui.

A second female shaman stepped closer, her face a dark landscape of intricate, tribal tattoos. "We also appeal for the opportunities to teach our beliefs. To erect new Ghe-sui temples with schools holding the best monastic libraries."

"They will be the finest libraries in all of Jyn." Ozyan stepped forward to address them all. The king watched her. The minister had run away. "Those accepted into the Ghe-sui way of life will possess a more stable, more privileged life than any ordinary citizen of Burnya. I swear it as your new Queen."

"All in Burnya must accept our authority," the male shaman said. "Dissent will be treated harshly. And you, the monarchs, will hold no exception to this authority. We expect you to respect us and communicate with us. And, above all, swear your allegiance to the new Magshaa."

"The Magshaa?" the king asked, his voice urgent. "I thought he'd been killed."

"We have a new Magshaa," replied Corsika. "A young woman. You will know her as Sarna. You will covet her as your superior. As will every king and Queen after you."

Quiet fell over the abbey. The battle outside had paused or stopped completely. Ozyan noticed the abbey had filled with other citizens seeking shelter. They looked on, wide-eyed, halfway interested by what the grand ceremony had been reduced to. Or that it was still happening at all. These were some of the poor who had been forced to stand in the street, trapped by barriers when the attack happened. Yet their moods did seem impossibly lifted by what they were witnessing. Ozyan even saw a small smile here and there, even among the men. Long, skinny motes of begrimed light fell in slats around them.

Ozyan looked into the eyes of shamans and saw something there she didn't like. "How do I know you won't kill me?" she asked them, not meaning to ask aloud.

"You're pregnant," Corsika answered. "You're giving this kingdom its first heir. We need you."

"How special is that?" asked another female shaman, smiling with yellow teeth, her green dreads tied into a tangled coronet.

Ozyan held her breath, thought it over—were they playing with her? They couldn't see with their psychic whatnot that she wasn't pregnant? As soon as she thought this, the shamans smiled. The moment stretched with their smiles, and she saw the truth: They knew. They had her. Why kill someone so valuable?

Ozyan tipped her dress to the attending citizens. She bowed. "I am yours," she said to them. "All of you, as your Queen, my life is yours."

The king knelt beside her. He placed his hand on her stomach, then his ear. In turn, she touched his dusty hair. She ran her fingers over his coarse, crownless scalp, and a fine white powder spilled loose over his shoulders.

"Our baby," he whispered. He wiped his eyes and looked up at her. "It's a boy. By all my authority, I am sure of it. I've never been more sure of anything."

EPILOGUE

SARNA

The siblings rode horseback with a procession of twenty shamans trailing them. Brother and sister rode side-by-side. The morning air was cold, so Sarna felt momentarily grateful the Ghe-sui had adapted their attitude towards killing animals. This way, she could wear a fur pelt around her shoulders rather than a straw blanket. At some point, she knew she would be expected to decide about such things. Like, should they still kill animals anymore.

Why had such a crucial role been left to her? She still didn't want it. She felt flattered that people thought of her as someone so incredibly special, but she had a hard time accepting this. Who in the world would want to be a leader? Who even decided such things? She only wanted to go home.

Seeing the sky blend from lavender to cobalt blue at its edges, she thought about the drakksuk she'd met, and how friendly he'd been. He'd given her the knowledge that magic came from within and without. That death was not the end. She figured the beast himself must've been dead, slain with all the rest, and this saddened her. She thought of all the death they were leaving behind, sparked off by a desperate ex-soldier's basic need to survive, following a betrayal by the only kingdom he'd ever known and loved. Luca had been a discarded piece of meat once, so he thought of the biggest plan he could, and he kidnapped a princess. The ultimate affront to the kingdom he'd once fought for. Lost friends for. He hadn't deserved what she'd done to him.

Sarna sighed. She had to let it go and move forward. To be what she needed to be. From what she could tell, living had little to do with who deserved what anyway.

She looked over at her brother, noticing that he hadn't shaved. The shadow of an approaching beard accentuated his jawline, making him look more masculine but also older. His hair had grown back, skin-short but even. Despite his habit of getting injured, he would have little problem finding a wife before long. He was still a young king. And he was still alive.

In this moment, though, he looked pensive and weary, the morning sun giving the side of his face a golden line. Watching him as he rode with his arm in a cotton sling, head held high, she realized it was Shayan who should've been the Magshaa, not her. Doubtlessly, she would be seeking his counsel in matters of absolutely everything. She pondered if she could even bequeath the job over to him. At least, he had some experience leading. She knew nothing about what she was doing.

On Shayan's right rode two older men and four soldiers, survivors of the battle. In fact, they appeared mostly unscathed, which caused Sarna to wonder where they'd spent the fighting. She assumed they must have hidden, and she couldn't blame them. The scene yesterday had been nothing short of horrific, and Sarna knew she had many restless nights ahead to replay the images of what had happened. The gore. The screaming. The burning eyes of the Fiend as he focused his hate onto her. The dark majesty visions he had shown her.

The siblings hadn't spoken much in more than two hours. There was too much to say. They were headed back to the refugee encampment of Tartarian survivors. Sarna felt both sad and joyful upon learning that some of their people had survived. They were sustaining. The hope now was to go collect their people and march back into Tartaria, subduing the current occupants with their powers. After what had happened to their entire military and its chief, there was the assumption that resistance would be weak. They would take their kingdom back, either way.

Sarna certainly wanted no part of more slaughter, but Tartaria belonged to them. She'd been informed that Burnya was hers if she wanted it, but she wanted nothing to do with that place anymore. She didn't even remain there to punish Queen Ozyan and King Montrose for what they had done to them. The apocalypse of their home had been punishment enough.

Sarna snapped from her thoughts when she realized Shayan was saying something to her. She leaned over to hear him better. Before them lay the Orgoon Plains, wide stretches of flat, wheat-covered grasslands containing few trees.

"There's something I have to tell you, Sarna," he repeated. "I killed an advisor. Back before we were attacked."

"Which one?"

"It was Zov. He insinuated we get rid of our father, and I snapped."

"You're forgiven."

"Am I?" Shayan laughed. "Is that why I told you? Because my sister is an actual goddess now who bestows forgiveness?"

"*Joppa*, I'm not a goddess."

"Why else are all these smelly, homeless people following us then?"

She slapped her leg, incensed. "How can you call them that?" she fumed, her voice strained and hoarse. "Did you not see what they did?"

"Didn't blink once during the whole event actually."

"Why would you insult them? You should love them."

"Guess I better learn to, right? They'll melt me with their minds."

Sarna sat back in her saddle and sulked. Her brother would be more of a challenge than she'd hoped.

No one could match his skepticism and stubbornness. She'd never considered he might feel jealous, emasculated by her status. The Ghe-sui would mostly rule Jyn, as some of them felt they should've done all along.

"What's going to be your first act as the Boshgosh?" he asked her.

"*Magshaa.* I'm going to erect a memorial to Lalya."

They rode a while in silence before he said, "That would be nice."

"Why did you let her come with you, Shayan? Why did you place her in danger like that?"

"Because she begged me."

"You liked her."

"I did. A lot."

She swallowed, her hand going to her throat. "I didn't even know she was still alive."

"Me either."

"What she did was incredible. Where did she come from?"

"Where did Lalya ever come from?"

Sarna laughed a little as thoughts of Lalya held the air between them. Sarna hoped dearly that her friend was in a happier place. Anything was better than this. She'd suffered enough.

Sarna noticed Shayan looking worried.

"You'll still be the king," she said to her brother.

"Thank you," he said. "It's what I want finally."

She bit her lip. "I didn't ask for this, you know."

"Then how did it happen?"

"I was chosen by the Magshaa Bells."

"The what?"

"Never mind."

Shayan sighed. "It's all right, Sarna. You'll do fine."

"I'm scared."

"Of what?"

She paused to formulate. It was a huge question. "What if Baal returns?" she asked. "A shaman told me Baal only went away because we annoyed him enough."

"You mean he's not dead? What are you saying exactly?"

"It means he could come right back if someone else conjured him here."

"Then I guess we'd better make this new world in the right way. That way, no one ever feels the need to go looking for him again. *Joppa*, what is that?"

He halted, and she turned her attention ahead. They had reached a small hill and watched as a black mass of marching men filled the fields below them. There had to have been thousands of them. They created an undulating carpet of moving bodies, peppered with those red, glowing eyes. As they drew closer, the white over their upper bodies and bald heads became more visible, as did their blue abdomens. Shayan stopped his horse in front as the entire group of shamans dismounted, taking up a defensive stance, their fists turning blue. At the sight of this, the tribal beings slowed their march. They shifted their spears.

Sarna held her arms out. "No," she told the shamans. They looked at her, confused, their clenched fists dimming but still covering the ground in a blue-ish glow. Uncertain, their eyes darted between her and the advancing mass of strange beings.

"No," she repeated. "Do nothing." She bounced her hands down as a way of demonstrating that she wanted them to drop their fists. They still didn't understand, though, so she approached the nearest shaman. She took his wrist and guided it downwards. She looked at each of them until they dropped their fists, their brightness dimming until gone.

She walked to the edge of the hill. When the tribal beings saw that the shamans had relaxed and were merely walking towards them as if to greet them, they appeared to relax as well, though they didn't lower their spears. Sarna could sense, through their collective minds, that they were finished with humans. Through their spirit, she felt how their health had been affected since joining the outside world. Their migration was due to the segregation and discrimination they'd encountered after helping the Cathyrnee invade Tartaria, an involvement resulting in nothing less than their physical, emotional, and psychological defilement.

Sarna motioned for everyone else to stay behind while she walked forward. Shayan started to ride after her, but she spun on him, stopping him with a frown. After some hesitation, he nodded, but with a hand kept on his sword handle.

Sarna knelt and leaned forward. She bowed, which she hoped might be seen by the beings as a demonstration of respect. A gesture of peace and honor. She held her breath as she heard the shamans doing the same. Or she trusted they were. She cheated by peeking under her left arm, and indeed she saw the tops of their bowed heads. They held their horse's reins in one hand, as she did.

Shayan and his men stayed where they were. She looked up and gave her brother a scowl.

He shrugged, showing her his sling. "I'm injured."

"Get down," she hissed.

Shayan and his men exchanged looks. The king told them, "Do what she says."

The men dismounted and shifted their armor-infused tunics to get onto their hands and knees, then their faces. This wasn't quite what Sarna had in mind, since what they were doing resembled playing dead rather than bowing.

She looked up and nearly yelped when she saw the beings had walked right up on top of them already. She offered a serene smile to the ones who were closest. She placed her face to the ground again, reforming her bow. She felt the ground vibrate as the beings moved around them. She clenched her teeth, fearful she had maybe, just maybe miscalculated. Now that throngs of evil-looking cryptids moved among them, she grew hyper-aware of how utterly helpless they were should the beings decide to hack away and slaughter them. It would be all her fault.

She felt her horse pull at the straps she held, bucking a little, spooked but staying put. She knew if they stayed calm, the horses would stay calm. She forced every muscle to go slack.

The beings kept walking. As each one went by, she reached out in her mind to read their thoughts. She couldn't make out anything in particular, except for a shared desire to simply go home. They'd been led to believe the world of the many was better than that of the few. Only, they were better off existing where they'd come from. For all their intelligence and adaptability, humans held no more superiority over nature than they did.

An hour later, when the entirety of the army had passed, Sarna lifted her head to find herself and everyone else coated in dust. They had been spared by a forlorn sense of resignation among the beings. They had likely not killed them because they didn't possess a need to. As novel a reason as any.

Sarna watched her brother slapping at his clothing to get the dust off. When he noticed her, he gave her a look of extreme relief. He whistled. That was lucky. Meanwhile, the shamans grinned broadly at her. *Magshaa, yes, The Magshaa.*

She knew that ultimately, men would be men, and as long as they were around, there was only so much peace one could expect. Perhaps it made perfect sense that a young woman should take over. The alternative was apparently evil and mass death.

The siblings, the shamans, and the countrymen regrouped, remounted their horses. They continued onward.

Shayan steered his horse closer to Sarna's. He reached over and tried to take her hand, but the reach was too far. She noticed what he was doing and met his reach. The siblings held hands until the strain became too much, and they dropped them.

"So..." Shayan cleared his throat. "What comes next,...my Magshaa?"

She looked at him, expecting to see the sarcasm on his face. But his expression was serious, grim even.

"I have no idea," she said.

As a single body, their procession rode into the north and veered west, brother and sister remaining by each other's side. The twin moons lit their way.

Before you go…

Thank you for reading!

Stories only survive because readers share them with others. If you enjoyed this book, the best way to support our work is to leave a review and tell a fellow reader about it.

For news on upcoming releases, exclusive previews, and special subscriber-only content, visit:

palmcirclepressbooks.com

We hope to see you again in another story.

OTHER BOOKS BY LEE ANDERSON:

WHAT HAPPENED AT SISTERS CREEK

A small-town sheriff sends a search party into the woods to hunt two escape convicts. What they find instead is a savage, unthinkable horror...

"I squirmed, I cringed, I gritted my teeth and held my breath…And that ending…. I just…. WHAT? I don't even know what to say. Amazing? Exhilarating? Total WTF moment? It was soooooo good!" Jessica Scurlock, author of **Pretty Lies**

Available now on Amazon, Barnes & Noble, and other major retailers!

DARK LORDS OF THE TRAILER PARK

Dark Lords of
the Trailer Park

Short Stories
by Lee Anderson

This gripping collection of stories will take you on a thrill ride through a morally bankrupt landscape of desire, desperation, and constant danger. Dark Lords of the Trailer Park is an exploration of redemption in unexpected places. A riveting deep dive into the complexities of human nature, the triumphs and challenges of society's outcasts. Lee Anderson's riveting tales will leave you breathless, yearning for more, long after the final page has turned.

Available now on Amazon, Barnes & Noble, and other major retailers!

THE ATROCITY BELLS
The Lost Books of Jyn, Book One

Sarna was never meant to wield magic. Now it's awakening inside her—and it may destroy everything she loves.

Kidnapped by ruthless outlaws, she finds herself bound to Luca, their scarred and enigmatic leader. He should be her enemy. Yet every clash between them ignites a connection neither of them can escape.

Back home, Prince Shayan struggles to hold their kingdom together as their once-great father descends into madness, haunted by the spirit of a vengeful war god.

But a far greater threat is rising from another world…

Available now on Amazon, Barnes & Noble, and other major retailers!

ABOUT THE AUTHOR

Lee Anderson is an American novelist, short story writer, and playwright. He is the author of the horror novel *What Happened at Sisters Creek*, the short story collection *Dark Lords of the Trailer Park*, and the fantasy duology *The Lost Books of Jyn*, titled *The Atrocity Bells* and *The Apocalypse Wedding*. His two plays, *Supper's Ready* and *Little America*, were staged in New York City, off-Broadway.

www.leeandersonbooks.com